THE GLASS SLIDE WORLD

ALSO BY CARRIE VAUGHN

The Naturalist Society

The Naturalist Society

The Kitty Series

Kitty and the Midnight Hour

Kitty Goes to Washington

Kitty Takes a Holiday

Kitty and the Silver Bullet

Kitty and the Dead Man's Hand

Kitty Raises Hell

Kitty's House of Horrors

Kitty Goes to War

Kitty's Big Trouble

Kitty Steals the Show

Kitty Rocks the House

Kitty in the Underworld

Low Midnight

Kitty Saves the World

Kitty's Greatest Hits (collection)

PRAISE FOR *THE NATURALIST SOCIETY*

"Vaughn's historical fantasy captures both the science and the magic of the natural world, as well as 19th-century sexism. With a unique magic system and engrossing character arcs, this novel will speak to fantasy and lit fic readers alike."

—*Library Journal* (starred review)

"Vaughn's prose is captivating and the story begins slowly, almost meditatively, echoing Beth's own grief and solitude while building a compelling magical system . . . perfect for anyone who enjoyed the science and magic parts of the His Dark Materials series and longs for more."

—*Booklist* (starred review)

"Vaughn spins a moving tale about the hardships that women faced in the late 19th century, while also introducing an inventive magic system that hinges on the pursuit of knowledge. The result is an adept and provocative feminist fantasy."

—*Publishers Weekly*

"*The Naturalist Society* is beautifully written. Characters are complex and multi-dimensional, and observations of fauna and animal behavior are detailed and astute."

—*Historical Novels Review*

"An historical fantasy whose author has raised a fun read to an impressive level of literary elegance."

—*Midwest Book Review*

The Immortal Conquistador (collection)

Kitty's Mix-Tape (collection)

The Cormac and Amelia Case Files (collection)

Other Books

Questland

The Wild Dead

Bannerless

Martians Abroad

Dreams of the Golden Age

After the Golden Age

Discord's Apple

Steel

Voices of Dragons

Amaryllis and Other Stories (collection)

Straying from the Path (collection)

Water Fire Fae: Stories (collection)

THE GLASS SLIDE WORLD

CARRIE VAUGHN

47NORTH

This is a work of fiction. Names, characters, organizations, places, events, and incidents are either products of the author's imagination or are used fictitiously. Otherwise, any resemblance to actual persons, living or dead, is purely coincidental.

Published by 47North, Seattle

www.apub.com

Amazon, the Amazon logo, and 47North are trademarks of Amazon.com, Inc., or its affiliates.

EU product safety contact:
Amazon Media EU S. à r.l.
38, avenue John F. Kennedy, L-1855 Luxembourg
amazonpublishing-gpsr@amazon.com

ISBN-13: 9781662530500 (paperback)
ISBN-13: 9781662530326 (digital)

Cover design by David Drummond
Cover images: © Techzaka, © Flipser, © VectorShow / Shutterstock; © MirageC, © Felice Placenti, © mikroman6 / Getty

Printed in the United States of America

To my first and greatest supporter, Jo Anne Vaughn.
I miss you, Mom.

The recognition so long refused to bacteria was now ungrudgingly given, for it was realised at last that, in the words of M. Duclaux, "Whenever and wherever there is decomposition of organic matter, whether it be the case of a weed or an oak, of a worm or a whale, the work is exclusively performed by infinitely small organisms. They are the important, almost the only, agents of universal hygiene; they clear away more quickly than the dogs of Constantinople or the wild beasts of the desert the remains of all that has had life; they protect the living against the dead."

—Grace Frankland, *Bacteria in Daily Life*, 1903

ONE

Vibrio cholerae

October 1902
London
The New Hospital for Women

Ava Stanley checked the petri dishes on the shelf, observing and recording progress. Her crops were coming along nicely. In each glass circle, microbial life propagated, spots of fuzzy white on pink agar backgrounds, a strange sort of impressionistic art suggesting snowflakes or a dusting of cotton. Deceptive images disguised the reality: The dishes housed colonies of bacteria, millions of cells reproducing, spreading. A whole mysterious world unto itself. One species of these tiny creatures had caused the death of millions. Had steered the course of human history. It seemed unthinkable that these little nondescript things held so much power.

She needed to determine which of these was her quarry, revealing the infected water source that had caused an entire neighborhood to fall ill.

The procedures were painstaking but rewarding. Harvesting the cultures—the yellow spots were the ones she was after; transferring them to glass slides; staining with the dye, methylene blue, that would reveal them, allowing her to identify, classify. One by one, she collected and prepared the samples, and finally, with all due anticipation, she arranged the microscope, fitted the first of the slides to the bed, and tilted the mirror to direct light to the lens.

The moment of truth followed. Looking through the eyepiece, she gave the focusing dial a gentle twist to bring the sample on the slide into view, revealing chains of cells, dyed blue, twisted together in a tangle of the most simple form of life. A veritable zoo of microbiology found a home in London's water supply. *Escherichia coli*, *Salmonella*, *Shigella*. She would recognize any of them without consulting her reference books. This time, she was looking for something specific.

And there it was. On the fifth slide the pattern emerged: Under the microscope, the smear of color resolved into the image of a hundred separate cells, splashed out like inked commas on a page, an abstract picture full of meaning. Each cell was visible, a stubby curved shape with a flagellum trailing. Magnified, they were a swarm, trapped on glass. *Vibrio cholerae*. Without the microscope they were invisible.

She compared the label on the dish where this sample had been grown to those on the jars of water she had collected from sources in Southwark. The source: a well on Stoney Street. She'd bet water from the Thames was leaking into it, and the *V. cholerae* had found a ready breeding ground. She felt like a detective out of a story, a scientific Sherlock Holmes, following clues until she identified the culprit. *There, you are the murderer. I've got you, and now your reign of terror is over.*

She'd raised eyebrows the previous week, walking the slums by herself, scooping up vials of water and carefully labeling them. A gang of very young ragamuffins, pickpockets, had followed her, and washerwomen and laborers had glared at her. With her neat walking dress, new coat, and proper hat, she clearly didn't belong. But she'd learned from Dr. Anderson and the other physicians at the hospital how to approach the suspicious. "I'm working with the doctors at the New

Hospital. You know the sickness that's spreading? The cholera? We're going to stop it."

They didn't always believe her. She was too young, too female, and maybe even too American. Her accent blared like a horn here. To be fair, twenty-one was awfully young, and she wasn't *quite* a doctor. She still had to take the exams. Then, maybe. If nothing else, the declaration made clear she had friends and would be missed if something happened to her. Now, if they could plug up the well and get clean water to the residents, stop the outbreak, maybe people would trust them a little more.

Ava wrote up her notes, drew a sketch of the bacterium as it appeared under the microscope lens, and put the slide in a sample case with the vial of water from the offending well. Covered the microscope, put the cultures back in place on their shelves, wiped ink from her hands and cleared off the desk. Then, she cleared it again. Motes of dust, bits of detritus smaller than the eye could see, fallen hairs, flakes of skin . . . A surface might be freshly dusted and still be grimy with pollen, mites, their droppings, and other microscopic debris. It was just as well no one could see it all without the help of a microscope. Every housekeeper in the world would scream in terror.

Ava had a tool that they didn't: Arcane Taxonomy, a deep study that gave one access not just to knowledge of the natural world but also to its power. With it, she could clean a surface without a splash of alcohol or wipe of a cloth. A hundred and fifty years before, Carl Linnaeus, in the course of developing a system of taxonomy, of classifying all the living creatures of the earth, inadvertently did more than that. Over the following decades, a handful of naturalists, from Alexander Wilson to Mary Anning to Charles Darwin, had gone beyond classifying the natural world to become something like magicians. The sharp eyesight of a falcon, a seal's ability to keep warm in the frigid cold, the heat of flame evoked by the fiery red plumage of a tanager—an Arcanist's imagination could give them great power. *If* they understood what they were doing. *To name a thing is to know a thing,* Linnaeus wrote. The limitations of Arcane Taxonomy were that so many Arcanists didn't understand as much as they thought they did.

Scarabaeus sacer. The sacred scarab, a holy insect in some parts of the world, and an efficient collector of waste. As a girl she had watched one of the beetles roll a ball of dung larger than itself, gathering unspeakable particles and burying them away. Taking a cloth, carefully wiping down the lab bench while channeling that power, she swept all the unseen dirt and grime into a single point, a lump the size of a blueberry, easily disposable.

In nature, the scarab beetle would eat the ball of waste it had collected. This was one of the contradictions, the uncertainties, of Arcane Taxonomy: The beetle's purpose in collecting waste was not the same as that of a young medical student clearing her lab bench. So much of Arcanism was metaphor, and metaphor was slippery.

While the *Scarabaeus sacer practicum* was very useful, it wasn't very impressive to look at. Not like starting a fire with a touch. She was the only Arcanist she knew who had to use a match to light a candle. At times, Arcane Taxonomy seemed little more than a parlor trick. Some said that in the modern world, with its electricity and dynamite, radio and telegraph, Arcane Taxonomy was less useful, less relevant. It couldn't mend wounds. It hadn't stopped war. She still needed to culture bacteria to track the source of cholera. No one had yet found an Arcane *practicum* to cure disease. Some said that all the spaces of the world had been mapped, that every species of animal had been discovered. Surely, all the uses of Arcanism had been discovered.

Surely not, Ava thought. The microscope revealed new worlds all the time. She swept up the pellet of waste and dropped it in the bin.

Down the corridor, an office door stood open. Ava looked in, but Dr. Anderson wasn't at her desk. At this hour, she must have been doing rounds in the ward. Ava went upstairs, to the first of the large rooms lined with patient beds. A row of windows let in sunlight, making the place seem spacious, airy. An antiseptic, chemical smell lingered, along with the unavoidable smells of illness: soiled bandages, bodily fluids. Discomfort had its own scent.

All the beds were occupied. The New Hospital never had enough space for everyone who needed it, even after expanding. The patients were mostly women and children. In this ward, they were on the mend from whatever injury or illness had brought them here, thank goodness. Resting peacefully or sitting up and reading, talking quietly to their neighbors. Ava smiled at a young woman with a broken arm she'd helped treat a couple of days earlier. The arm was splinted, bandaged, and her expression was no longer twisted in pain. The woman smiled back.

She found Dr. Anderson in an examination room down the hall, bent over a woman in a chair who lay in a swoon, soaking with sweat, overcome with fever. Curious, Ava stepped closer for an impromptu examination of her own. The woman's left arm was grossly swollen, an angry red, the skin tender and stretched almost to bursting. An infection, trapped and festering. The duty nurse was putting a damp cloth on the patient's forehead, and Dr. Anderson touched the woman's neck to find her pulse while studying the watch on her wrist.

Dr. Elizabeth Anderson was an icon, the first woman in England to qualify as a physician, and founder of the New Hospital for Women. In her sixties now, she was both matronly and intimidating, her light-gray hair pulled back in a prim bun, collar up to her chin, her gaze studious. She'd announced her retirement for next month. The end of an era.

"You should have come in sooner, my dear," Dr. Anderson said, looking up from her watch. "As soon as you knew it wasn't healing."

"Have to keep working or I'll lose my job," the patient answered in a thready voice. Her gaze was half lidded, and she seemed only partly aware of the proceedings. The heat of fever was so strong it seemed to rise off her.

"We need to operate, to clean out the infection. Do you have someone here we can speak to?"

"Sister. Downstairs."

Dr. Anderson nodded smartly to the nurse. "Prepare for surgery. We'll operate right here, I think."

"Yes, Doctor." The nurse bustled off to the supply cupboard to gather sterilized instruments, bandages, washbasins, and on and on.

Against all sense, the woman tried to straighten, pushing off from the chair's arm. Her whole frame shook. "I can't, have to get home . . ."

"My dear, you must stay here or you'll die," Dr. Anderson said bluntly. The woman whimpered but settled back. She didn't have the strength to argue further.

Dr. Anderson finally noticed Ava lurking behind her.

"Can I help?" Ava asked.

"Miss Stanley, I thought you were off by now."

"Just about to leave, but I can stay."

With a gesture, she guided Ava to follow her to the nearby washroom, little more than a closet with running water and a basin, and clean surgical gowns hanging from hooks. Dr. Anderson's sleeves were already rolled up. She commenced scrubbing her hands and arms up to the elbow.

"Miss Nash is on duty—no need for you to linger. It's a simple enough procedure," Anderson said in her brusque, precise English accent. "If everything goes well, we'll save her life. I'm not hopeful about the arm."

"It doesn't look good."

The smile Anderson threw over her shoulder was wry. "We'll be sure to get a culture for you."

"Thanks." Ava hadn't wanted to be so ghoulish as to ask for one. "I've found the source of the cholera. It's on Stoney Street."

"Oh, excellent! Put the samples in my office, won't you?" Dr. Anderson at least let Ava help with putting on her apron and tucking her hair under a cap. "You're still off to Nassau next week?"

Ava felt the weight of her attention. Speaking with her always felt like taking an exam. "Yes. I'm looking forward to the project." This was a collection trip, surveying bacterial diseases across the Atlantic.

She had a case full of petri dishes waiting for cultures, to compare to the catalog of cultures collected here in London. Were they different? Similar? How far could one strain spread? She could hope to at least start to get answers.

"And when you get back, you'll schedule your exams, yes?" There it was, the steady piercing look.

Ah, Ava had hoped she could scurry away before the conversation turned to this topic. "I've got a couple more months of practicum first."

"I thought you'd arranged to work at the hospital in Nassau."

"Well yes, I hope to, but there's the collecting project, and I've promised a report to the Linnean Society as well as to the medical journal."

Dr. Anderson couldn't cross her arms or put her hands on her hips, not with them scrubbed clean. She should have seemed ridiculous, standing there with her hands raised, studying Ava like she was a culture in a petri dish, fascinating and frustrating. A little squishy and unsettling. "Miss Stanley. Do you want to be Miss Stanley your whole life, or would you like to be Dr. Stanley?"

Well, that laid things out clearly, didn't it? "I should be back in three or four months. Plenty of time to study for exams in the meantime."

The doctor seemed skeptical, and Ava tried to put on a hopeful smile.

"I've said this before, but I must say it again. I fear you're dividing your time and attention," Dr. Anderson said. "The days of the great physician Arcanists like our good Sir Joseph Hooker are over. These days, there's simply too much knowledge required in either subject to do both well." Dr. Anderson was one of those who saw Arcane Taxonomy as more of a parlor trick than a useful skill. A way for naturalists to compete, seeking out rarer and rarer creatures, not for knowledge so much as to claim their names and power for themselves. Medicine—now there was a noble profession.

This was an age of specialization. Of professionalism. But Ava didn't want to have to choose.

"You're not the first person to say so," she answered. "I keep hoping . . . to find a way through. I've got this talent—I ought to try to use it for good."

"You can do a great deal of good in medicine."

"Yes, ma'am. I'll think about it. I'll have an answer when I get back."

"Very good. And Miss Stanley? My condolences on your loss. To your whole family."

"Thank you. We appreciate it."

Dr. Anderson nodded and hurried to her patient, now surrounded by nurses and instruments. Ava fled before the first cut of the scalpel.

TWO

Lactococcus lactis

Ava's next challenge was fast approaching: how to tell her family about her research trip to the Bahamas. She had intended to much earlier. But Sir Archibald fell ill, and it hardly seemed appropriate to drop the news on them then. Then her step-grandfather passed away, the family was preparing for his funeral, and they still didn't know. This really shouldn't have been such a crisis. And yet here she was, avoiding the argument she was sure was coming.

Her parents worried about her. They wanted to help, and she appreciated them, she truly did. But the line between advice and criticism seemed awfully thin sometimes. Their interest in her career aspirations had become a bit oppressive—ever since her certification in Arcane Taxonomy with the Treasury Department. That episode hadn't gone as well as any of them might have wished. Ava had all the right references from her instructors at Radcliffe. She had demonstrated and documented an array of Arcane *practica*. But the board knew very well who her mother was, and no doubt suspected who her father was, and had made clear that they expected more from Ava. *Practica* based on fur and feathers and scales, the obvious representatives of the natural world. Botany, at the very least, as was more traditional. More acceptable. They hadn't quite known what to do with her crawling creatures, or worse, the mites and spores she'd found through her microscope lens. Using Arcane *practica* to *clean house.* Not to clean house, she'd insisted. To sterilize—a very useful *practicum* for a medical Arcanist. On the advice of nearly everyone, she hadn't even brought up her hopes of finding *practica* based on the biological class of bacilli. Words like *unproven* and *questionable* would start to get thrown around, jeopardizing her attaining any Arcanist Rank at all.

And then, of course, they'd asked her to light a candle. Every Arcanist could light a candle with a touch, or a mere thought. Except for Ava. The candle remained dark, and there was a vague implication that her Fourth Rank was only granted at all out of respect for her family's reputation and not anything she'd done on her own. Beth and Bran had insisted they weren't disappointed, but they'd offered lots of suggestions about what she could do to improve that rank at the earliest opportunity.

The next step of her career, she needed to accomplish on her own.

Late afternoon she boarded the train for Winchester and got off at the closest station to Sir Archibald's estate.

Ava tipped the porter and waited with her stack of luggage at the end of the platform at Barleydale. She had no idea who was going to come pick her up. It might be a hired coach, any one of the parental figures, or all of them together. Whoever it was, they were late. She began to think she'd forgotten to tell anyone what train she was on when the sound of hoofbeats and the squelch of wheels on the damp road came up from around the bend in the road, and the carriage itself emerged. There was Archie Torrance, her youngest brother, age seventeen, driving a single-horse trap by himself. He was lean and athletic, and over the last year had decided he was all grown up, wearing smart trousers, a vest over a crisp white shirt, and a straw boater on his dark hair. He'd been out in the sun, his skin darkened to brown. She would have considered him good looking if she didn't have memories of him flinging mud at her when they were smaller. She'd fling it back, and he'd start crying and get all the sympathy. She was the oldest and ought to know better. That was always the line.

He pulled the bay gelding to a stop right at the platform and leaned back, smiling a big grin, obviously pleased with himself.

She put her hand on her hip. "They let you out all by yourself?"

"I've been practicing. I'm a very good driver!"

"If you say so. Are you going to help me with my bags or just sit there?"

He checked the brake—a point in his favor—and swung off the seat. "Good to see you, too, Ava."

She had to admit she'd missed him. She'd missed them all and wanted to be home, right now. He opened his arms, and she walked into his hearty embrace. She hoped he was done growing, but probably not. She remembered when he was a baby, tiny. She'd been taller than he was until just a couple of years ago. Then he'd shot up to six feet tall. He was so smug about it, looming. He lifted her off her feet to prove the point.

"Here, get off me." Usually she would have laughed, but she was out of patience just now and pushed away.

"Huh. What's got you in a snit?" His expression fell. His feelings actually seemed to be hurt.

"Never mind," she sighed. "I just want to get home."

Archie frowned at her pile of luggage. "What is all this?"

"My microscope, lab kit, books. I'm supposed to be studying." She shrugged. It hadn't seemed like a lot when she had a porter to help.

"You look like you're packing for an expedition."

"Maybe I am."

"I don't think it's all going to fit."

True, she'd been expecting a bigger carriage. "It'll be fine."

They wedged the valise and lab kit under the seat and strapped the trunk to the back. She held the case with her microscope on her lap. And they were off, the bay trotting briskly. She restrained herself from telling Archie he was driving too fast. It would have only made him go faster.

"Anything I should know before entering the scrum?" Ava asked.

"I suppose everyone's a bit quieter than usual. Especially Dad. That whole mortality thing getting to him."

Ava's stepfather, Anton Torrance, had spent most of his life willingly plunging headlong toward death. Or at least danger. Mountaineering, polar exploration, expeditions into the most remote wildernesses. She supposed he'd been able to do so by simply ignoring the possibility of dying. It had begun to seem as if her stepfather's father, Sir Archibald, would live forever. He'd made it to eighty-four.

"I imagine it'll be better once the funeral is done. The finality," she said, without knowing at all what she was talking about. This was new territory for them.

After a turn or two down country roads, they were home. Somewhere between a fancy cottage and a proper manor house, Barleydale Croft had been in the Torrance family for four generations. Now that the elder Torrance was gone, Ava wondered what would become of it. She couldn't imagine anyone in her family settling down. Maybe with Archie at Cambridge, the rest of the family would stay put for a while. Everyone but her. That thought felt strange, her going off without them. Reality hadn't quite sunk in.

She really ought to tell them she was going.

The house had a staff. A groom came out to take charge of the horse and trap. Archie gave the bay a friendly pat on his neck before helping Ava with her bags.

Harry Torrance, Ava's middle brother, sat on the stone steps leading up to the front door. He was playing his violin. Ava didn't catch the tune; he stopped when he heard the rattle of the carriage.

"Have you retrieved the pilgrim?" he asked, leaning back on his elbows and stretching out his legs. His brown hair was parted in the middle, brushed neatly over his ears. His light-colored jacket was open, the shirt under it wrinkled. He was light skinned, with some pink stains of scarring on the sides of his face from a bad bout of the measles when they were children. The scarring had spread to his eyes, blinding him. He could see light and dark, but not much else. His shaded, round-framed glasses helped stave off headaches when the light got too bright. He was clean shaven this week—that might change next week.

"Lo, she has arrived!" Archie replied grandly, and Ava felt like they were making fun of her.

No one would ever guess that Harry and Archie were brothers, even half brothers, until they started arguing and bantering, striving to one-up each other with exactly the same tone of voice and verbal jabs. Harry losing his sight hadn't stopped them from coming to blows sometimes, even when Archie gained two inches in height over Harry.

"Hello, Harry." She set the microscope case down when he came at her with his arms spread. She intercepted him. They teased because they cared. And because it was easy to annoy her. "Kick you out, did they?"

"Kicked myself out." His expression turned sour. "The vicar is here talking to Mr. and Mrs. Torrance about the service. Mr. West has made himself scarce. To not cause *excessive discomfort*." Harry said these words with a smirk. The three siblings were well aware of what *excessive discomfort* their mere presence could cause.

"Ah," she said. "Where is he?"

"Round back, I think."

Harry opened the door so she and Archie could stash her bags in the vestibule, along with his violin; then they went out searching for their other father, since they didn't want to talk to the vicar any more than Harry or Brandon West did. Ava hooked one arm around Harry's, and Archie claimed her other arm. Suitably escorted, they walked around to the lawn at the back of the house.

Autumn was well underway. The rosebushes growing along the edge of the drive were shedding petals. In the garden beds, the last of the dahlias and asters valiantly brought in some color. A few bees were still exploring the dahlias, and Ava started to veer toward them to have a closer look. Her brothers steered her back on track.

They found Bran West seated on a stone bench at the end of the veranda, a pair of opera glasses in hand, peering through them to the hedgerow marking the boundary of the estate, fifty yards down. Ava immediately looked to what had caught his eye, but whatever it was—some bird, most likely—was hidden.

Bran was fifty-one, worn from a life of fieldwork, exploration, risks taken, illnesses weathered. An acclaimed naturalist, he'd been Anton's partner in exploration for most of their careers. They'd met on an Arctic expedition back in 1876. These days, he walked with a cane, though his back was still straight, his eyes still clear. His mustache and sideburns were graying, closer to salt than pepper, thinner than in the old photographs from the expeditions that had made his reputation.

He glanced over when they approached. His broad smile took years off his face.

"Ah, here you all are. Ava, darling, how was the train?"

"It was a train," she said, amused. "Glad to be away from it and here instead."

"I've got a *Falco columbarius* on the hedge. Want to take a look?"

This was a ritual from her childhood. Ava joined him on the bench, and he handed her the glasses and pointed, explaining which section of hedge the bird had settled on. The speck came into focus, but she only knew it was a merlin because he said so. Something about the coloration on its face, the proportional length of its tail, made it different from a falcon or a harrier. He identified it through instinct and experience rather than a careful assessment of its traits. They'd seen lots of merlins together, but he treated every one like the first, with wonder and excitement.

"Female?"

"Yes," he answered approvingly. He patted her shoulder affectionately. "Does your mother know you're here?"

"Not yet. Since everyone else fled the house, I figured I'd wait before going in."

He chuckled, then cocked his head, listening. Had he heard some bird in the trees? No, because he frowned. "They're discussing who should give the eulogy. Sir Archibald was prominent enough that there's apparently a question of appearances."

Bran West was eavesdropping. The ears of an owl, the hearing of a fox that could track mice under a foot of snow. He borrowed that power. Ava felt some stray annoyance—he'd used this Arcanist *practicum* on them when they were younger. They couldn't keep secrets around him.

"I thought Anton would do it," Ava said.

"So did Anton."

Appearances. Right. Anton Torrance, Sir Archibald's mixed-race son. However progressive Britain had been on banning slavery, it wasn't quite reconciled yet to a brown-skinned man speaking to a high-ranking respectable audience. Ava didn't need to eavesdrop to guess that Anton would win the discussion, one way or another.

"What are you using?" she asked.

"Bubo scandiacus."

Snowy owl. Bran was famous in Arcanist circles for his knowledge of ornithology. Settling herself, she gave it a try. Her *practica* were not her father's *practica*. She didn't have the affinity for birds that he did. She'd always been more interested in beetles, worms, creatures she had to turn over rocks to find, the bees tucked in bluebells, the water striders balancing delicately on the surfaces of ponds. To eavesdrop, to spy, she reached for these smaller creatures, the ubiquitous species that went unobserved in the nooks and crannies of everyday life.

Common earwig. *Forficula auricularia.* An annoyance, found everywhere. Ambient sounds drifted; Ava focused, and whispers came to her. A hint of voices. She didn't recognize the first one she caught.

"You understand that there will be men of rank in attendance—"

"Am I not a man of rank?" That was Anton, his voice tight, drifting to the edge of anger. He never stepped over that edge, but he sounded like he might this time.

"Sir, with all due respect, think of your father's legacy."

"I am my father's legacy."

"Anyone offended by Mr. Torrance doesn't have to stay." That was Mother, in her blithe, brash American accent, which probably offended the English vicar as much as Anton's brown skin.

Harry made a dismissive huff, which jolted Ava out of her concentration. She blinked confusedly, returning to herself. Such a strange feeling, splitting her attention like that. She wasn't used to it. Bran would tell her she needed more practice.

"Bad luck that Mr. Cadwell died before Sir Archibald," Harry said. "This shouldn't even be a discussion."

Mr. Cadwell, the old vicar, had been a lifelong friend of the family and supported Sir Archibald's marriage to Margaret, a Bahamian woman.

"Damn it all, anyway," Archie said. "That's what Grandfather would say. 'Put me in the ground and be done with it!'"

"Language," Bran said, but he smiled, because they could all hear the old man's voice in the words.

"Should we go in and help them?" Harry asked.

"They're almost done, I think," Bran said. "Another minute."

"Hey, Harry. You're it." Archie slapped Harry's shoulder and ran. Archie could always be relied on to disrupt any situation, especially if he was tired of waiting.

But Harry didn't run after him, as he usually did. He crossed his arms, and though he didn't have sight to glare with, everything in his expression conveyed annoyance. "No."

Archie stopped and turned mid-stride. "What do you mean, no?"

Ever since Harry was well enough to climb out of his sickbed, they'd played a modified version of tag. It had always started with Archie teasing; at the time, he'd been too young to realize Harry had lost his vision. Harry had cried at the way Archie had poked and prodded and taunted, calling from one direction and another. Then, Archie had cried when Harry lunged at the sound and punched him outright. The game went on for years, the teasing and jabbing ranging from good natured to fiercely competitive. "You're blind, not lame. Come at me, why don't you!" Archie would call, and Harry would counter, "I only need one chance." As long as Archie kept making noise, Harry could get in a good blow.

Until now, and Archie seemed nonplussed.

"I mean *no*," Harry said.

"But—"

"Archie, grow up."

Archie might as well have been punched, given the stunned look on his face.

"Hey there, settle down, boys," Bran admonished.

The brothers pouted and postured, no matter how grown up they were.

Harry cocked his head—judging sound, adjusting his mental map—and walked right over to the bench. Bran scooted over to make room for him. When they were side by side, the resemblance between them was plain, Harry's unruly wavy hair matching Bran's, the matched set of their shoulders as they slouched.

Archie kicked a divot out of the grass and shoved his hands in his pockets. Full of energy and no place to put it if Harry wouldn't roughhouse. Some balance had shifted. As if Sir Archibald's death had tipped some scale. The world would never be the same, and the change rippled out.

The French doors in the back of the house opened. Arm in arm, Mr. and Mrs. Torrance stepped out on the flagstones. Beth was frowning, and Anton's eyes were shadowed, tired.

Anton Torrance was tall, imposing, a physical presence with an elegant polish that should have been a contradiction, but he somehow encompassed both ideals. He'd made a name as a polar explorer, attacking and conquering both the Arctic and the Antarctic, and had led scientific expeditions all over the world. His close-cropped hair had a dusting of gray. Not as gray as Bran's, but they both looked weathered. He still gave an impression of strength, with a clear dark gaze that missed nothing. But he moved slowly. Ava only just now noticed how careful his steps were. Arthritis, missing toes, worn-out joints. She'd only been away for a couple of months, but Anton had never looked old to her before now.

Elizabeth Torrance, Beth, was in her late forties and had an elegance to match Anton's, wearing a walking dress in the black of mourning, her pale-brown hair pinned up under a simple hat. No vicar could possibly argue about their appearance except for the difference in skin color.

When Ava was born, Beth had been Elizabeth Stanley. Ava kept the name at her mother's request, a memory of that long-dead and apparently beloved first husband who wasn't Ava's father. She'd done the math on that one. Beth had met Anton and Bran right after her first husband died. The three had been fast friends ever since. More than friends, really. Anton and Bran had loved one another before they'd fallen in love with her. She'd married Anton for reasons of money, inheritance, and making sure they were all legally taken care of. *And* because she couldn't legally marry both Anton and Bran. She would if she could, Ava was sure. They were the fathers of her children.

It made for awkward moments whenever stodgy vicars and the like came to visit.

"Didn't go well, did it?" Bran asked.

"Listening in, were you?" Anton said.

"All but the last bit. I got distracted." He nodded at Ava beside him.

Anton's face lit up. "Ah! Dr. Stanley has returned!"

Him calling her *doctor* had been endearing when she first started her medical studies. A vote of confidence. But after three years and all the procrastination over exams, it had become annoying. Mocking, almost. He didn't mean it that way, but that was what her ears heard.

Ava went to meet them, to get swallowed up in their hugs.

"My darling girl," Beth murmured. "It's so good to see you."

Harry stood to meet them, and Archie was drawn back to the family. "How did it finally turn out?" Harry asked.

"Mr. Brown will *not* be conducting the service," Beth said firmly.

Anton scowled. "My father wouldn't have put up with such nonsense."

"If he were here, they wouldn't indulge in such nonsense in the first place," she answered. "You boys, you're going to have to change for dinner—"

"Beth, that merlin's back in the hedge," Bran said. He held up the opera glasses.

She was completely diverted. "Oh, wonderful." She settled on the bench next to Bran to look at birds.

Well, here they all were, her whole family. Maybe it would be nicer to wait until supper, when they were sitting and relatively quiet. Or after supper in the parlor, with a couple of glasses of sherry . . . No, this would only get more difficult the longer Ava waited. When Beth lowered the opera glasses, finished admiring the merlin in the hedge, that was her moment.

"I have some news," Ava said, voice lifted. She noticed she was kneading the fabric of her skirt and stopped.

"Oh, you've scheduled your exams!" Beth said, brightening.

Well, at least that got everyone's attention. "No," Ava had to admit. Her mother's smile dropped away. In disappointment? Resignation? "No. I'm going on a trip. I got a research grant to collect samples in Nassau. I leave . . . well, right after the funeral."

They all just stared at her. Even the boys seemed nonplussed and oddly quiet. Ava wasn't sure what she'd been expecting. Really, she must have known they'd have doubts, or she'd have told them weeks ago.

"*Alone?*" Beth finally exclaimed, with some amount of horror. "You can't possibly. You're too young to go so far by yourself. I won't allow it."

Ava was an adult in medical school. She'd traveled the world—in the company of her family. Which part of this was Beth responding to? "It's already settled, Mother. Nassau's hardly the other side of the world, and I'll be staying with the cousins."

"Collecting what? Insects? Worms?" Bran's tone was accusing rather than curious. Professional doubt?

"Bacteria," she said.

Bran sighed, and there it was, the professional doubt. "Do you really think this is the best use of your time? If you want to advance your rank in Arcanism, I'm not sure bacteria is the route you ought to be taking—"

"This is more of a medical study," Ava insisted. "Collecting samples, comparing varieties. Exactly the kind of thing you do, isn't it? I'm convinced there's some Arcane knowledge to be gained here."

Beth and Bran were standing now. She was wringing her hands; he leaned on his cane, the other hand on his hip. The boys were both gawping, like they were watching a cockfight. Ava felt the pressure of all their attention.

"I'm just not sure you've considered all aspects of such a trip," Beth said. "The difficulties of a young woman traveling alone."

"Oh really, Mother! How old were you when you hopped on a train and traveled to the other side of the country by yourself? Pregnant, no less!" This was the story of how Beth, a New York socialite turned ornithologist and Arcane Taxonomist, had ended up alone in Colorado with a baby.

Beth brushed away the observation. "To be fair, I didn't know I was pregnant then."

Ava huffed and rolled her eyes.

They'd all traveled, they were professional adventurers, and it was rank hypocrisy for them to complain about her wanting to do the same. But they were protective. She could travel the world and get into any trouble she liked, as long as they were right there with her. Going abroad by herself? Did they think she wasn't capable?

On the other hand, Anton had remained silent, his expression neutral. Considering.

"Your first real expedition," he said then, his smile breaking open. "I think that calls for a celebration."

"Anton!" Beth said accusingly. "She's too young! She doesn't know what she's getting into! What if something happens?"

Anton glanced at Bran, and their gazes met. Finally Bran flashed a smile. Their expressions hinted at a story none of them had heard.

"What if it does?" Anton said. "That's usually the point of going on a trip, isn't it?"

Beth huffed a little. "We'll talk about this later," she said, then swept back to the house with a swish of her skirt. Bran shrugged a little and followed.

That left Ava regarding Anton and the boys, who still seemed flummoxed.

"What's got Mother all riled?" Archie asked.

"We've all been to Nassau before," Harry said. "It isn't like you're going to Borneo or Shangri-la or someplace like that."

"But I've never gone alone," Ava said. Apparently that made a difference. The conversation had gone worse than she'd expected. She had expected argument, but not outright denial. "Does she think I can't do it?"

"I think she's worried, that's all," Anton said. "I'll talk to them. It's a worthy trip, my dear."

She gave him a wan smile.

After dark, the house fell quiet, and Ava crept off to the boys' room, carrying the book she'd promised them. Ridiculous, that she still felt like a child sneaking in secret, when they were all adults or nearly so. But after the conversation—argument—on the lawn, Ava couldn't help but feel like a child. They didn't trust her—not to travel, not to do good science. How was she ever to make her way in the world?

Ava didn't need a lamp to find her way around the corner to the room that Harry and Archie shared—she'd gone this way in the dark so often when they were younger and getting up to clandestine missions.

She passed the library on the other side of the landing and noticed light shining there. Within, soft male voices spoke. If she stood at the top of the stairs and leaned in, she could see around the edge of the doorway while remaining mostly hidden. She didn't need Arcane *practica* to eavesdrop.

Bran and Anton were on the sofa in front of the fireplace. Bran nestled at one end, his arms around Anton, who reclined against him and held his arms tight. They went without coats, their sleeves rolled up. The oil lamp on the side table painted them bronze.

"I'm sorry you still have to deal with this . . . this *garbage*." That was Bran, murmuring. He freed one of his hands to stroke Anton's hair.

"And I'm sorry that you end up outside it all. On the fringes," Anton said, sounding tired.

"I don't mind."

"Yes, you do. Don't think I don't notice you skulking about not talking to anyone."

"You shouldn't notice. People might notice you noticing."

"I swear to God, Bran, if people haven't noticed the two of us by now, they never will."

Bran chuckled and drew Anton's hand to his lips.

Ava was about to creep away and continue to her destination when Bran said, "I'm worried about Ava."

Anton chuckled. "Of course you are. It would be unnatural if you weren't. But she'll be all right. The chick must fly the nest someday, you know that."

"But there's so much that can go wrong. I think of all the times we almost died on our trips—"

"She's only crossing the Atlantic."

"Yes, I know. But . . ."

"But what?" Anton asked patiently, almost condescendingly.

"I worry that she's taking a wrong turn. Wasting her talents. I only want her to succeed."

"She's very young. Give her time. Give her space."

Bran huffed. "Easier said than done. Beth doesn't want to let her go."

"You really think we have a choice?"

Ava chose that moment to leave. Her cheeks were burning, and she didn't want to hear any more. It was her life, not theirs. She feared she'd never be able to convince Bran and her mother that her studies were valuable.

Collecting herself, she turned the corner to the boys' room and shoved open the door without knocking.

"Hey! Some warning!" Archie called in a forceful whisper.

She'd always come in without knocking, and he always made a fuss about it. "You were expecting me—what's the problem?"

"We might have been . . ." He trailed off in a shrug.

"Throwing a party? Summoning demons? I hope you'd tell me about it first. Let me in on the fun."

"Like we could ever hide from you," Harry said.

The room used to be the nursery and playroom, but most of the toys and furniture, the cribs and little chairs, had been moved to the attic. A few traces remained: an ornately carved rocking horse that had belonged to Grandfather when he was a boy, with a real horsehair mane and tail; the blankets and quilts that had kept them warm as children, now neatly folded and stacked on a cedar chest; childish drawings pinned to the walls. The place seemed only half lived in, a transition from the past to somewhere else.

Now, Harry and Archie shared the room when the family came to visit. A pair of beds sat against one wall under the windows; the rest of the space was taken up with desks, shelves of books, and wardrobes, all in pairs, one for each. All of it was unerringly neat so Harry could find what he needed.

They both sprawled on their respective beds, still in shirts and trousers, though they'd taken off their jackets and shoes. A lantern burned on the nightstand between the beds. The house hadn't been installed with gas or electricity, that's how old it was.

"Did you find it?" Harry asked. He lay back, hands behind his head, his glasses on the bedside table.

She revealed the book from behind her back, the title printed on the cover in glaring red, along with a flowery looping border design.

"Oh my God, it's ridiculous," Archie declared.

"Title, please?" Harry asked.

Ava complied. "*Torrance and West and the Terror of the Zambezi*. By Conrad Zane."

Harry laughed. "Can't wait to hear what this one's about."

"How many of these can this Zane fellow possibly write?" Archie exclaimed.

"As many as people will buy, I expect," she answered.

The first Torrance and West adventure, *Torrance and West and the Fires of Mount Erebus*, had appeared four years earlier, and a new one had come out annually ever since, each more outlandish than the last. Anton had been startled by their existence, and Bran furious—he seemed to think they should be getting royalties—and their mother quietly amused. She'd said, "Making a fuss about this Mr. Zane will only draw more attention to it. It would be better to be flattered, don't you think?"

The author had clearly read Anton's and Bran's memoirs and drawn from them. And then . . . embellished. Fancified. Turned them into supernatural melodramas. The novels sold well, by all accounts. Ava wondered what Zane would think if he knew that the intrepid Torrance and West were across the landing, taking comfort in one another's arms.

Their parents had banned the dime novels from the house. But then Ava left for school and got hold of a copy. The secret nighttime readings had become a tradition.

Archie drew his feet up, and Ava hurried to sit on the foot of his bed and open to the first page. The frontispiece showed an extravagant engraving of the story's heroes: The larger and more imposing Torrance wore a comically fierce expression and wielded a pistol; the more bookish West held his hands raised, haloes of light bursting from them in a wash of lines, a fanciful depiction of Arcane Taxonomy in practice.

She assumed a deep, melodramatic voice and began to read. "'It was in the harbor marketplace of Maputo where Anton Torrance first heard the tale of a treasure of such vast wealth that it was difficult to even speak of.'"

"And yet the author's written what, two hundred pages about it?" Harry said drily.

"Hush! 'One assumes the treasure of these stories was gold, jewels, priceless artifacts handed down from the pharaohs of Egypt or mysterious kingdoms of this vast continent lost to history. But others say this treasure was more intangible. The secret to eternal life. A source of unlimited power with which to rule the armies of the world. Or even a gateway to other worlds.'"

Archie leaned in, interested. "Gateway to other worlds, I like that."

"Would certainly make traveling easier," Harry added.

Ava closed the book. "Now, children, do you want me to read this or not?" This was a game whose patterns had sunk into their bones. Grinning, the boys urged her on.

The passage went on to introduce the intrepid heroes to the reader, telling of Torrance's great strength and presence of mind, how he quested to unravel the mysteries of the world's farthest reaches and so on. How West was brave and clever and could bend the forces of nature to his will as a master of the art of Arcane Taxonomy . . . "It's science, not art," Ava muttered in an aside.

A merchant—trembling with fear, of course—told them the tale of the distant mountain that hid untold riches and of how everyone who went looking for it died. But Torrance and West would not be dissuaded, and on and on . . .

Harry groaned. "Stop, stop. I can't take any more."

"Hey, I want to know what happens," Archie said. "The Zambezi—that's in Rhodesia or someplace, isn't it? Have Anton and Bran ever even been to Rhodesia?"

"No," Harry said. "At least not that I know of."

"It's all pure fiction right from the start," Ava said. "Not a grain of truth in any of it."

Harry shifted around to lie on his stomach and prop himself up on his elbows. "Here's the question. Why them? Why make up stories about Anton and Bran when this Zane fellow could have picked a dozen other explorers? Richard Burton or Henry Stanley, say. Or someone who's dead and wouldn't complain about it."

That laid it out quite bluntly. Anton and Bran both wrote memoirs about their explorations—any information about them was public knowledge, and Zane's stories were clearly fictional. But he could have invented characters, like Sherlock Holmes and Allan Quatermain.

Maybe that was the point. If Conrad Zane had invented characters, they would have been just like a dozen other adventure stories. Anton and Bran were real.

"Because Bran's an Arcanist," Ava said.

"And Anton isn't white," Archie said, frowning. "It makes them . . . special."

"Exotic," Harry added. "Would it be better or worse if the fictional versions resembled the real thing in any way?"

The problem was too much knowledge. Anton and Bran weren't famous explorers to the three of them. They were simply the men who'd taught them to fish and shoot and sat up with them when they were sick and kissed their bumps and scrapes better. That wouldn't be nearly as interesting a story, would it?

"Well, that's taken some of the fun out of it." Archie took the book from her and began flipping pages to look at the pictures, a handful of engravings even more ridiculous than the text.

"You might as well keep it," she said. "I'm bringing along too many books as it is."

"That's going to be strange, you going away alone," Archie said.

"You'll hardly miss me," she said lightly. But she was afraid she missed them both already, in anticipation.

"I thought the parental figures were going to burst," Harry said. "They took it personally, didn't they?"

"What do they think is going to happen?" she said, exasperated. "It's a simple Atlantic crossing, with a whole flock of cousins waiting on the other side. Now if I were going to try for the North Pole, that would be another thing."

"Yes, Anton at least would insist on going with you to the North Pole," Harry said.

"I hope they don't decide they need to go to Nassau with me." Wouldn't that be just like them. *Change of plans, dear—we're all coming along, what a nice holiday!*

Ava needed to do this alone.

"We'll miss you," Archie said simply. Right to the heart of it, and from Archie no less. Ava nearly cried right there.

"I'll write," she said. "It'll be a grand adventure. You both will have to plan your own adventures so the parents can blow up at you next."

"Bah," Archie said. "Too early to be making plans for myself. I've still got a few years of skipping lectures and messing around. After that, I can do anything I like. Go into politics. Write books on philosophy—that seems to be fashionable these days."

"Political philosophy?" Harry asked, brow raised.

"Just so! Or maybe I'll go back to New York and play baseball."

"For a living?" Ava asked.

"It'll drive everyone crazy. Sounds like fun."

Harry had rolled onto his back. He tapped his fingers against his chest, some rhythm the rest of them couldn't hear. "I'm trying to think of what that looks like. For me, I mean."

"What, baseball?" Archie said.

"Leaving the nest."

"You could play violin in any orchestra in the world," Ava said, hoping to pull Harry back before he went too far down this line of thought. In general, he was good spirited. He must know he'd be looked after his whole life, if it came to that. But she knew that was part of the problem.

"A violinist who can't see the conductor? Nice try. As far as performance goes, I'll only ever be a trick pony. The blind violinist."

"But you're good!" Ava insisted. "You really are."

Harry made like he was going to argue, but the tension in his brow faded. "Well, thanks for that. Look, don't worry about me. I'll figure it out." He always said that when they got to talking about fates and dreams. He put his hands behind his head, snuggled into his pillow, and seemed content. She worried that if he was struggling, the rest of them would never know it. He'd never say a word. Then again, when he said he was all right, maybe she should believe him.

"I don't worry about you," Ava said. "Not really. We've got our whole lives ahead of us."

"Plenty of time to make lots of mistakes," Archie said, and Ava groaned.

"More material for the memoirs," Harry said, chuckling.

"This family already has too many memoirs," Ava said.

"Letters, then. Write us all the letters, and we'll publish them," Harry said.

Archie seemed taken by the idea. "Better make them scandalous."

She couldn't even imagine. "A lady doctor and Fourth Rank Arcanist? I can't think of a more boring tale. And that doctor part is only if I pass the exams. It sure isn't *The Terror of the Zambezi*."

"Ah," Harry said, smiling wryly. "You never know, do you?"

Torrance and West and the Terror of the Zambezi

It was in the harbor marketplace of Maputo where Anton Torrance first heard the tale of a treasure of such vast wealth that it was difficult to even speak of.

One assumes the treasure of these stories was gold, jewels, priceless artifacts handed down from the pharaohs of Egypt or mysterious kingdoms of this vast continent lost to history. But others say this treasure was more intangible. The secret to eternal life. A source of unlimited power with which to rule the armies of the world. Or even a gateway to other worlds.

Torrance and West were just the men to discover the true secrets of this ancient mystery. To introduce the players of the story you have begun: Anton Torrance had the gift of camouflage. He could pass as any sort of man in any sort of place, as at home in the slums of Mumbai as in the mountains of Peru. With a powerful grip, broad shoulders, and an aim that never missed, he was always ready to confront the mysteries of the world–and unravel them. Anton Torrance's constant companion and partner in conquering the far places of the globe was Brandon West, a brusque and unassuming man. While of only average height and build, he had the blazing intellect and bravery of a master of Arcane Taxonomy. He was one of the great practitioners of that mysterious art, of binding the forces of nature to his very will. What need had he for physical prowess, or the unstudied elegance of his good friend? Indeed, he had the rough edges and unkempt manner made famous by the frontiersmen of his native America. And did not apologize for it.

"No one returns from that mountain, great sir!" The merchant trembled with fear. "A great spirit guards the place and hates intruders!"

Torrance narrowed his gaze thoughtfully in the manner of one considering a great puzzle. "I do wonder—do these tales have some core of truth, or are they put out to dissuade men from some great treasure? What do you say, my dear Mr. West?"

"Well, Torrance, I reckon I don't rightly know," West replied in his distinctive American drawl. "Just when I think I've seen it all, the world up and surprises me all over again."

"I'm inclined to investigate these stories. Just to satisfy my own curiosity, mind you. As you know, I am not so much interested in the treasure as I am in the mystery."

And the two men were not in the habit of paying heed to the warnings of natives.

They did not make much of gathering supplies and making plans for their next expedition. Even in those early days they were well known enough that even the quietest preparations would have drawn attention. They did not want attention. So much of their prowess lay in subtlety. They did not need the long baggage trains of other explorers, the hundreds of porters attempting to carry civilization with them into the unknown. Rather, they brought only what they needed to survive and depended on their knowledge of the land to carry them through. They knew by experience and common sense what they needed, and in a matter of days set off with no fanfare. They had maps, charts, and the stories to guide them. And so they slipped into the jungles of Rhodesia to seek their quarry. Either they would succeed, and the story of their victory would spread. Or they would fail, and they would vanish, and no one would ever know what travails they had faced.

THREE

Clostridium botulinum

The funeral took place, as inevitable as the movement of glaciers. They all wore black. Black dresses, black suits, black armbands, black gloves, the black netting of veils on black hats. They were like crows.

In place of Mr. Brown, a vicar from Winchester had been recruited to conduct the service, held in the village church where Archibald Torrance had been baptized and would now be laid to rest. Full circle. Imagine, spending a whole life out in the world and then ending up back where you started. How did the miles count, then? Ava's step-grandfather was buried in the churchyard next to his wife, gone ten years now. Lady Margaret Torrance was buried several thousand miles from where she'd been born, in Nassau. Ava wondered if it mattered, or if something in a person's soul would grow restless, separated from its origin. Millions and millions of people died far from home. She thought of Arctic explorers like Franklin, vanished into the ice. Countless sailors lost at sea. They were all born and all died on the same planet, so maybe that was the only location that mattered.

Harry played "Ave Maria" on his violin, as sweetly as any of them had ever heard it played. Ava glanced at Anton, who squeezed shut his eyes until he let out a shuddering breath, and was himself again. Bran and Beth stood on either side of him, as if holding him up.

The luncheon back at the house seemed crowded. So many people, they spilled into the garden. All of them were stitched up in black, a flock of crows, milling and murmuring.

The receiving line was excruciating. Mr. and Mrs. Torrance and the three offspring lined up in the parlor, accepting condolences, mostly from people Ava didn't know. They shook Anton's hand, nodded politely at Beth, started to bestow sympathies and admiration on the children—and hesitated, skepticism creeping in. They couldn't help but notice that only one of the children resembled Anton.

Beth addressed every person by name, for Harry's benefit, so he would be sure to know whose hands he shook. In return, they raised their voices at Harry, who bore it patiently, used to the absurd paradox of people yelling at someone whose hearing was perfectly intact. Many of them complimented his playing, at least. Meanwhile, Bran lurked. Just another guest, another friend, while everyone politely pretended not to notice that two of Beth's children looked like him. Ignored the implication that Anton's good friend and exploration partner was perhaps more than that. Anton glanced at him frequently, brow furrowed, worried, and Ava recalled the conversation she'd overheard. No one ever said anything about their family, but there was just so much to *notice*.

Most of those in attendance were neighbors and old friends of the family. A handful were colleagues of Anton, Bran, Beth, or all of them together. Members of various naturalist and scientific organizations, Explorers Club members—Anton was a founding member, though that hadn't seemed to impress Mr. Brown. There were writers and professors, some of them famous, even. Sir Henry Morton Stanley had graced them with his presence—no relation to the Stanley Ava had been named for, and people asked. (The truth was, Stanley was his adopted name. It rather brought up the whole question of what names meant, when one could simply choose. The entire realm of Arcane Taxonomy, which depended on accurately labeling the world, might become suspect if she thought too deeply about it.) He was white haired, typically distinguished in a suit and tie, long past his days exploring the African interior. Most of the photographs of him from that time showed him in a pith helmet, carrying a rifle. Hard to tell where the reality of him lay, after all the storytelling of his adventures. He did like to trade stories with Anton, though. His American accent was rounded with a bit of Welsh.

Ava listened in—mundanely, with her own ears—on the pretense of bringing a cup of tea to Anton.

Anton introduced them. "Sir Henry, may I introduce my stepdaughter, Miss Ava Stanley."

"No relation, I assume?" he said predictably, chuckling.

"Not that I know of, sir," she said.

"She's studying to be a doctor," Anton said proudly.

"A lady doctor? Well! How exciting." He didn't frown at the idea, at least.

Ava faded to the background while Sir Henry turned back to Anton. "I'm surprised Lord Curzon didn't recruit you for this expedition to Tibet he's cooked up."

Anton raised a brow. "Who says he didn't try? Younghusband can have it."

"What? You, refusing an expedition into the unknown?" He made it sound like the Conrad Zane novels.

"It's not unknown to the people living there," Anton said. "The politics of this one are too fraught for me. Is it truly a journey of exploration if he's bringing an army with him?"

Talk between two of England's best-known explorers drew attention. Ava wasn't the only one who lingered to listen.

"Part of the attraction of Antarctica is that no one's already living there," Bran said. He had enough adventuring credentials of his own to insert himself into the conversation. "By the way, who's their Arcanist?"

"Not sure," Sir Henry said. "Have you seen the list, Torrance?"

"It's the usual, the medical officer doing double duty. Fellow named Mackie? I don't know him."

"I do," Ava said. "Percival Mackie. He's published on infectious diseases, tropical fevers transmitted by insects and parasites. I attended a lecture he gave last year. He does good work, I think." He'd seemed young and earnest. She could picture him off adventuring in the high mountains of the Himalayas.

"Well, if you say so, my dear," Sir Henry answered, and Ava bristled. She might wish herself where Percy Mackie was right now.

"They'll need that know-how in that part of the world," Bran said. "But how is his Arcanism? I've never heard of him."

"I'm sure the expedition is more concerned with his skills as a doctor," Anton said. This was a long-running discussion between them. Anton brought along on his expeditions only Arcane Taxonomists who had plenty of other skills.

Bran turned to Ava. "Is he as obsessed with bacteria as you are?"

She didn't want to have this argument here in public. "And why not? It's a whole other world of species that need cataloging, just waiting for the right people to do it." It just wasn't as exciting when you needed a microscope, not to men like these. If you couldn't shoot it with a rifle, was it worth mentioning?

Before Bran could fire back, a bearded man in a dark-gray jacket butted in. "I've heard stories of Arcanism in that part of the world. Indian fakirs, Tibetan priests. They don't just use the power of the natural world. They can actually transform themselves. Make themselves birds or fish or whatnot."

"I don't put stock in that sort of thing," Bran said. "Just because we don't understand what they do doesn't make them supernatural."

Another man whom Ava had never met, though she recognized his name as that of a botanist and Arcanist from Oxford, said, "Torrance, if it isn't too forward, might I ask if any of your children have exhibited any talent in Arcanism?"

Anton and Bran both looked at Ava, along with the rest of the cluster. It was a lot of attention thrown at her at once.

"I take after my mother," she said. "Practicing Arcane Taxonomy, I mean. Not studying birds. I study bacteria. And insects. Anything, really. Maybe I'll be a medical officer Arcanist on an expedition someday."

The botanist, Sir Henry, and the others chuckled at this, as if she'd told a joke. Anton smiled thinly, and Bran just sighed.

"Not the boys, then?" Sir Henry asked, in what might have been a hopeful tone.

"Their interests lie elsewhere," Anton said tightly, a sign he was losing patience. No one else seemed to recognize it.

"That's what we all hope, isn't it? To have our sons follow in our footsteps?"

"Of course! You can't expect, but you can hope!"

Ava didn't need to see where the thread of this conversation was going. "If you'll excuse me, I think I'll get myself a cup of tea." One thing about England—you could always use that excuse for an escape.

She plunged through the gathering on a search for . . . for anything other than old men looking at her askance. Tea would give her hands something to do, so she made her way to the dining room sideboard, where a service was set out, and accepted a cup from the maid there.

Her mother was in the next room over, sitting in a chair by a window, drinking her own cup—they all needed the shield of a cup of tea today. She was watching the birds at the trays of seed in the garden outside. Everywhere they went, Beth put out food for the birds, whether plates of fruit for the toucans and honeycreepers in the jungles of Costa Rica or cakes of suet for the nuthatches and woodpeckers in the forests of Maine. This afternoon, the offerings appeared to have attracted blue tits and chaffinches.

When Ava approached, Beth glanced up and smiled. "How are you holding up?"

Ava pulled a nearby chair closer. "Oh, I'm all right. It just makes for a long day."

"It does. I can't say I knew Sir Archibald well. But I was always grateful for the way he took us all in without question. He was so happy when Anton finally married, he didn't seem to care how it happened."

"Cheerful," Ava said. "He was always so cheerful. I'll miss that."

"Yes."

They sipped quietly while Ava waited for her mother to say something about the trip. To argue again, but Beth stayed frustratingly quiet. The argument simmered until Ava couldn't stand it anymore.

"Do you think I can't do it?" she asked. "Is that why you don't want me to go?"

"No, that isn't it at all," Beth said, forcefully enough that Ava believed her. "It's just hard, letting go." She dabbed at the corner of her eye. Ava hadn't even seen the tears gathered there.

"I'll be fine. It's a simple trip to a place I've already been to. Hardly a real expedition, not like Anton and Bran have done."

"You don't have to go to the ends of the world to find danger," Beth said. "I'll worry no matter where you go."

It was so much like the conversation she'd overheard the other night. She had taken their worry as a sign of doubt. Maybe it was more a sign of love. Ava would try to regard it as such. "Can I ask you something?"

"Of course."

"Nobody ever talks about daughters following in their fathers' footsteps. Or their mothers', for that matter. It's all about fathers and sons. Why is that?"

Beth smiled, sphinxlike. "You know that doesn't really matter for any of us? I was under the impression you're not following in anyone's footsteps. I believe you'll be the family's first doctor. We're all very proud of you."

Ava gave her a look, brow raised, skeptical. Of course her parents, all three of them, would say they were proud of her. "Dr. Anderson has suggested I'm distracted. That I can be a doctor or an Arcanist, but not both."

Beth Torrance had traveled the world, studying birds and delivering lectures on the natural sciences. She adopted something of that lecturing tone now. Ava wasn't sure she appreciated having it directed solely at her.

"Arcane Taxonomy is the study of life. The essence of life. I can't think of any subject more suited to that than medicine. Hundreds of doctors have practiced Arcane Taxonomy."

"But what if . . . what if I'm not good enough at either? What if I am splitting my attention?"

"You're much too hard on yourself." Beth set down her cup of tea and glanced around the room, and Ava's heart sank. She knew what came next. With an elegant swish of her skirt and a determined stride, Beth retrieved a candle in a brass candleholder from the sideboard, a bit of light abandoned in the room for some forgotten reason. Beth set it on the table between them and crossed her hands in her lap, looking on expectantly. "Have you been practicing?"

Practicing suggested that Ava knew what she was doing. "I can't honestly say that I have."

Beth was undeterred. "Then draw on your instincts. Let go of rationality. Consider the *idea* of heat, rather than literal heat."

This was like trying to explain a poem to someone who didn't speak the language it was written in.

Beth went on, "When I think of the idea of fire, I only have to remember the fiery plumage of—"

"*Piranga olivacea*, I know." The bright-red plumage of the scarlet tanager would suggest fire to anyone. They'd had this conversation before. Maybe dozens of times. "But I deal with water, creatures that need dampness to survive. There's nothing about my work that suggests fire."

"You need metaphor, Ava. It's metaphor as much as it is power."

She could think of red, but so many of the specimens she studied were translucent, the color of water, or no color at all, because they existed in a world where color meant so little. Or they were the color of dirt, drab browns and tans designed to blend in with their surroundings.

The bright-red caps of *Amanita muscaria*, the famous mushrooms that instantly came to mind when anyone thought of mushrooms, the classic toadstool. Fanciful paintings of fairies using them as parasols. That wasn't a metaphor for anything, that was pure fancy. These mushrooms were toxic, and Ava supposed there was some fire there, an instrument of harm. She focused on this, hoping to form some solid *practicum* that she could deploy. Fiery red, the power to burn from within; she worked to impart this to the wick of the candle—

Toadstools needed damp to grow, and this overpowered all. A dewy moisture dripped down the side of the candle, a parody of the wax that would have dripped down if the wick had actually caught fire and burned.

They both regarded the sweating candle. Ava felt dejected; Beth seemed bemused.

"Well," Beth said. "That's not something I can do."

The only reason she wanted to be able to light a candle with a thought was that everyone expected her to be able to do so. "This'll come in handy if I'm ever stranded in a desert, I suppose."

"That's the spirit. But please don't get stranded in a desert—I'm not sure my nerves could take it." Beth licked her lips, a prelude to a serious observation. "There's quite a bit of talk in the journals that drawing Arcanism from microscopic life, from bacteria, simply isn't possible. There's never been a bacteriologist who practiced Arcanism. How can you possibly know a thing if you can't hold it in your hands, if you can't really see it?"

Ava almost pointed out that Beth's hands were likely covered in bacteria, or at least her gloves were, after she'd been standing in that receiving line shaking hands. "Bacteriology is only what, twenty years old? There's hardly been a chance for anyone to develop Arcanism around it." Her Fourth Rank came from her work with insects, invertebrates, and the odd fungus.

"Maybe you'll be the first." It was such a kind, motherly thing to say.

"Bacteria are everywhere," Ava said. "Even if we can't see them, we see the effects of them every single day. In a slice of cheese, a cup of wine." This line of reasoning wasn't going to make any headway with her. Beth studied what she could *see*. Not just that, she studied what was flamboyant, full of color and obvious behaviors. "Think of Darwin. Of evolution. All life evolved from some simple organism. The simplest. From tiny, microscopic scraps of life, like bacteria. It's where we all came from. It's all connected. Someone ought to be able to tap into that. Maybe not me, but someone."

Beth flicked her fingers like she was brushing lint off a tablecloth. The wick of the candle hissed and flared, and a yellow flame burst to life, settling into a steady light, exactly how one expected a candle to behave.

"You make it look easy."

"I've been doing this for quite a long time," Beth said. "Have you considered . . . you're trying to catalog branches of life with thousands of species. Perhaps if you specialized."

Ava shook her head. "I just need to find the right species, make the right discovery. Then all the pieces will fall into place. It'll all make sense." She had a suspicion, though—call it a hypothesis—that she shouldn't *have* to specialize, not when all life was connected, when one group of animals preyed on another, when fungi grew on trees and algae depended on water and bacteria grew everywhere. But this was an old discussion that always seemed to draw them into the weeds until they were cross with each other. "I'll figure it out. I'll just . . . figure it out. Somehow."

FOUR

Saccharomyces cerevisiae

Southampton

Ava paid the carriage driver an extra tip when he grumbled about how much luggage she was bringing to the dock. She didn't feel the need to explain that it wasn't all hats and gowns. Then she would have to explain her work, and he would either be confused or disgusted.

There was the ship, the *Penelope*. Though its single funnel was quiescent, it bustled with preparation, horses and wagons bringing loads in and out, porters carrying crates and carts full of supplies, luggage, cargo up on deck and down into the hold, crew scurrying everywhere. The scene was familiar, but it somehow never got old. It was an overture, a prologue: the start of a journey, the beginning of something new. She had boarded plenty of ships, but this time was different. She was on her own, not trailing along with her swarm of a family.

She missed them, just then. The pier felt emptier than it should, despite all the activity. She was both thrilled and melancholy, and the contradiction was strange.

The farewells that morning had lingered. There at the end, Ava wondered if they would even let her go. Everyone had hugged her hard.

Archie got in a few of his favorite jabs one last time, how she was too serious and bossy and he wouldn't have her any other way. Harry implored her to write, and she promised, as soon as she could. Beth cried a little, and Bran gave her well-meaning but confusing advice about studying hard and practicing her Arcanism but also not losing herself in the work.

Out of all of them, Anton's farewell had been simplest. He'd kissed her on the forehead and said, "I'm so very proud of you." Only then did Ava feel like she wanted to cry. She flashed on a memory, one of her earliest, the first time she'd met Anton, when he returned from his Antarctic expedition. Only an image, this great man looming over her, held in Bran's arms, and his big beaming smile. All these years later, that had never changed.

God, she was going to start crying. Time to move forward.

Other passengers lined up at the gangplank, and she looked them over, curious. In the back, a stern-looking man with a full mustache wore a worn suit and carried a leather case in one hand, a cane in the other. He wore a bowler cap low on his head, which made it hard to see his eyes. Next came a man and a woman. The man was giving instructions to one of the porters and seemed urgent about it, speaking loudly and slowly, as if he doubted he was being understood. The woman—his wife?—seemed young and stood quietly aside, her gaze downcast. Ahead of them, an older woman was moving up the gangplank. Well dressed, serene, she seemed to be an experienced traveler, unaffected by the bustle.

The couple was occupied, so Ava moved past them to the gangplank, a narrow walkway with sturdy railings. There, she hesitated. An uncertain moment, the inner contradiction taking hold. Well, here she was. She still had time to turn back. Gulls wheeled and called over the ship. A horse nickered somewhere, and a stevedore shouted. At the top of the gangplank, a man in a felt coat and sailor's cap leaned on the railing of the ship, gazing over it all like he wouldn't wish to be anywhere else. The captain?

Valise in one hand, microscope case in the other, Ava marched up. Her hollow footsteps on the gangplank changed to more solid steps when she reached the main deck of the *Penelope*.

The man who must have been the captain was greeting the older woman.

“Mrs. Monroe, are you traveling alone?”

Ava listened for a tone of surprise, disapproval. Or was it merely a question, and she was reading too much into it? It must have seemed odd, such an elegant and obviously well-to-do woman traveling without even a maid.

“I am, Captain. I’m being met in Nassau.”

“Very good. Jones, come and help Mrs. Monroe to her cabin.”

“Yessir.” A young man trotted up. He was broad shouldered enough that his jacket seemed stretched across his back. Hard to judge his age; he seemed young, but was also frowning, serious.

On the main deck, she looked right at the captain. “Miss Ava Stanley. Also traveling alone.”

His lip curled in a wry smile. “Indeed. Welcome aboard. Captain Hallern, at your service.”

As with the deckhand, his age seemed hard to judge. He seemed too young to be a captain. His light-brown hair, crushed under his brimmed cap, was a bit long and windblown, even though the air was still. His face was clean shaven, with crinkles at his eyes, like he was always at the edge of laughing.

The sleeves of his jacket were rolled back, and his left hand was missing. A dinged-up, well-used metal hook of a prosthesis took its place. Out of professional curiosity, she wondered what had happened: an accident or a congenital condition?

Mrs. Monroe lingered, studying her appraisingly, and Ava stood for it with what she hoped was an open, engaging manner, demonstrating that she was the kind of girl who could make friends. She wanted to make friends.

"Miss Stanley, how lovely to meet you," the older woman said finally, allowing a smile. Ava could pin her just by the way she spoke. English, very English, smooth and full of upper-class society. Her friends probably had titles and estates. Mrs. Monroe offered her gloved hand.

Ava was glad her mother had reminded her to wear her own. They shook. "Likewise, ma'am."

"You see, Captain?" Mrs. Monroe said smoothly. "We've already made friends. No need to worry about us lone women in the slightest."

"Never doubted it," Hallern said, clearly amused.

Jones, the deckhand, didn't meet their gazes as he picked up Mrs. Monroe's valise and started to reach for Ava's. She kept the microscope case, holding it with both hands. "I'll take this one. It's no trouble. Scientific instrument."

Jones shrugged and tipped his head along the deck. "This way, ma'am, miss."

Another sailor came up along the deck from the stern. Taller than Hallern, he had dark skin and short-cropped hair. He didn't pay the passengers any mind. "Cargo's settled. I'm headed to the wheelhouse."

Ava couldn't place his round, drawn-out accent, but she would bet it wasn't from the Caribbean. She'd try to find out where he was from.

"Very good, Mr. Suminwa. If you'll excuse me, ladies." Hallern tipped his hat and turned to follow his crewman.

Jones guided them to the stairs and up to the starboard row of cabins.

"You're American?" Mrs. Monroe asked Ava, falling into conversation with the ease of a lady used to moving in society.

"Mostly, yes," Ava said.

"Well, that's an intriguing answer."

"My family traveled a lot when I was growing up. I've spent as much time abroad, I think. I was born in Colorado."

"Ah, the Wild West."

Ava merely smiled and didn't mention that her mother had taught classes on natural history at a local college. Not very wild.

"And what takes you to the Bahamas?"

"Family. I've got cousins there. Also work. A little of everything."

"Work?" As if the idea startled her.

"I'm studying bacteria and collecting samples. Yellow fever, cholera, that sort of thing. I'm a doctor—well, I'm studying to be a doctor. I'm almost a doctor." Would Mrs. Monroe be horrified or merely disbelieving?

She nodded thoughtfully. "That sounds rather complicated. And also a worthy subject, if you can save lives."

"That's the plan."

Jones stopped at the first door, Mrs. Monroe's cabin. "I look forward to hearing more. I hope to see you at tea?"

"Yes, of course."

Mrs. Monroe disappeared within her cabin, carrying her air of mystery with her.

Ava's cabin was on the next row, smaller and not nearly so nice. Which was fine—all she needed was a desk to work at and a bed to sleep in. The rest of her luggage was already here. She snapped open the microscope case and checked it over. The packing was good; it hadn't budged, everything in order. The instrument had been a truly extravagant gift from her family two Christmases ago, and she was determined to take good care of it. She'd been making do with magnifying glasses before then until she got to school. It was a beautiful piece, the brass eyepiece and fittings contrasting with the blued tube, arm, and stand. A newer model, it had two lenses that rotated on the turret at the bottom of the tube, offering a range of magnifications. She could see more than ever.

After securing the case in the closet, she collapsed on the bed, a narrow bunk tucked up against the wall. She was here, she'd made it. The first step of the journey was finished. Staring up at the ceiling, she let herself be tired for a moment before getting a book on zooplankton out of her valise to read until departure. At the shouts of deckhands and the blast of the ship's horn, Ava emerged and made her way to the upper deck to watch the ship's departure, steaming away from Southampton. Since she was little, leaving every port, she'd hung on the rail and watched the dockyards recede, the stretch of ocean between her and the shore growing wider. She wasn't the only one watching. Passengers lined up along the starboard railing, many of them holding their hats on their heads against the breeze with one hand and waving with the other.

The *Penelope* carried both cargo and passengers. She wasn't a large ship, but she was trim and fast. They'd make the Atlantic crossing in about ten days. Her hull was painted black, with a white stripe around the top. The rails and cabins were white, and the funnel was brick red. As it picked up speed, the vessel cut through the water, and a mild chop crashed against the hull, a fine mist rising up. Gulls and terns followed, hunting for fish. She watched for curious dolphins, but didn't see any playing in the wake.

As the ship left the shelter of port, its speed increased, and smoke billowed up from the funnel, smelling of coal. It settled into a rhythm, a gentle, rocking pitch, the shape of the waves it traveled through. Around this time, passengers new to sea travel discovered if they were prone to motion sickness. At least a couple of those on deck started looking a little green.

Ava wasn't one of them. She turned her face to the breeze of their passage and filled her lungs. She relished the salt mist, the rushing sound of water, even the thump of the engine and screws. The shifting expanse of the sea surrounded her, and she thought of all the life hidden within it.

They'd been underway for a couple of hours when she headed for the passengers' salon, where an afternoon tea had been promised. A group had gathered in chairs clustered around a table. A tea service and trays of cakes and sandwiches had been set out.

Mrs. Monroe was there; she'd changed from her traveling clothes to a prim walking dress of gray with rose accents. She smiled graciously at Ava. "Come over and join us, my dear. Everyone, this is Miss Ava Stanley."

The others murmured greetings. Ava recognized several of them from boarding. The loud man and his quiet wife, memorable because of the contrast, were Mr. and Mrs. Brannock. He worked for an investment firm in London and had business in Nassau and Florida. The stern-looking man with the impressive mustache was French, also traveling for business interests: Mr. Luis Marchand. He gave Ava a polite bow when they were introduced and seemed unmoved when she greeted him in French. Another woman sat in a chair by the window, gazing out, a cup of tea in her hands. Mrs. Bell, also traveling by herself, had apparently been adopted by Mrs. Monroe as well. She gave Ava a quick flash of a smile, then turned back to the window.

Ava accepted a cup of tea and took a seat by Mrs. Monroe.

"Another woman traveling alone?" Mr. Brannock said, grinning. "We've got a regular suffragette society on our hands."

Ava was planning to ignore him and ask Mrs. Monroe about where she'd traveled, which seemed a much more interesting conversation. But Mrs. Monroe smiled serenely. "Does that frighten you, Mr. Brannock? A whole squadron of independent women?"

Mrs. Brannock revealed no emotion. Her husband chuckled, a moment of confusion dimming his gaze. "Where are all your husbands? What must they be thinking, letting you all loose like this?"

"Dead," Mrs. Bell said. "My husband is dead."

If not for the distant pounding of the engine, the silence after that would have been absolute.

Brannock could only stammer. "Hm. Yes. Well then."

"It's wise to not ask questions to which you might not like the answers," Mrs. Monroe said. Ava decided she'd do well to stay on Mrs. Monroe's good side.

"I'm sorry for your loss, Mrs. Bell," Ava said politely, hoping she sounded kind.

"Thank you," Mrs. Bell answered, and sipped her tea.

Marchand rescued them from further awkward silence. "I have never been to Nassau. I hear it is hot? Hotter than Marseille in summer?"

"Oh, it's beautiful," Ava said. "Ocean, beaches, palm trees—it's as pretty as a picture. It isn't so very hot when the breeze is blowing off the water. But you probably don't want to wear a wool coat."

"Good advice," Mrs. Monroe said. "You're quite familiar with the islands, then?"

"My stepfather was born in Nassau. He still has family there, and I'll be visiting them."

"You seem well traveled for someone your age," Mrs. Bell said, her voice soft. Easy to miss, if you weren't listening.

"I suppose I am."

"Where all have you traveled, then?" Mr. Brannock asked.

"Oh, all over the States. Also Alaska, Costa Rica, Peru, Australia, Egypt—"

"Oh my," Mrs. Monroe said. "You really have been around the world."

Twice, in fact. "My parents are naturalists. They travel for their studies and brought us kids along when we were growing up."

Mr. Brannock issued a huffing interruption. "Your mother, a naturalist? Well, that explains things, I suppose. Next thing you know, you'll all be wearing trousers."

Blushing, Ava suppressed a scowl, too annoyed to think of a good response. Mrs. Monroe didn't have that problem. "You object to women pursuing professions, Mr. Brannock?"

"I simply don't understand why you think you need to," he said, with sneering confidence.

"Because we can," Ava said. "That's it. We're able to, so why not?"

Mrs. Brannock stood, setting aside her teacup with a clatter. "I think I need to get some air. If you'll excuse me."

"If you aren't feeling well, I have some ginger candies," Mrs. Monroe said. "They've always helped when I feel a bit of seasickness."

The quiet woman seemed thrown off by the offer. She hesitated, hand on the door. "Oh . . . thank you, but I'll be all right, I'm sure."

Mr. Brannock didn't acknowledge her departure, just kept drinking tea and chewing on a bit of cake.

As she left, Captain Hallern passed her on the way in, glancing back with curiosity. His jacket was unbuttoned, his stride loose. A picture of professional nonchalance.

"Well, here we all are." He had a light East London accent to go with his easy manner. "Everyone settled in?"

"Smooth departure, Captain," Marchand said. "I commend you."

"Why, thank you, sir. If you need anything at all, please come to myself or my first mate, Mr. Suminwa."

"The African man on deck earlier?" Brannock said.

"He's Congolese, yes."

"Can you trust him?" Brannock said.

For just a moment, Hallern's ease tightened, his smile thinning. "I trust him with my life. And so do you, since he's helping run the ship."

"Trust the men to do their jobs, why don't you," Mrs. Monroe said, her voice a purr. Brannock had the grace to look awkward, shifting in his seat and grimacing over his cup.

Hallern was about to tip his cap and take his leave when Ava spoke up.

"Captain Hallern, if the weather's good in the next few days, might I drop a sieve over the side to collect samples?"

His response, a baffled, brow-furrowed expression, was entirely predictable. "I'm sorry, what?"

"A sieve. A net made of muslin attached to a hoop and line. To collect plankton."

"Plankton—"

"Very small sea creatures. I study them. Well, I study lots of things, but I thought I might as well take advantage of the opportunity."

"That box you were so protective of—that was a microscope, I assume?"

She brightened. "Yes, sir."

"Well, I suppose. But don't fall overboard." He said this so good-naturedly, with such obvious amusement, she couldn't be offended. He might have been confused by her, but he didn't question her. It was the best she could hope for.

"Of course."

"I'll assign one of the deckhands to help."

She didn't need help, but it was easier to accept the offer and stay in the captain's good graces than argue. "Thank you."

"You follow in the naturalists' footsteps, then?" Marchand asked.

"I do."

"Fascinating," Mrs. Monroe said. "Just fascinating. May I pour you a bit more tea, dear?"

Days on a ship involved a certain amount of tedium, a sameness to the schedule. Ava and her brothers had learned early on how to entertain themselves and each other. She was missing them now, the way they'd egg each other on to trouble or settle in for card games and reading. Now, she had only herself to rely on. She wrote the first of her letters to them, describing the ship, the other passengers, and the usual excitement of setting out on a new voyage.

She encountered the Brannocks several times, but hardly ever together. Mrs. Brannock was apparently prone to seasickness and would travel between her cabin and the rail. She refused any offers of help or tricks. Ava told her it was better to stay outside in the fresh air, to watch the horizon, which was stable, to diminish the feeling of stomach-turning rocking. Mr. Brannock seemed to spend a lot of time at the stern, watching the wake churn behind them, or going up to have a look at the wheelhouse.

Mrs. Monroe spent much of her time in the salon and library. She always seemed to know just what to say, asking polite questions while offering select details about her own situation. Her husband was in the Foreign Office and had had postings in India and the Caribbean. While she didn't go into details of his exact job, Ava could speculate: She was a diplomat's wife. Her easy manners and cool demeanor would make her perfect for the role. That raised the question: Where was her husband? Was she going to meet him in Nassau? She managed to deflect direct questions.

After breakfast on the second morning, Mrs. Monroe invited Ava to take a walk around the deck with her. Ava accepted, and they paused by the railing to watch the sea. The rippling, steel-gray sameness was hypnotic, intriguing. Ava could study the water for hours.

"It looks to be a good day for fishing," Mrs. Monroe said, holding the railing with a gloved hand. "That's what you proposed to Captain Hallern, yes? A kind of fishing?"

"I suppose so. Though you wouldn't want to eat the catch."

"Well, I approve. Pay no mind to Mr. Brannock and his ilk. Girls should find things to keep them busy."

Most women Mrs. Monroe's age looked at Ava askance when they learned that she'd gone to school, that she studied medicine, that she had *ambition*. They disapproved. They couldn't imagine a young woman in such a role. But Mrs. Monroe seemed unconcerned.

"You remind me of my mother," Ava said, thinking of the way her mother was also unconcerned by what others thought and yet was so self-possessed no one could criticize her. Ava could never learn how to maintain a respectable public face, and she blamed that on growing up in a household full of friendly men. "The way she holds herself. Very precise."

"One has to be precise, moving in some arenas. When one must demand respect, to be taken seriously. Your mother likely understands that."

"I never learned the knack of it," Ava said. "I never needed to."

"There's always time."

Mrs. Bell came up the deck toward them, hesitating, uncertain. She gripped the rail, pursing her lips. "Do you mind if I join you?"

"Of course not, my dear," Mrs. Monroe said, smiling. "We lone women must stick together."

Mrs. Bell slouched a little, sighing. "I confess, I haven't felt . . . comfortable. So many strangers. I'm not used to this." By *this*, she might have meant travel, being on a steamship, or being alone, a widow. Maybe all three. She seemed nervous. She wasn't wearing gloves and wore no rings. Her dark hair was wrapped in a tight bun, and the straw hat she wore was simple, with a narrow, undecorated brim.

Mrs. Monroe spoke gently. "You must forgive me—you aren't in mourning, so may I assume Mr. Bell died some time ago?"

"It was last month, but I didn't want to draw attention. I . . . I don't like to speak of it."

She didn't seem to like to speak of anything.

"My mother's first husband died quite young," Ava said. "She said nothing felt right for months after. She still misses him, I think."

"Did she love him?" Mrs. Bell asked.

Ava tilted her head. "Yes."

"Well then." Mrs. Bell turned back to the water, impassive.

Pressing her lips in an expression of sympathy, Mrs. Monroe exchanged a glance with Ava. She seemed to understand more than she was saying.

The three of them walked together until lunchtime, talking of this and that, but nothing of consequence.

After lunch, Ava found the library in the next compartment over from the parlor and dining room. Of course she scanned the shelves, looking for interesting field guides or expedition journals. What she found was a complete set of Conrad Zane's Torrance and West adventures. From the first, *Torrance and West and the Fires of Mount Erebus*, to *The Karakoram Quest*, *The Secret of the Incan Tomb*, and *The Beast of the Red Sea*, right up to the latest. All right there with the rest of the novels, everything from Jane Austen to Charles Dickens to George Eliot. Not that the dime-novel adventures rated such august company. The books seemed well read, the spines loose and the edges of the pages soft. In spite of herself, she reached for *Torrance and West and the Terror of the Zambezi*. She'd left her copy with her brothers. She might as well find out what happened next. Just for the sake of completion.

The weather held through the next morning, so Ava brought out her sieve, a shallow basin, and vials and found a spot on the main deck, starboard side, close to the water. The quiet, serious deckhand named Jones appeared a moment later, shirt buttoned up, neat and presentable, as if he'd been ordered to clean up. Hallern had warned the crew what she was up to.

"Hello," she greeted him.

"Miss."

She shook out the sieve and checked the line on the fishing reel she'd rigged up for it. Bran had helped her put the device together a couple of trips ago.

"Miss—" Jones reached for her, clearly thinking she was about to tip over when she leaned on the railing.

"Don't worry, I've done this before." Her feet never left the deck, though other times she'd climbed up on the railing to get the best angle. She didn't want to give the poor guy a heart attack.

The reel spun, and the cloth sieve dropped and hit the water with barely a splash. Water passed through the cloth, which skimmed the surface like a water-laden flag. She counted to sixty, watching the cloth merge with the water, rippling along with the speed of the ship.

She gathered a small audience. Mr. Marchand watched from the rail toward the bow, smoking a cigarette pinched between thumb and forefinger. Mrs. Bell was taking a walk but stopped, hand coming to her face in apparent surprise when she saw Ava leaning over the rail. Mr.

Suminwa gazed down from the deck above, outside the wheelhouse, as if he watched a street magician of dubious talent.

The ocean was a protean realm of chaos. Gray, interrupted by bursts of chop and broken waves, elemental, indecipherable. But it was not featureless. Seabirds dove because they saw fish. In the distance, an elusive spout from a whale's blowhole indicated that the immense creatures lurked close by. A dolphin's dorsal fin broke the surface and vanished. Observing these things, one must know the ocean contained worlds.

The tiniest drop of its water contained worlds. There was power here. Even a pint of seawater might contain something new. Some larval form, some scrap of life somewhere between plant and animal, or something else entirely. If only the creatures could tell her what they were. Sometimes, this felt little better than drawing up a ton of earth from a mine without having any way to differentiate the minerals.

After a minute, Ava reeled in the line. The cloth sieve rose dripping to the railing. She set it in the basin she had filled with seawater and turned the cloth inside out, releasing whatever was there into the water. A few specks showed up against the white ceramic of the basin.

Jones knelt on the deck next to her to see what she was doing. Some bits floated, and on first glance one might have thought they were just scraps of seaweed or debris. A second look revealed a couple of fluttery specimens no bigger than her little fingernail, scudding jerkily in the water. Some crustacean larvae or daphnia species. The insubstantial film of a tiny jellyfish. Not much, but enough to make the exercise worthwhile.

"Would you look at that?" Jones murmured.

"Some species of Copepoda, I think. And a Pelagiidae." She scooped the tiny creatures into glass vials to have a better look at them under the microscope.

Suminwa called down to her from the upper deck. "Most young ladies on the ship read books or paint watercolors to pass the time. The sea is a very popular subject for watercolors." His shirtsleeves were rolled up, and he wore a kerchief around his neck. Gave him a rather roguish air, and he almost seemed to be laughing at her.

"Well, I paint sea monsters," she replied. "Very small sea monsters."

"We used to gather up clams and things in Dover when I was growing up," Jones said. He was still studying the vials of seawater, and the little bits of life within. "Never thought much about what the little buggers ate till now."

"They suck their food right out of the water. All kinds of things go on that we can't even see."

"Why're you so interested? If you can't even see them?" Jones asked.

Kneeling there on the deck, she had to think. What seemed obvious to her was more difficult to articulate. "Our whole lives are affected by things we can't see. All the diseases caused by bacteria. The cells in our own bodies."

"The decisions made by blokes in suits a thousand miles away," he said wryly, and she nodded in acknowledgment. Yes, so many unseen powers in the world.

"To name a thing is to know a thing," she said, quoting the tenet of Carl Linnaeus, father of Arcane Taxonomy. "And I would like to know more."

She'd collected enough samples to keep her busy for the next day or so, so she packed up her things. Jones helped her carry the equipment back to her cabin.

He took her by a back route, a narrow stairway that deckhands used to keep out of the way of the passengers. At the turn at the base of the stairs, he hesitated. Ava nearly ran into him. Peeking over his shoulder, she saw what had caught his attention: Mr. Brannock was there, speaking with another crew member, a stout man with a beard. An item the size of a cigar box changed hands, and they parted.

Jones and Ava kept out of sight, just inside the passageway where the stairwell let out. She wondered why all her instincts insisted that they not be seen. Maybe it was the way Brannock was looking over his shoulder, as if watching for onlookers. For spies. She held her breath, waiting, but the two men left by another way.

"Passengers don't usually come this way, do they?" Ava asked. "Who was he talking to?"

Jones shook his head. "He's from the engine room. Don't know him well. He just started this trip."

"I wonder what it was about."

"Smuggling happens sometimes. Passengers paying crew to carry things they shouldn't, to put things in the cargo hold. I wouldn't worry. I'll tell the captain."

Mr. Brannock, a smuggler? He seemed ordinary, if a bit boorish. Ava wondered if his wife knew. She couldn't very well ask.

Outside her cabin, they rigged up a hook where she could hang the sieve to dry. Jones bowed himself out, maybe a little less reserved than he had been before.

With the promise of smooth sailing, she'd already set up her microscope on the cabin's small desk. If the seas got rough, she'd pack it back up again before it could tumble over. She gave the mirror a quick polish and tilted it to bring in the light.

Starting with the copepod, she used a pipette to draw it out of the vial and set it, along with a drop of water, on a glass slide. Next, she pressed a coverslip, a thin glass square, over the drop to flatten it. She then clipped the slide onto the stage under the lens. A bit of focusing . . . and the minuscule scrap of life came into view, filling the lens, its every detail revealed.

A tiny little crustacean, it had a segmented body and collection of fuzzy limbs. Antennae almost the length of its body protruded from its front, and from its rear a kind of tail, narrow and pointed. *Calanus finmarchicus*? Maybe. She'd have to consult her books. Its limbs twitched, propelling it around in the thin layer of water that was its whole world.

Near the front of its body was a tiny, near-transparent organ, rapidly thrumming. Its heart. What intrigued her was the sheer ethereal nature of its physical form. It hardly seemed to have a body, its flesh transparent, its internal organs mere shadows.

She sketched every part of it made large by the microscope, from its whole shape to separate detailed drawings of the branching antennae, the curve of its digestive tract. She didn't need to attempt a dissection—not that she could; small enough scalpels didn't exist. If she had more time and space, she might try picking it apart with needles. Imagine it, so perfectly adapted to water, traveling through the ocean as insects traveled through air. So vulnerable, but it had evolved effective defenses: Invisibility. Stealth.

Light passed through Ava's hand. She gasped and nearly dropped her pencil. Taking a breath to steady herself, she tried again. *Calanus finmarchicus*. Invisibility. Stealth.

Her arm seemed to disappear—no, the outline of it was still visible, but only because she knew where to look and saw the blurred edges of it against the paper of her sketchbook. But she could see her pencil through her fingers. If she stood in front of the light, it would shine right through her. An observer who didn't know she was there wouldn't see her.

She set down the pencil and pressed her hands flat to the desk. Her heart raced, a flush making her sweat. Closing her eyes, she calmed herself. When she opened them again, her arm appeared normal, solid flesh.

She made notes, breathless scribblings of what she was thinking, how she had managed to take in the creature's most visible trait. She crossed out "visible" and wrote "prominent" over it, not impressed with the accidental pun she'd made. What was she feeling? What had she been feeling during the last few days, the first few days of her adventure? Thrilled, excited, daunted.

She glanced at the thin curtain over the porthole in her cabin. The light was low and diffuse, gold falling to gray. Dusk. Nearly suppertime. She'd lost track of the hours, so occupied with the thumbnail creatures under her microscope. She ought to clean up and change clothes.

Right then, she felt small. Lonely. No one around to remind her to eat, if she didn't do it herself. She dropped *Calanus finmarchicus* back in its vial and secured the microscope in its case.

FIVE

Escherichia coli

The group of them who'd met that first day had come together again at supper and coalesced around the same table in the dining room. They'd returned every night since, finding company via familiarity rather than any common feeling. No matter, they'd all go their separate ways at the end of the trip.

Mrs. Monroe might not have had a maid, but she appeared perfectly turned out in appropriate dinner wear every evening. Ava recognized the signs of independence—a stiffened bodice rather than a corset, all the buttons and fasteners in front. Beth Torrance dressed the same way. The elegant older woman reached for Ava and bade her sit next to her.

Mrs. Bell sat on her other side. At Mrs. Monroe's inquiry, she said that she'd spent the day on deck, resting. "I used to make drawings when I was young. I haven't had the urge to draw in a long time, but I feel it coming back to me," she said.

Ava jumped in, eager to encourage. "If you need paper and pencil, I have lots. I'd be happy to give you some."

This seemed to startle Mrs. Bell, and she regarded Ava with blinking uncertainty before finally answering. "That's very generous. Thank you."

Mr. and Mrs. Brannock entered, along with Mr. Marchand, to fill out the table. Though Mr. Brannock held the chair out for his wife and assisted her, they hardly looked at one another.

"How are we this evening?" Brannock said after he'd seated himself. Polite affirmations went around. Mr. Marchand merely shrugged, then waved to the waiter to bring him a whiskey, part of his routine.

An empty chair had been added to the table, and the answer as to who it belonged to appeared shortly. Captain Hallern strode in, still buttoning his coat up deftly with his one good hand.

"Good evening to you all. I've been rotating tables among the passengers, and tonight it's your turn." He slumped into the chair without further ceremony.

"I've always liked the tradition of a captain dining with his passengers," Mrs. Monroe said. "It rather gives one a sense of belonging. Makes one feel that much safer in the middle of the wide ocean."

"Glad to hear it," Hallern answered.

Once he was seated, the waitstaff took that as the cue to begin the soup course. Small talk about the weather and the route they traveled continued. Hallern even coaxed Mrs. Brannock into saying a few words. She replied that her mild seasickness was much better, thank you very much.

"Miss Stanley, what did you find on your fishing expedition?" Hallern asked.

The trick to talking about her work in society was to go into enough detail to sound intriguing without saying so much that her audience became bored. Or disgusted. "*Calanus finmarchicus*. They're a type of crustacean. Think of them as tiny little lobsters, no bigger than a fingernail." She held up her thumb and finger, almost touching, as if that would give them any idea.

"It's amazing to think of it, isn't it? All that life just teeming, and we have no idea what's there." After Brannock's previous contempt, Hallern's enthusiasm was a comfort. She couldn't help but think well of him.

"Exactly," she answered. "We'll never come to the end of it." She was in danger of launching in on a lecture, but Mrs. Monroe spoke up.

"Miss Stanley," Mrs. Monroe said. "I had a question about your name, if it isn't too forward of me."

Ava was sure she'd happily answer anything Mrs. Monroe asked. "No, I'm not related to Sir Henry Morton Stanley."

Mrs. Monroe laughed. "Oh my, I hadn't even considered that. No, my question is rather more personal, I'm afraid. You mentioned that your stepfather was born in Nassau. Am I to understand that you didn't take his name when your mother married him?"

"No. She has a . . . sentimental connection to Stanley. So I kept it."

"I couldn't help but wonder if our paths have crossed, if I might have met your mother or stepfather, as well traveled as they are."

The question was leading, and Ava began to be suspicious of her tone. "I suppose it's possible, if you know any naturalists or explorers. They belong to a lot of societies and give lectures. They're Elizabeth and Anton Torrance. Anton is originally from Nassau. My mother is from New York. I got my accent from her."

Mrs. Monroe sat back in her chair, giving the slightest nod, her smile thin and knowing. Ava realized—she'd already known who her parents were. Or she'd guessed and was too polite to come out and ask. But Ava had the vague feeling that she'd been trapped into something.

Hallern's fork hesitated above his plate. "*The* Anton Torrance? The man who sailed around Antarctica in '82? Who nearly made it to the North Pole in '91?"

"Um. Yes," Ava said.

"Why didn't you say anything?" Hallern demanded.

"Was I supposed to?" she said, annoyed, trying to keep the edge out of her voice. "No one else has mentioned their parents' names."

"This Mr. Torrance, he's quite famous, then?" Mrs. Bell asked.

"He's made a name for himself in exploration," Ava said.

"And on the lecture circuit, if you're intrigued by natural history, adventure, that sort of thing," Mrs. Monroe said.

"Isn't that *exciting*!" Mr. Brannock declared with too much enthusiasm. "A real celebrity among us!"

"By proxy only, I think," Ava argued. Her first time traveling alone, she hadn't expected to be followed by her parents' reputations. Maybe she should have.

Mrs. Monroe tapped her finger thoughtfully. "Who was his partner on his travels? The Arcane Taxonomist. What is his name—"

"Mr. Brandon West," Hallern said, before Ava could.

"You must know him as well?" Mrs. Monroe asked.

"He's a good friend of the family, yes," Ava said as neutrally as she could.

"Well, no wonder you have a sense of adventure about you."

"Both Mr. Torrance and Mr. West encouraged my mother in her own studies," Ava said. "And my mother encouraged me in mine. Really, we're all just trying to learn more about the world."

The fish course arrived. Hallern pushed away his soup bowl. "There's a whole series of novels about them, if you want to know more. I think we've got a few in the ship's library."

Ava waved her hand dismissively. "Really, neither of them is anything like the characters in those ridiculous books."

Hallern studied her. "Ah. Then you *have* read them."

She'd said too much. "Only bits and pieces. Out of curiosity."

"Surely they aren't so bad." He leaned back in his chair, and she blushed. This was too much attention.

"They're sensationalized. Melodramatic. If you really want to know about Anton Torrance, you should read his travel journals."

"I have," Hallern said.

"Ah, you're a fan, then," Ava countered.

Now Hallern might have blushed, though it was hard to tell around his windblown complexion. "I appreciate a good adventure story. I . . . don't suppose you'd like it if I asked what Torrance and West are really like?" He scooped up a bite of fish and waited expectantly.

How could she even begin? More importantly, how could she divert the conversation to something less personal? "I expect my report would be rather biased."

Mrs. Monroe saved her just then. "I think what I'm most looking forward to in Nassau is the fresh fruit. Tell me, have any of you ever had mango? I very much recommend it."

The conversation moved on from there, to other foods of the Bahamas and how long it took to teach parrots to talk. Ava flashed Mrs. Monroe a grateful smile.

Dr. Anderson might have been right. Ava was spending too much time on her small Arcanist collection. She could fill up her sketchbook with drawings of what she'd seen under the microscope and be no closer to understanding anything. No power that she was drawing from these studies would help her pass her medical exams. But these creatures were ubiquitous, living all over the world. The oceans were connected, without boundaries. There might be no limit to their influence.

She could maybe use some boundaries. A better-laid-out path rather than hacking her way through the weeds. She was trying to map the whole globe rather than the country that was right in front of her. She put away her sketchbook and pulled out a physiology text. When her attention drifted and she found herself reading the same paragraph over and over, she set it aside and, almost against her will, reached for the copy of *The Terror of the Zambezi* she'd borrowed from the ship's library. These characters really were nothing like the men who inspired them; she couldn't imagine them teaching small children to swim, as Anton and Bran had. And yet she kept reading. Unlike those of the physiology text, the words just flowed.

She tilted her head, looking away from the desk. Something had caught her attention, without her realizing it had even been caught. Silence. The ship had fallen silent, the thrum of the engine gone still.

The motion of the ship changed, rocking with a lateral sway as forward movement ceased. The waves pushed the hull, instead of the hull cutting through them. They were adrift.

And then the lights went out, the electric dynamo shut down. Combined with the silence, the darkness felt absolute, and ominous.

She opened her cabin door. The night was partly cloudy, a little yellowing moonlight shining through. The air held a chill. The ship rocked disconcertingly. Captain Hallern must know something was wrong. He didn't need her rushing around asking for news. She would close the door and wait—

A gunshot banged out toward the stern.

Torrance and West and the Terror of the Zambezi

The great roar ahead of them, akin to a never-ending rumble of distant thunder, could only mean one thing: waterfall. Caught in the current, their small native canoe veered inexorably toward the rising mist, where the river plunged into an abyss.

"Pull for all you're worth, West!" Torrance called out.

"Without a doubt!" West shouted back.

With West working on the right, and Torrance on the left, the pair drove their paddles into the water again and again, straining to make progress against the current. The canoe turned, inching ever so slowly toward one side of the riverbank—and then was caught again, spun around, and sent back toward the deadly falls. The roar of water was now like the stampede of a thousand buffalo.

No one would ever deny the strength and determination of the pair of men, the supremacy of their wills. But they were growing tired, and relentless water was perhaps the most deadly element on earth.

"I have a suggestion," West called over his shoulder. "You won't like it."

Torrance grinned back. "You think we should let the canoe ride over the edge and hope for the best."

"Exactly!"

"Well, only one way to know how this turns out," Torrance said, drawing his paddle from the water.

They took these final few moments to tie lines to their gear, strapping it all down as best they could. From the front and back of the canoe, their gazes met one last time as they once again plunged together into the unknown.

The canoe drifted over the edge of the falls and followed the river down, to the mist and rocks below.

—

West was the first to rise gasping back up to the air. His hat was missing. His hair was soaked, and he shivered in the water. Around him, oilcloth-wrapped bundles of supplies drifted. He thought he might as well start to gather them up. The canoe was in pieces, shattered into bits of wood that floated around him.

"Torrance! Where are you?" he called.

No answer came. West called again, to no avail. He began searching the river, sweeping his arms through the water. Torrance might have been knocked out, trapped by debris. A hundred things might have happened, but there might still be time for a rescue.

Suddenly, a brown hand reached up. The body followed, Torrance bursting from the current and taking in air. Wildly, he looked around until his gaze rested on West. Then he laughed.

The pair trudged against the current to the boulder-strewn shore, hauling the boxes and bundles they'd managed to save.

"You gave me quite a scare just now, friend," West admonished him.

"Gave myself quite a scare," Torrance replied. "Now then, how are we doing?"

"The canoe is finished," West said, picking up a split piece of wood and throwing it aside. "We've got some food. Looks like one of the guns made it."

"Well, if we have a gun, food will take care of itself, I wager. Shall we continue on?"

"We've come this far," West said, determined.

For the moment, they rested, making camp by the riverside and building a fire to dry their clothes. They sat side by side, passing a flask back and forth, discussing their good fortune that the whiskey had survived. They watched the sun set over the jungle as birds and monkeys howled in the canopy overhead.

SIX

Streptococcus thermophilus

The crack from the gun echoed in the still air. Confused voices emerged from cabins. Someone toward the stern shouted. Running footsteps echoed on the deck below.

Something was wrong, but no bells or whistles rang, no alarms sounded. The engine remained silent, and the ship continued drifting. The funnel overhead was dead, not a lick of smoke coming out of it.

Ava shrugged on her jacket, buttoning it up as she headed for the stairs to the wheelhouse. Filled with foreboding, she rushed to find Captain Hallern or Mr. Suminwa, when she maybe ought to have been more concerned with stealth.

A silhouetted figure stood at the top of the stairs. With all the lights off, the ship was overcome with darkness; only moonlight and starlight backlit the figure, obscuring details. But then it spoke.

"Stop right there." Mrs. Brannock held a pistol aimed at Ava.

Ava froze, right there on the middle of the stairs, even as she vaguely thought that she ought to raise her hands in a show of surrender. She was gripping the railing too tightly and couldn't seem to let go.

"What is our little adventurer up to, hm?"

"It's just . . ." she stammered. "There's something wrong. With the ship."

"Yes, I know. Now, turn around and go back to your cabin, why don't you?"

Still, Ava hesitated, even as the back of her mind screamed to move, to do something, anything to get away from that looming pistol. It stood out, its metallic barrel reflecting the scant light.

"Go on," Mrs. Brannock ordered, crowding down the stairway toward her. Ava stumbled back obediently and let herself get herded toward the cabins. Another passenger opened a door and stuck his head out. Mrs. Brannock showed him the weapon.

"Get back in, lock the door, and don't come out again." The man obeyed instantly, much more alert than Ava currently was.

Her mind was spinning at the wrongness of this. She was a scientist, an Arcane Taxonomist—she must have some trick, some skill she could use to get out of this situation, to . . . to do what?

Famously, Bran could freeze time for a few seconds. Alter the function of compasses. But alas, she wasn't Bran. Being the child of two Arcanists didn't count for much when she could apparently only stand there gawping.

"What are you doing?" she finally burst out, rather stupidly.

"Never you mind. Now, get in there." They'd reached Ava's cabin door, still standing open. Mrs. Brannock planted a hand on her and shoved. Startled, Ava stumbled back into the room.

The cabin door slammed shut, and the clack and thud of a tumbler indicated the lock locking—from the outside. Mrs. Brannock must have a key. Must have all the keys and control of the ship, somehow.

Ava rattled the doorknob, which didn't budge. The door was well built and didn't move a millimeter in its frame. She was caught. Stuck. She leaned her forehead against the door and let out a shuddering sigh. Outside, shouting continued, along with footsteps. Some organized mayhem taking place, led by . . . Mrs. Brannock? That made no sense.

The woman who'd pointed a gun at Ava was nothing like the quiet, mousy thing she'd eaten supper with the last few nights.

That was the point, wasn't it? It had all been a ruse.

Ava needed to be able to hear what was happening. The earwig, *Forficula auricularia*. Stay hidden, stay quiet. She closed her eyes, steadied her breathing. She wouldn't be able to do a thing if she wasn't calm. Think of infestation, of getting in everywhere, unseen until it was too late.

Her senses reached out, becoming shadow, infiltrating.

". . . a few passengers started a fuss, but they're no worry now . . ."

". . . then the ship is ours . . ."

". . . did you find it?"

"No, blast it. We'll search the bitch's cabin—it has to be somewhere . . ."

That was Mr. Brannock. So they were working together. But to what purpose?

The rumble of the ship's engine returned, jolting Ava out of her concentration. Once again, the ship shuddered with the usual background noise and movement. The lights stayed out. She had a vague sense of the ship turning, and a look out the window confirmed the stars overhead shifting, a change in direction to a new course.

She tried again, summoning the quiet, ubiquitous presence of *Forficula auricularia*, but the engine noise drowned out the distant voices, and without a target to focus on the power slipped away from her. Where was Captain Hallern? Mr. Suminwa and the rest of the crew? A terrible thought: They were dead. The gunshot had been aimed at someone.

Where was the *Penelope* being diverted?

She was under no illusions that she could stop whatever act of . . . of piracy was happening. Pirates! Like something out of a Conrad Zane novel. Ridiculous. Wouldn't Harry and Archie be impressed?

She also couldn't just sit here and wait. Apprehension overcame her—what had become of Captain Hallern and Mr. Suminwa? The rest of the crew? They wouldn't have given up the ship without a fight. Mrs.

Brannock seemed willing to kill. Who had that gunshot been meant for? Ava needed to get help. Maybe she could get to the radio room and send a distress call over the wireless. She would simply have to find a way to stay out of sight while she did so.

The first step was breaking out of her cabin.

She wasn't large or physically powerful, and this wasn't a matter of brute force but rather a targeted application of just the right effort. She felt around the doorknob, the lock. Painted wood, good condition. In time, all things decay. The fate of all wood on the planet was to someday rot away into nothing. *Cryptotermes domesticus* could bring down a whole house, given enough time. Even more insidious, undetectable until it was too late: *Serpula lacrymans*. Dry rot. A fungus, actually, but what mattered less than its classification right now was its effect on wood. An infested piece of wood would simply crumble under one's touch.

Ava gave the handle a sharp tug. The wood around it fell apart, crumbling into a stinking mess. The entire lock mechanism dropped away.

Well. Wasn't that satisfying?

She traveled along the deck by feel, scant starlight, and the nighttime gleam reflected off the sea. Every noise made her flinch. With every turn she expected to find someone ready to shoot her.

Calanus finmarchicus. She mouthed the words, attempting to use what she'd recently learned, to take in the creature's transparency. To move without anyone knowing she was there. The invisibility only took hold on her hand, then her arm, then her other hand. Coming in and out of focus, inconsistent and useless. It was an ambitious *practicum*. Maybe now wasn't the time to practice something she wasn't sure of.

Her mother would be able to do something like this straight off.

She managed to reach the upper deck, and then had to explore a bit to find the wireless room. It would be near the wheelhouse, which she very much wanted to avoid. If the ship had been taken over by an enemy, they'd be there. She could be quiet, even without Arcanism. She'd sneaked around her family a thousand times. Nothing to it.

Turned out, the wireless room was helpfully labeled by a brass plaque. The cracks around the door were dark. No lights inside. She paused to listen and heard nothing. All she had to do was get in, lock the door, and send a message to someone, anyone, calling for help.

She went in, pausing to let her vision adjust to the darkness—and a despondent weight nearly overcame her. The wireless device had been shoved off its table, the innards pulled out and strewn aside. No way to call for help now. Unless she could think of some *practicum*, some way to use Arcanism to send a message across hundreds of miles—

Something grabbed her from behind, and she cried out for half a second before a gloved hand covered her mouth. Arms wrapped around her, pinning her.

A light appeared: Mr. Brannock, holding a lantern. And yes, there was a pistol in his other hand. Soft yellow light filled the room but only clarified the scene a little. The person behind her was a burly man in crew's clothing, securely restraining her no matter how hard she struggled, kicking and twisting to wriggle out of his arms. He was implacable.

Whatever the Brannocks had planned, they'd had help among the crew. She wondered how much and if Hallern had been in on it. She hoped not.

"You were right, love," Mr. Brannock said. "Waiting here brought out all the troublemakers."

Mrs. Brannock stood outside the doorway, her arms crossed. Ava would very much have liked to spout curses at her.

"Put her with the others," Mrs. Brannock said, and Ava's captor hauled her out of the room.

"What in God's name is this about?" she exclaimed. She didn't get an answer, not that she expected one.

They didn't drag her far. Just to the other end of the deck. Another door opened, releasing a musty, soapy smell. Some kind of a supply cupboard, large enough for a rack of rain slickers, boots, life preservers and lines, buoys and flags, buckets and mops, all manner of useful items for running a ship. It was also large enough to keep a half dozen prisoners secured, and Ava's questions about who was in on the conspiracy and who wasn't got an answer.

A few gasps and exclamations of protest greeted her, from captives who'd come before her. The conspirator threw her to the floor, wrenched her hands over her head, and tied her wrists very snugly to a cleat attached to the wall. Struggling, she tried to twist free, but it was a good sailor's knot. By the light of Brannock's lantern, she had a chance to look around.

Mr. Marchand was tied up beside her. A bruise was blossoming below his right eye. Gilda Bell was to his left. She wore a coat over a walking dress, and her hair was coming out of its bun. Both were disheveled, clearly from a fight. On the other side of the room were Mrs. Monroe, who somehow seemed as serene and elegant as ever, not a hair out of place, wearing the same neat dress she'd had on at supper; Mr. Suminwa, who regarded the proceedings with a watchful manner; and Captain Hallern. They were each tied up, out of reach of the others. No chance of mutual assistance.

Hallern's prosthetic had been taken from him, so one hand and the stump of his arm, amputated some three inches below the elbow, were tied over his head. The rope around the truncated arm was so tight it was cutting off circulation, causing swelling. Hallern seemed sanguine about it. He grinned at Brannock with contempt.

Apparently unaffected, Brannock regarded them with a narrowed gaze until he stepped over to Ava. She could kick him, trip him. Bust up his knee. She tried, aiming the solid heel of her boot as she struck. He was ready for it and deftly sidestepped.

Then he grabbed her chin and forced her head up.

All the prisoners reacted. "Leave her alone!" Suminwa called, and Marchand cursed in French.

Still, Brannock seemed unaffected. He squeezed her jaw, pinching the skin. She wondered: If she tilted her head just right, could she bite him?

Chuckling, he shoved her away, glancing over his shoulder at his wife. Was she even his wife? "This one might be worth some ransom."

"Hm, perhaps," Mrs. Brannock replied.

"Tell me, Miss Stanley. Is Anton Torrance the kind of man who loves his stepchildren or resents having to care for another man's brats?"

Anton Torrance had been a father to her her whole life. "You seem determined to find out, don't you?"

He kicked her leg, an obvious threat that he could do whatever he liked with her. This inspired another lurch of protest from the other prisoners—all for nothing. They were all tied up, helpless. Of them all, Mrs. Monroe never moved, didn't even flinch.

"I'm not afraid of you," Ava said brazenly, stupidly, when it was so clearly a lie. Fear inspired the declaration in the first place.

"Well, bloody good for you, you chit." He made a slow circuit of the room and stopped next at Mrs. Monroe's feet. She met his gaze calmly. "This one is definitely worth some ransom if she can't help us any other way."

"You overestimate my value," Mrs. Monroe said.

"I don't think I do, madam. It's such a little thing, after all. If you tell us where you've hidden it, you'll be much more comfortable in the long run, I assure you."

"I've no idea what you're talking about," she said.

Ava was sure that she did, in fact, know what he was talking about. She was also sure that no threat would make her tell.

Brannock leaned in, grabbed a chunk of her hair, and twisted her head back. The men in the group shouted, attempting some chivalric defense despite their helplessness. Mrs. Monroe bore the abuse like a seasoned soldier.

"Enough of this," Mrs. Brannock said. "We'll find it without her and tip the lot overboard when we don't need them anymore."

"It's worth trying for ransoms," Brannock insisted.

"Yes, yes. Later. Come along." She held the door open and gestured Brannock through. Obediently, he marched on. And wasn't that a switch?

She banged shut the door, and the light left with them. A couple of portholes let in the unsatisfying nighttime aura. It was just enough to let her see the shadowed faces around her, silvered like ghosts in a photograph. Ava shut her eyes and tipped her head back against the wall, focusing on her breath, ignoring the racing beat of her heart. There must be a million Arcanist *practica* she could use to get out of this. If only she could keep her mind still enough to think of them.

How aggravating, that her mother was so worried that something terrible would happen, and she turned out to be *right*.

"Miss Stanley, are you all right?" Hallern demanded.

"Well," she said thoughtfully. "I'm tied up in a smelly room, so not particularly. But I'm not injured, if that's what you mean."

"Why us?" Marchand complained. He sounded more frustrated than scared. As if he'd spilled wine on his shirt and not been kidnapped. "I'm not worth any ransom, I can tell you."

"We're the ones who broke out of our locked cabins," Mrs. Monroe said wryly. "The troublemakers."

"They put on quite an act, didn't they?" Hallern said. He seemed almost amused. Maybe even impressed. "We all thought she was so meek."

"Yes, it was quite the act," Ava muttered, yanking uselessly at the ropes binding her. The knots were so secure they'd have to be cut. She regarded them thoughtfully.

Suminwa glanced over. "Mrs. Monroe, what exactly are those two looking for?"

"Really, I couldn't say." They might have been having tea in a parlor, as steady as she seemed. How did she do it?

"I beg your pardon, but I think you could say," he replied. "The ship's been stolen out from under us, and I'd like to know why."

"I think a much more pressing issue is how do we escape from this," Mrs. Monroe said. Suddenly, she looked across the room. "Mrs. Bell, are you all right? Are you hurt?"

Mrs. Bell hadn't spoken yet. She opened her eyes and looked. She might actually have been sleeping. "Yes, I'm all right, thank you. Apart from being a bit uncomfortable."

Ava could have laughed. They were all being so . . . so *English.*

Hallern started picking at his ropes, trying to loosen them, or slip out. He winced with pain; his injured arm was clearly swollen.

"Captain, stop," Ava said. "You'll hurt yourself."

"Dammit," he muttered under his breath.

"They're good seamen's knots. Alas," Suminwa said.

"Are anyone's ropes the least bit loose?" Hallern asked. "Is there a chance of getting out?"

Ava could. She was certain. Almost certain. "Do you have a plan? For when we get free?"

"Honestly, I hadn't thought that far ahead."

"What I mean is that I can break us out of here if you have a plan to confront the Brannocks and retake the ship."

He stared at her. They were all staring at her, or whatever shadow of her they could see in the dimness. They must have thought she was mad. How could she ever make good on such a claim? Well, if she couldn't, this was going to be awfully embarrassing.

"Yes," Hallern finally said. "I think I do."

Serpula lacrymans had worked on the door; no reason it wouldn't work on rope as well. She had studied the fungus's cells and branching tendrils under a microscope. Such a tiny thing, and so destructive. Six sets of ropes. If she really concentrated, she could destroy every rope in the room. But she only needed to disintegrate these six.

The power surged. When she gave her arms a sharp tug, the strands of rope snapped apart. Rotten pieces fell away. The others followed her lead. The captain, Suminwa, and Marchand. Mrs. Monroe and Mrs. Bell. It could have been done more spectacularly, the ropes disintegrating into nothing so that they fell free without effort. But this was good enough. Suminwa rushed over to help Mrs. Monroe and Mrs. Bell to their feet. Ava was up before he could get to her.

Hallern was back to staring at her. "You're an Arcanist."

She shrugged a little. "Only Fourth Rank."

"Well, it's good enough for this. What else can you do?"

"Some eavesdropping. A bit of cleaning. I'm not really sure what else. I've never been in a situation like this before."

Hallern stifled a laugh. "Neither have we."

Mrs. Monroe put a hand on Ava's shoulder. "Dear, why didn't you say anything? To have such a talent—"

"It usually isn't relevant."

Mrs. Monroe donned a wicked smile. "Anything's relevant if you make it relevant. So, Captain. How do you plan to take back your ship?"

SEVEN

Mycobacterium tuberculosis

"First thing's the wheelhouse, I think," Suminwa said softly. They all spoke softly in this terrible game of hide-and-seek.

Hallern was poking around. From the corner he pulled out a couple of oars and set them in the middle of the room. A coil of rope, a life preserver. Anything that could be used as weapons in a pinch. He did this one-handed, keeping his amputated arm tucked against his chest.

"Captain, does your arm hurt?" Ava asked.

"What?"

"Your arm. It's swollen. If it's injured, I can look at it. I'm a doctor. Well, I'm almost a doctor."

"You're not quite a doctor, not quite an Arcanist," Hallern said. "I wonder—what are you?"

Marchand took one of the oars from him and hefted it like a club. "I will fight."

"Miss Stanley," Suminwa said. "If you have any way of finding out where our thieves are and how many of the crew are working for them, that would be most useful. Meanwhile, you ladies should wait here."

"I think not," Mrs. Bell said, and Mrs. Monroe's stance, straight and glaring, said the same thing. If the men expected the women to be weeping in terror, they must have been surprised. "We will not wait if we can be of help."

"We're in this as much as you are," Mrs. Monroe said.

Sighing, Suminwa shut his eyes briefly, as if he was marshaling an argument. "Then perhaps you can keep a lookout? One on either side of the upper deck."

Giving him an annoyed look, Mrs. Bell picked up the other oar.

Meanwhile, Ava was ransacking her memory for all the ubiquitous bugs and mites and fungi that might give her access to other parts of the ship. Her parents had been known to see through the eyes of birds on the other side of the world. They had scouted for Anton's expeditions from hundreds of feet in the air, through the eyes of arctic terns, *Sterna paradisaea*. Surely she could find a way to see other parts of the ship.

In the end, she'd used *Forficula auricularia* before, so she used it again. The difficulty this time was settling her mind enough to be of any use. She kept rubbing the rope burns on her wrists, some part of her astonished that Brannock had inflicted pain on her on purpose. She kept edging close to panic and having to haul herself back. For all her adventures she'd encountered very little real danger in her life. The other five seemed supernaturally calm, as if they faced pirates or similar dangers every day.

Maybe they did.

"Miss Stanley?" Mrs. Monroe prompted, as if she could tell the state of Ava's mind.

"Please, call me Ava. I'm sorry, I just need a quiet moment."

"You have it. Stay right here with me." Mrs. Monroe edged up to the railing and looked out to the decks below.

Ava leaned up against the wall and closed her eyes.

Earwigs got everywhere. They crawled into the walls and burrowed into curtains, infested food stores. Now, she tried to do the same. To listen all over the ship, to make her way into every corner to learn anything that might be of use. What she sensed first was what was happening right here on the upper deck.

The darkness benefited them now. Hallern and Suminwa stuck to the wall and crept toward the bow, to the wheelhouse. One man was inside, the crewman who'd helped Brannock lock them up. A pistol rested on the surface next to him, in easy reach. Hallern and the others might be able to overcome him before he could shoot. Or they might not.

Ava had a sudden thought, one of those bolts of inspiration that were so welcome and so rare, the insight could jostle itself right out of her head. She held on to this one and tried, just tried. The most useful thing she could do would be to disable whoever was in the wheelhouse. Remove any need for a fight before the men even got there. Knock them all over.

She had never used Arcanism directly against another person. Conventional wisdom and training discouraged such direct attacks—they tended to backfire. But indirect . . . knock them over without touching them. Maybe she could do this. If her life, if all their lives depended on it? She steeled herself to try. No, she *must* do this.

Imagine the slimy trails left behind by *Deroceras agreste*, garden slug. Imagine a floor covered with them, so thick and gooey one couldn't take a step without sliding. One couldn't hold onto the wheel, unable to grip anything without slipping. Make it all slippery.

The door to the wheelhouse cracked open. A startled shout and the thud of a body hitting the floor followed. More thunking and knocking continued, the sounds of a man scrambling and failing to get to his feet, reminiscent of someone very bad at ice skating. The next ruckus was Hallern and Suminwa storming in. Ava dropped the *practicum.*

The fight ended quickly, and the wheelhouse was secured. There was one part taken care of. Meanwhile, Ava was supposed to find the Brannocks and their henchmen. Dividing her attention only made her more flustered. The ship had a hundred or so crew and passengers to search through. Likely, the Brannocks weren't even trying to hide. They thought they had the best of the situation. They'd said they were searching for something—something belonging to Mrs. Monroe.

Ava sat right there on the deck and covered her ears to block out everything else but what *Forficula auricularia* was telling her. "*. . . there's nothing here . . .*" "*. . . then she's hidden it somewhere else . . .*"

Snatches of noise, conversation, urgent and out of place on a ship in the middle of the night. The sounds of boxes being knocked over and smashed, steps running across the hold. A crowbar wrenching open some crate. If only she could *see*. She had no context, only scraps of sound, from which she tried to build information. This was what Harry experienced all the time, she thought suddenly.

Harry seemed very far away just now.

"Miss Stanley?"

She startled awake, as if shaken from a trance. "What? Did it work?"

Hallern knelt beside her, close enough to touch. She almost reached out to grab his arm, relieved that she wasn't alone in this. But she refrained.

He'd acquired a gun, either from Brannock's man in the wheelhouse or one of his own. "We've recovered the wheelhouse, if that's what you mean."

Mrs. Monroe and Mrs. Bell knelt on her other side, all of them looking at her with concern. Had she fainted? Had some kind of fit? Insight fell on her, the bits of noise piecing together to form a picture that, if not entirely clear, at least started to provide clues.

"I think the Brannocks are in the hold," Ava told Hallern. "Smashing up cargo. Looking for whatever it is they're looking for."

"Any idea where the rest of the crew is?" Hallern asked. "I refuse to believe that every single one of my men was bought off."

"Is that what happened with the man in the wheelhouse?" Mrs. Monroe asked.

He shook his head. "He was a newer man. Seems the company brought on a lot of newer men for this trip. All secretly working for Brannock."

"So this was planned," Mrs. Monroe said. "A conspiracy."

"I suppose you would know better than I," Hallern said to her accusingly. "What exactly do they think you have?"

"Later, Captain." Mrs. Monroe's tone brooked no argument.

Hallern ducked into the wheelhouse, where Suminwa was checking charts on the table. "Suminwa?"

"Things are well in hand here. You go find our men."

"Yes, sir," Hallern said, stepping out again to where Marchand stood keeping watch at the railing. "Marchand, with me."

Ava prepared to follow them down to the lower deck. The other women were right with her.

Hallern turned on them. "No, you three are staying here."

"I don't think so, Captain," Mrs. Monroe said with studied pleasantness. "I know you mean well with your chivalric impulses, but do trust us to be of some assistance."

"Bloody hell," he muttered predictably. "All right. I suspect whoever of my crew is loyal are locked up in the bunks or galley. We won't try to confront anyone until we get more people on our side. You take this—I suspect you're the better shot." Hallern handed his pistol to Marchand.

Marchand grinned, his shifting mustache changing the whole shape of his face. "Indeed I am."

"He was a sniper in the French army," Hallern helpfully explained to the others.

"You never told us that!" Mrs. Bell exclaimed.

"Eh, I am on holiday," Marchand said, shrugging. He didn't seem entirely disappointed about getting unexpectedly called to action.

"Marchand, Mrs. Bell, you take the port side. Call out if you find trouble. You two, this way."

Ava went with Mrs. Monroe and Hallern down the starboard side of the ship. She worked very hard to be quiet, keeping to the same shadows Hallern and Mrs. Monroe seemed to cling to naturally. She didn't want to give anyone a reason to rebuke her. And why did all the others seem to take to this situation so naturally? Ava was swept along like a leaf in a storm. After this, her medical exams wouldn't seem nearly so daunting.

If only she really could be of some use. She mentally gathered the collection of *practica* she'd already used, as if they were arrows. She need only to deploy them, while also moving cautiously, while also being aware of every pop and creak of the ship around her, the thud of the engines and the near darkness that made moving around so much harder.

Forficula auricularia, Forficula auricularia . . .

A commotion intruded on her awareness. Footsteps moving up stairs, from a couple of decks down.

"The Brannocks have left the hold," Ava whispered. Not that anyone needed her *practicum* to know this; the footsteps grew audible quickly enough. Hallern urged them to the wall and waited.

If Ava could make them all quiet, invisible. There were *practica* that could direct someone's attention elsewhere, like a killdeer feigning a broken wing to lure hunters from her nest. Like butterflies with the images of giant eyes on their wings to mimic predators and frighten off attackers. Goodness, it was fascinating to think of; she ought to be writing all this down.

Focus, she must focus. She recognized the Brannocks' voices.

"Set a watch, there and there . . ."

"If we threaten the woman . . ."

"I don't think that will work. She's been at this game a long time."

"Blast it all . . ."

The conversation drifted away, and Ava's attention snapped back to her present self.

"Miss Stanley?" Mrs. Monroe was studying her. Hallern was looking ahead, out and around, for the enemy.

"I can almost hear them." She shook her head, unwilling to explain how she could almost but not quite understand. "They're setting a watch."

"I don't suppose you have some Arcanist trick that can, I don't know, put them all to sleep? Freeze them in their tracks?" Hallern suggested.

She threw him a glare. "That sort of thing only happens in those terrible dime novels." Of course, an hour ago she would have insisted she couldn't possibly overpower an enemy with her Arcanist *practica.* But she had.

"They're not *that* terrible," he argued.

"Captain," Mrs. Monroe urged softly.

"Right. We'll go around, then."

Hallern knew all the ins and outs of the *Penelope* and led them on a roundabout way beyond the passenger cabins, into a narrow passage the crew used. A metal ladder rather than stairs led down. Hallern gave the two women a skeptical frown, then must have thought better of saying anything. He simply started climbing, deftly balancing with his one hand. Monroe urged Ava to go next. She also thought better of arguing. Mrs. Monroe seemed to be the type who rarely lost arguments. Twice they heard voices, and Hallern paused. Ava wished for shadows to hide in. For the attribute of being tiny, invisible. *Calanus finmarchicus* might have worked for herself; she had no idea if she could affect the rest of the group. Could she extend the invisibility of this *practicum* to anyone else?

Belowdecks, they met back up with Marchand and Mrs. Bell. Marchand kept the pistol held at his side and seemed eager for the hunt they were on. Mrs. Bell was alert, interested.

Hallern led them to a section with a steel door. The crew bunkroom. Without a word, Marchand took up a watch position at the end of the corridor. Monroe and Bell stood out of the way. Hoping to be useful, Ava parked herself against the opposite wall and once again tried to keep track of the Brannocks and their pirates.

Footsteps seemed to travel up the stairs. They were going back to the upper decks. Suminwa had locked himself in the wheelhouse; he should be safe. But Ava wished she could warn him.

"If we can't threaten her, perhaps one of the others. That Stanley girl," Mrs. Brannock said.

"I thought we were going to hold her for ransom."

"Well, we've got to do something, and I don't hear you making suggestions!"

What on earth were they looking for?

"The Brannocks are going back to the upper deck," Ava said. "They'll likely discover we've broken free soon."

The hatch had a simple sliding bolt across it. It was for securing bulkheads in case of flooding, not locking in prisoners. Hallern slammed open the lock with his right hand; the left stump remained tucked up by his chest, as if it pained him. The steel door fell open of its own weight, and the men inside pressed forward. Even with a few portholes, the room was nearly dark.

"Captain!" one of them called, others murmuring and rumbling around him.

"Quiet, all of you!" Hallern looked around until his gaze settled on one man in particular, a burly deckhand. "Rafe, report."

"God, where do I start?"

Hallern replied patiently. "How many of the crew does Brannock have working for him?"

"If you count who's missing from here, it's ten."

"All from that new batch?"

Rafe hesitated at this, which seemed to bode ill. "Not sure, I'm afraid."

"Anyone hurt?"

"No, sir. They caught most of us asleep and had their own people on watch. I'm sorry they got us so easily."

"We were all caught flat footed," Hallern said. "It's supposed to be a bloody passenger cruise, not a naval expedition."

He ordered the engine chief and his men to the boilers to protect the ship's bowels. The deckhands, he organized into units to confront the pirates. It sounded dangerous and messy.

"You want to turn the bilge into a brig?" Rafe suggested. "Or just toss them overboard?"

"Isn't that tempting?" Hallern said. "Let's get through this next step. Ladies, can I please beg you to get to your cabins and stay there?"

"We're going to see this through," Mrs. Monroe said. "And I think you need Miss Stanley."

"Well then. Let's get a move on."

Ava was rather thinking she'd like to go back to her cabin. Hallern was beginning to look harried, with shadows under his eyes and a stiffness in his shoulders. Ava was still worried about his injured arm.

Hallern mapped out a plan that placed his loyal crewmen at various points on deck and at stairs. They would sweep each deck, take custody of any enemy crew they encountered, and prevent the Brannocks from leaving the upper deck. Hallern planned to corner them and demand their surrender. To Ava, the plan seemed to offer lots of opportunities for people to get hurt. She'd rather not have to use her medical skills tonight.

"You're absolutely sure they've moved to the upper decks?" Hallern demanded of Ava.

She flushed. "I'm mostly sure. The Brannocks, yes, I think so. I don't know about the rest of them. It's . . . Arcane Taxonomy isn't an exact science. That's rather the whole point of it."

"I didn't know women could be Arcanists," one of the crewmen said blankly.

"Well, you were mistaken," Hallern explained before Ava had to. He flashed her a smile, and she beamed back at him in spite of herself.

"Would the plan be any different if you didn't have Miss Stanley's advice?" Mrs. Monroe said.

"No, I suppose it wouldn't. The tactics remain the same."

"Well then."

Ava tried to help where she could, drawing on stealth, a dozen creatures she knew of that moved silently, from spiders lingering in the corners of a room to the mold that overtook a piece of fruit. She hadn't thought of any of those things as stealthy. What she thought of was the surprise felt by anyone who turned around and saw an arachnid crossing a pillow or lifted the lid off a dish to find their food spoiled.

Exactly what their adversaries felt when they turned around and found a whole gang of men ready to overpower them.

In trying to influence what was happening elsewhere, she lost track of the Brannocks. Her attention strayed—rather, she couldn't pay attention to this many *practica* at a time. Not many could, she reassured herself. Still, this wasn't a time she could afford to fail.

They had once again split up, Marchand and Bell on one side, Hallern and Monroe with Ava on the other, each with crewmen to stand watch and take custody of anyone they captured. They were two decks below the wheelhouse when Ava stopped and leaned on the railing, grasping for the ability to eavesdrop and struggling to listen. All she heard was the ocean, waves rushing against the ship's hull, scuffles between sailors a deck down, audible to everyone. She winced at a sudden ache in her head; her overstretched power had fallen still.

Mrs. Monroe noticed her distress. "Miss Stanley?"

"I've lost them," she confessed. "I can't hear anything."

Hallern looked up past the railing of the upper deck, which was empty for the moment. What lay above was a mystery. "Well, nothing for it but to push on."

He plunged ahead with what Ava thought was rather reckless abandon. Mrs. Monroe charged after him, fearlessly. What could Ava do but run after them?

Then a voice called, "Stop!"

Reflexively, she turned. She shouldn't have, she shouldn't have hesitated in the slightest. But her body reacted before her mind could make the decision.

Mrs. Brannock stood halfway down the row of cabins, holding an axe in both hands. A gleam in her eyes revealed an eagerness to use it.

Help. Ava's lips mouthed the word but made no sound. Not so much as a scream to alert Hallern and Mrs. Monroe that she was in trouble. Her throat was frozen.

"You," Mrs. Brannock muttered accusingly, threatening with her soft English accent. "You, stop right there."

What would Bran or Anton do, caught in this situation? Freeze time, swing a cane to crack against an enemy's skull? For that matter, what would Torrance and West do? Ava's mind scattered, thinking of three different *practica* she might deploy to hinder Mrs. Brannock and get away. Make the floor slippery, raise the temperature of the air, put holes in her shoes. The Latin turned over in her mind in a jumble. *Calafin auriflorae* or some such nonsense that didn't mean anything.

"I . . . I'm no threat to you. I don't have any weapons." Ava backed away but ran into the railing by the stairs.

"You're leverage. Hold a gun to your head, and the others will fall into line, I wager." Mrs. Brannock's leer seemed so odd and out of place on her. So unlike the woman Ava had first seen by the gangplank back in Southampton.

"You were so quiet," Ava said lamely.

"Discounted me completely, didn't you? You of all people should know better."

Mrs. Brannock took a step forward, and Ava crept back along the railing. She had so few options of where to flee. The deck was narrow, and Mrs. Brannock would be on her before she could get up or down the stairs.

"Now, dear, why don't you go back to your cabin and stay there? You don't have to be involved in any of this."

"I already am, I think." She backed up again.

"Yes, well." Mrs. Brannock raised the axe and charged.

The handle was wood. This was something Ava knew how to do. In fact, by now, she'd had an awful lot of practice at it. But her targets before this had been stationary, not coming right at her with speed.

She had nothing to lose, and so lashed out with the *practicum*, even saying the words out loud as if that might help. *"Serpula lacrymans!"* Crying out, she ducked and raised her arms to protect herself.

As the axe swung down, the head went flying, a missile spinning over Ava to land and slide away on the deck beyond. Stunned, Mrs. Brannock stared at the remaining bit of handle, which was crumbling at one end, the wood turning to a rotten mess.

"What? How—" She was only bewildered a moment before swinging the remaining length of handle like a club, right at Ava.

The blow struck Ava's shoulder, and she yelped, stumbling to the deck. Rotten all the way through, the rest of the wood crumbled.

Ava scrambled to her feet and ran. Not that it did any good when Mrs. Brannock lunged forward, grabbing her skirt. Ava slammed back down, and Mrs. Brannock was on top of her, hands reaching for her jacket, her hair, her neck. She would have to ask her mother and Bran about how one was supposed to concentrate enough to use Arcane Taxonomy in a fistfight, assuming she ever saw them again.

In a sudden fury, she kicked up and caught Mrs. Brannock in the gut. She drew back, grunting. Ava tried again to run away, and again Mrs. Brannock lashed out, grabbing her, hauling her back and swinging a punch. She'd clearly been in fistfights before. So had Ava—with her brothers. But however rowdy they were, they'd never come at her with this ferocity.

Mrs. Brannock shoved. Ava's head struck the deck, inciting a ringing in her ears. Clawing her hands, she swiped, putting all her strength behind the blow, and managed to catch Mrs. Brannock's cheek. Mrs. Brannock snarled.

A cry distracted them both. A string of French curses that Ava hadn't learned but suddenly wanted to. Mr. Marchand raced up the stairs from the deck below, full of fury and determination. Pistol in hand, he aimed at his target. Mrs. Brannock threw herself behind Ava, denying him a clear shot.

Ava was getting tired. And frustrated. She took advantage of Mrs. Brannock's hesitation and shoved her in the chest, hoping to give herself time to run away. Get behind Marchand and his pistol, preferably. But the damned skirt provided lots of fabric for Mrs. Brannock to get hold of. Ava only got a couple of steps forward before her adversary dragged her back. Marchand shouted again. Mrs. Brannock was trying to get her arm around Ava's neck, and Ava just wanted to get *away*.

Ava shoved. With her whole body, she threw herself at the other woman, hoping to knock her over and gain a little time. Get Mrs. Brannock off her feet, just for a moment—that was all she needed. And it worked, sort of. Mrs. Brannock stumbled, losing her balance, and Ava pressed the advantage, digging in her shoulder, shoving again.

Mrs. Brannock went over the rail. And since she still had hold of Ava's skirt, Ava went too.

Ava shouted in shock and surprise. Mrs. Brannock did not. Somehow, in a flailing panic, they both grabbed hold of the edge of the deck, outside the railing. Gasping for breath, Ava scrabbled to get a better grip; her hands already ached, cramping. There just wasn't much to hold on to, and her legs were swinging in air. A couple of decks below was the main deck, a broad expanse of planking. Too far down to survive a fall.

"*Tiens*!" Marchand ordered.

Brannock was swinging beside her. Too close. Snarling at Ava, she kicked her legs up in an effort to dislodge her. Ava tried to dodge, her hands threatening to slip. Tried to return the blows. Then, just like that, she'd had enough.

"Deroceras agreste!"

Mrs. Brannock squinted at her, confused. And then her hands slipped. Just slid right off the edge of the deck, as if they'd been dipped in oil. She gasped out a bitten-off scream, and her skirt billowed around her as she fell.

Ava turned away, but she heard a bone-splitting thud that gave off a hollow echo. She kept her eyes shut tight, unwilling to see what the next moments brought.

"Miss Stanley. Ava, look at me. Take hold. Please." Marchand was leaning over the rail, reaching for her. She whimpered; she wasn't sure she had the strength to reach even that little distance. "Come along. You must." He gestured, urging her. His gaze was hard, determined. He would not allow failure, would accept no other option.

Giving an extra kick, she willed herself upward, reaching until she thought her shoulder would pop out of its socket, and Marchand stretched to grab hold of her. With her hand in both of his, he hauled her to the top of the railing, slinging her half over it before collapsing to the deck himself. She was able to spill over the rest of the way, nearly falling on top of him.

They lay there, gasping for air. Ava shivered. The night suddenly seemed cold.

Perversely, Marchand chuckled. "Is lucky she slipped."

Ava nearly started crying. "She didn't. I made her slip. I did it. I killed her." She was meant to be a doctor. *Do no harm*, that was the oath; she wanted to help people, to save lives. Who did she think she was? She rubbed her face to stop the sudden stinging in her nose and eyes.

"Ah." Marchand didn't ask for an explanation. Didn't need one. "Don't think of that. Not just yet."

"Have you ever killed anyone?"

"*Oui*. Yes. I have." He said it so matter-of-factly.

"Thank you. For saving me. *Merci*," she managed to get out.

He only flashed a smile. "Can you stand?"

She had to think about that. She didn't want to stand. She wanted to curl up right here and not think about anything. They had to find the others. Holding the railing, she pulled herself up. Marchand put a steadying hand on her shoulder, warm and comforting for all his brusqueness.

She happened to look over the side, to the main deck. The body sprawled there was little more than a dark shape, a black outline under starlight. A skirt splayed out, two booted feet stuck out at odd angles, arms curled. Mrs. Brannock lay face down. There must have been blood, but Ava couldn't see it from here. Just another strange shadow on the deck.

"Come. Miss Stanley, please come." Marchand urged her away from the rail. Slowly, she followed.

EIGHT

Rhizobium leguminosarum

Who were the Brannocks, and what were they after? This was certainly a more complicated mystery than the origin of an outbreak of *Vibrio cholera* in a London neighborhood. Ava couldn't solve this one with a microscope. At this point in a Torrance and West adventure, West would wave his hands to cast some Arcanist spell, and the prize the Brannocks sought would glow blue and rise from its hiding place to be discovered at the heroes' convenience. In one of Conan Doyle's Sherlock Holmes stories, Holmes would direct Dr. Watson to the culprit, and with a few Latin words, Watson would compel a confession from them. All would be well, wrapped up in a tidy package, everything making perfect sense.

Nothing about this situation on the *Penelope* made sense.

Once the crew spread out on the decks, the mutineers were outnumbered. In short order, Hallern's men captured them and put them under lock and key. In the end, they surrendered easily. None were willing to die for whatever cause the Brannocks had recruited them to.

Ava and Marchand continued to the wheelhouse, where Suminwa had control of the ship.

"Where's Mrs. Bell?" Ava asked as they climbed the next set of stairs. The last she'd seen of her, Mrs. Bell had been with the Frenchman.

"I do not know. I turned and she was gone." Marchand seemed unconcerned.

"What if she's hurt?"

Marchand merely shrugged. Ava desperately hoped she hadn't been tipped over the railing or knocked out somewhere.

When they reached the upper deck, Marchand paused behind the shelter of a wall, inching around to have a look, holding the pistol at the ready. Ava stayed back, suppressing a gasp when she realized she'd been holding her breath. She had to strike a balance between not making any noise and not passing out because she'd forgotten to breathe. Slow and careful. Just stay calm. She could panic once this was all finished.

Daring to close her eyes, she steadied herself and tried to throw her awareness out, to once again sense what was happening beyond where she could see. She heard footsteps, voices, but not clearly enough to make out what they were saying. A headache started pounding in her skull. She'd overextended herself.

"Come out or I will shoot them!"

Ava didn't need Arcanism to hear that: It was Mr. Brannock.

Marchand whispered a report. "They are outside the wheelhouse. Brannock has a gun. The captain is in front of Mrs. Monroe. Mr. Suminwa is still locked inside, I think. Do you think he will come out?"

To save the captain? "Yes," Ava murmured.

"I think I can get him." Marchand crept along the wall, sighting along the pistol. Ava really hoped he was a good shot.

But that little bit of movement was too much. Brannock spotted him.

"Monsieur Marchand, do put down your weapon. I can kill them before you can fire, I'm sure you'll agree."

"Might be worth it to get him to shut up," Marchand muttered. "You say you're a doctor, yes? Perhaps I only wound him?"

"Please don't risk it," Ava said. "I haven't passed my exams yet." As if passing exams would somehow magically give her the skill to treat bullet wounds. Not that she wouldn't try, if it came to it.

What would her parents do, what would her parents do . . . Ava was quite sure none of them had been shot at. They wouldn't know what to do in this situation either.

Marchand stepped from the wall, holding the pistol up by the barrel, hand off the grip. Slowly, he knelt and laid the weapon on the deck. Every movement slow and calm, so as not to set off Brannock.

"Ah, and Miss Stanley is with you. You come out, too, my dear."

The urge to simply turn and run, to hide away in some other part of the ship, was powerful. But that wouldn't do any good, would it? She ought to be able to do something to stop all this. Rot the deck out from under him. Summon a fog they could use to escape. Too many possibilities, and no chance to practice.

She stepped into the open with Mr. Marchand. Hallern and Mrs. Monroe glanced back briefly. The captain's expression was taut, gaze burning, lips pursed with anger. Mrs. Monroe revealed no emotion at all.

"Mr. Suminwa, this is a revolver," Brannock said. "I have enough shots for all of them."

The bolt on the wheelhouse door slid back. Suminwa emerged slowly, halfway between Brannock and the others, some twenty feet away. He showed his hands, empty, his manner nonthreatening.

Then Brannock grunted. Confusion crossed his features, his brow furrowing. His whole body stiffened.

Mrs. Bell reached around him and grabbed the revolver out of his hand.

She'd sneaked up behind him, with no one the wiser. Calmly, she watched as Brannock collapsed. The hilt of a chef's knife protruded from his rib cage, the blade inserted between his fourth and fifth ribs, right behind his heart. Blood rapidly soaked the back of his jacket. Quite matter-of-factly, Mrs. Bell regarded her gloved hand, rubbing the fingers together, smearing a bit of blood on the fabric.

"Captain?" She offered him the pistol she'd taken from Brannock. He seemed confused for a moment before taking the weapon and shoving it in his coat pocket.

"This . . . this isn't the first time you've done this," Mrs. Monroe observed, nodding at the body, her lips thin with tension, the first sign of nerves she'd yet revealed.

Mrs. Bell shook her head. "This was how I murdered my husband."

After everything else that had happened this night, the statement was far less shocking than it should have been. "Good lord!" Hallern leaned against the wall outside the wheelhouse, putting his truncated left arm against his forehead. "What a night."

Sweating, dizzy, Ava leaned on the railing and worked very hard at not fainting. She'd seen dead bodies before, hundreds of them. She'd dissected bodies, for God's sake. She'd never once fainted at the sight of blood, so what was wrong with her? She looked around at the others, at each of them, at how calm and unbothered they seemed. Even Mrs. Monroe regarded the dead Mr. Brannock as a small annoyance, not as a murder that had taken place in front of her.

"You've all killed people before, then?" Ava asked, her voice shaking a little.

At first, no one answered, which was itself an answer. Mrs. Monroe finally said, "Not so personally as this. Indirectly, perhaps."

And what on earth did that mean?

"Miss Stanley caused Mrs. Brannock's death," Marchand explained. "It has upset her."

"I didn't mean to," Ava said, pleading almost. "I didn't want to!"

"Oh, my dear," Mrs. Monroe said. "You mustn't let it overcome you. She would have killed every one of us in a heartbeat. You saved the rest of us."

"I'm pretty sure you all could have saved yourselves just fine."

Suminwa stood at the open door of the wheelhouse. "Charlie, are we secure?"

Hallern sighed. "I need to see how the mop-up is going, but I believe we are secure."

"Then come in—I have something to show you." He patted Hallern's shoulder and went back in. Hallern followed, and so did the rest of them, of course. Unwilling to be left out of any part of the adventure.

At the door of the wheelhouse, Ava hesitated, unable to look away from Brannock's body. He'd bled out quickly. His jacket was growing sticky as the blood cooled. If she turned him over, she imagined the look of surprise would still be on his face.

Mrs. Bell stared at the body as well, but instead of looking dismayed, she seemed satisfied. Her lips pressed in a line. She peeled off her gloves and tossed them on the body.

In the wheelhouse, on a table against the back wall, Mr. Suminwa arranged charts, putting the wide sheets of paper side by side and pointing.

"See here," he explained. "The new course they set goes south. I think they meant to take us here." He tapped a second page. Mrs. Monroe and Marchand leaned in to try to read it.

"What's our current position?" Hallern asked.

"Haven't had a chance to take a reading," Suminwa answered. "I think we are approaching Tenerife by now."

Well off course, then. "Where?" Ava said. "Where did they want to go?"

Suminwa looked up. "Cape Colony."

The very south of Africa. On the opposite side of the Atlantic from Nassau. Her stomach twisted at how far afield they were. "But why?"

"We'll find out," Suminwa said with determination. "Search the bodies and their cabin. Question their men. We'll find out."

"I think I might be able to help answer that question," Mrs. Monroe said. As poised as ever, she seemed . . . *authoritative* was the word. She took for granted that she'd be listened to. Ava would have liked to learn the trick of it. To be a doctor issuing orders, having everyone snap to attention.

Mrs. Monroe started unbuttoning her bodice.

"Hold on—" Hallern started, and Monroe merely raised her brow at him.

Undone, the top four buttons exposed the hint of a silk-and-lace camisole underneath and a packet of papers. This, she drew out, and deftly rebuttoned her bodice, a proper lady. The papers were folded in thirds and bound with twine. Handwriting marked one edge, but Ava couldn't make it out.

"I believe they were searching for this," she said.

Ava gaped. "And you had it the whole time?"

Mrs. Monroe was cool as a cucumber. Unflappable.

"But what is it?" Hallern asked.

She nodded. "Perhaps we could all sit somewhere to discuss. Order some tea."

Marchand laughed. "Tea, ah yes, that will fix everything. You English."

Perversely, a cup of tea sounded really nice just now. Ava almost laughed with him, but it came out as a gasp.

"Charlie, we should finish securing the ship," Suminwa said.

"Yes. And find our position. And search the Brannocks. God." Wincing, he rubbed the stump of his arm, still covered in rope burns and bruises. They all had bruises and abrasions, injured to some degree.

Mrs. Monroe left the wheelhouse. Gingerly, she knelt by Brannock's body and started tugging at his jacket.

"Oh, let me do that." Mrs. Bell rushed to her side. "You'll get blood all over you, and I'm already a mess." Mrs. Bell retrieved her gloves, rolled Brannock over, and started a thorough search of his pockets with Mrs. Monroe's guidance.

Hallern moved to Ava's side. "Are you sure you're all right?" His voice was low, full of concern.

She laughed a little, too high pitched, nervous. "It's like something from a Conrad Zane novel, isn't it?" She was trying to make a joke, but it came out sour. She felt wrong, from her scalp to her toes.

"Comforting in a way. In the dime novels the heroes always get out alive in the end."

"Are we the heroes, then?"

"I certainly hope so," he said, tapping the brim of his cap.

Over the next hour, dawn sneaked up on them, painting the sky gray and pink. They'd been awake all night, and yet no one made any move toward their cabins and sleep. Rafe, the crewman, arrived at the upper deck and reported that they'd caught most of the mutineers, but a couple were still in hiding. Mr. Suminwa continued to lead a search. Hallern said he would examine the Brannocks' cabins personally. Meanwhile, he ordered that the two bodies be secured in a quiet spot of the hold, and the blood cleaned up as best it could be. The rest of the passenger cabins needed to be unlocked, and the passengers reassured that all was well. Or at least as well as possible. Hallern ordered the cooks to prepare a good hot breakfast for everyone, right on schedule.

The ship had slowed to a crawl, just enough forward movement to keep cutting through the waves. Still determining their position before they changed course back to Nassau, Ava assumed. Her skin was thrumming with exhaustion, but her mind was too rattled to even try to sleep.

There was still the mystery to think of. The six members of their unlikely brigade gathered in the salon off the dining room, where they had privacy—and a fine tea service. Ava nearly lunged for a cup. Didn't bother with milk and sugar. Just drank down a hot cup and poured another. It cleared some of the fog and fear.

Hallern arrived and set a courier bag on the table, full of what he'd found in the Brannocks' room and on their bodies. He hadn't had a chance to interview their henchmen yet—he wanted to do it personally.

Suminwa came in with Hallern's prosthetic arm. It was grimy, the wood and hook smeared with something oily. "They'd tossed it in the rubbish bin on the main deck," he explained.

"Bloody hell," Hallern muttered.

"I'll get one of the deckhands to clean it up, shall I? There's one other thing," Suminwa said. "Jones is missing."

Jones, the unassuming deckhand. Ava hoped nothing had happened to him, but she feared the worst. The Brannocks had seemed like they'd have no trouble tossing overboard anyone they couldn't use.

"God," Hallern said, sighing. "Is he the only one?"

"Near as we can figure. We're still looking."

"Right." He sat heavily, jostling his amputated arm and wincing.

Ava pulled a bottle of lanolin ointment from her jacket pocket and offered it to Hallern. She'd briefly gone back to her cabin for it. "It should help with the rope burns and bruises."

He held out the bottle to read the label, then nodded. "Well. Thank you, Dr. Stanley."

"I'm not really—" She closed her mouth when he threw her a stern look.

Before Ava could think to offer to help, he got the bottle open one-handed, using some maneuver where he gripped it with his fingers while popping the cork with his thumb.

Hallern rubbed in some of the greasy stuff, covering the angry-looking rashes, and sighed. "Truthfully, it never really stops hurting. The injury goes deep."

The thick scars and bunched tissue told a story. "The surgery was rushed. An emergency?"

He didn't have to answer. But he did. "Back when I used to be Ensign Hallern in His Majesty's Royal Navy. Though it was Her Majesty's navy back then, wasn't it? Shot off in action. Stupid little shore skirmish in the Suez. Ruined the whole hand, and the surgeon decided it was easier to get rid of than try to fix."

"That probably saved your life."

He shrugged. "Got a pension out of it. And a discharge. Good Admiral Nelson notwithstanding." He waved the stump, a strange salute to the famous one-armed admiral from a century before. "Ah well. The merchant fleet took me quickly enough."

"The navy's loss," Suminwa said.

"Nothing of it. The Royal Navy never loses."

"The USS *Constitution*," Ava said, with a crooked smile.

He pointed with his stump, unselfconsciously. "Oh, we don't talk about that one. That was a fluke."

"The *Constitution*'s ship surgeon was an Arcane Taxonomist," she said, regarding the ship's victories against the British navy during the War of 1812. "No fluke."

"You Americans," he said with amusement.

Marchand came in next, washed up, his mustache trimmed, and wearing a clean jacket. For all his teasing about tea, he drank down a cup right away and sat heavily. "Is all well?"

"Well enough."

"But not good?" Marchand asked, brow raised. Hallern shrugged expansively.

"*Monsieur, merci pour votre aide,*" Suminwa said, offering a stylized bow with a salute. Marchand waved him off.

Last came Mrs. Monroe and Mrs. Bell. Mrs. Bell, who claimed to have killed her husband, and no one questioned it. No one demanded she explain. They never would have found out if all the rest of it hadn't happened. So what did it mean? Nothing. Maybe, right this moment, it meant nothing.

Marchand brought the women tea as they sat on a chaise. Monroe held her packet of papers in her lap. They all eyed it, curious.

"Well, here we all are," Hallern said. "To start, thank you for your assistance in recovering the *Penelope*. We owe you a debt, and I'll always be grateful. I trust we'll keep the ship well in hand from here on out.

"Next, I made some discoveries about our mysterious Mr. and Mrs. Brannock. I'm sure it will come as no surprise to learn their names were not Brannock. I wish I could tell you more, but half the papers in their cabin aren't in English. Care to make a guess what language they're in?"

"German, I'd wager," Mrs. Monroe said.

Ava's cup paused on the way to her mouth. Her mind had wandered, relishing the hot drink and the feeling of safety in the cozy little room. The word *German* crashed in on her. Suddenly, she was swinging over the main deck again, moments away from death.

She set the teacup on the nearby end table because her hand started shaking.

Hallern tilted his head, narrowing his gaze. "Yes. I also found a packet of German marks. Mrs. Monroe, I beg your pardon for phrasing it like this, but who the hell are you, really?"

"I do suppose I owe you an explanation, since you have all risked your lives in this endeavor. Whether you realized you were doing so or not." Even after everything, she seemed unflustered. She'd had time to smooth out her clothes and pin up her hair again. The rest of them still looked like they'd been tied up in a storeroom. "My husband works as an administrator for the Foreign Office. If I feel some kinship for you, Miss Stanley, it's because I too have spent most of my life traveling all over the world. China, Australia, the West Indies, Suriname. If I play some little part in Mr. Monroe's work . . . well then, isn't that the work of a wife?"

"Is your name really Monroe?" Hallern asked.

Mrs. Monroe gave him a look that would have been called coquettish if she'd been fifteen years younger. As it was, she seemed merely amused. Indulgent. "Really, Captain. You'll have us all questioning ourselves."

"That isn't yes," he said.

"My husband is Mr. Frederick Monroe. You can look him up. He's currently in Cape Town. Or at least he was the last I heard from him."

"Which was?"

"Several days before the *Penelope* left Southampton. By telegraph. You're probably aware that some work simply can't be done by telegraph or mail. It's too sensitive. The consequences too great if a message or document should be waylaid. Over the years I've acted as his courier, taking messages and papers to and fro. No one much bothers a respectable middle-aged lady among a raft of other passengers." She held up the packet she'd kept safely secured inside her dress. Not even the Brannocks had dared search there.

"This," she continued, "is a mining survey for a region on the border of Cape Colony and German South West Africa. The potential riches here will make the diamond mines and goldfields of the Transvaal look like a pittance. Britain has an interest in making sure those regions are indisputably in its territory of Cape Colony. Officials of the Foreign Office are ensuring that this happens. Whoever has the surveys determining exactly where the borders are will win the region. If Germany discovers the mineral potential and makes a competing claim, there is the risk of war. I'm sure you'll understand why His Majesty's government would rather avoid a war in the region so soon after the last one."

"Although a large part of that army is still in Cape Colony," Hallern observed. "It would be convenient, starting up another war."

The recent war against the Boers in South Africa had been all over the papers. It had been brutal, messy, and by many accounts, unnecessary. A matter of wealth and ego rather than the so-called higher principles of British sovereignty. Neck-deep in her studies over the last couple of years, Ava hadn't followed it as closely as she now wished she had.

Hallern had opened his mouth to make another jab when Mrs. Monroe cut him off. "Once again, I expect you to ask why you should believe me. If I can maneuver around the likes of spies such as the Brannocks, why should I not try to fool you? Here. Have a look."

She handed him the papers, an act of trust that couldn't help but win them over. They all leaned in to study the innocuous object that the Brannocks had been so willing to kill for. That they'd died for. Hallern used his good hand to open the packet and spread it out on the table in front of him, holding down one edge with his left arm. His eyes moved quickly.

"I was traveling to Nassau to divert attention," Mrs. Monroe said. "There, I was meant to hand the packet off to one of my husband's associates while I continued to lead any *interested* parties astray. But they cut me off at the pass, as it were. As I said, spies are everywhere. I believe the Brannocks meant to carry this straight to their masters in German South West Africa. We are most fortunate that that didn't happen."

Who was *we*, Ava wondered. Them personally? Or the British government? She and Marchand were not British.

Hallern searched through the pages, then searched again. "This is all . . ." He shook his head. "This seems very official. Is this really the foreign secretary's signature?"

"Yes. I was honored to dine with the Marquess of Lansdowne and his wife before traveling to Southampton. It was then that he entrusted me with these documents."

English aristocratic titles had a spell about them. It wasn't Arcanism; they still involved names and the power of names. But it seemed that so much of the power of these titles lay with the people hearing them. Did they respect the system that codified them or not?

The others seemed impressed. Ava wished she could ask Anton what he knew about this Marquess of Lansdowne, and if he was a man to be trusted.

"It's a geological survey," Hallern confirmed. "Whoever lays claim to this territory might become very wealthy indeed."

"Who's living there now?" Ava asked. "Is anyone living there now?"

"The Herero and Namaqua tribes live there, I believe," Suminwa said.

"No one who can develop the mineralogical resources of the territory," Monroe said. "And that is not my immediate concern."

It was an old pattern, seeing territory and resources, potential for profit, and not who or what was already there. The first lesson any naturalist learned was observation. See what was there, not what one wished was there, or what one assumed. But people like Mrs. Monroe seemed to want to remake the world into something else, more to their liking.

"You want me to keep that in the ship's safe for you?" Hallern said, folding the pages.

"That won't be necessary." Mrs. Monroe smoothly retrieved the packet. "Now, I must ask a great favor of you, Captain Hallern. I must ask you to continue to Cape Town. Then I can meet Mr. Monroe and deliver this to the colonial governor, where it will do some good. Perhaps even prevent a war."

Hallern stared at her. "I have a hundred other passengers on board expecting to go to Nassau. What do I tell them?"

"That it's for the good of the British Empire."

Hallern snorted, as if he didn't believe in either good or the British Empire. "How about this. We'll drop you off at Gibraltar, and you can find passage to Cape Town there."

"Gibraltar will be crawling with spies. A dozen more just like the Brannocks, or whatever their real names were. This is the only possible way by which I can reach Cape Colony without being discovered."

Hallern persisted. "We go back to Nassau, you meet your contact—"

"Same problem. If the Brannocks found me, whomever they're working for will find my contact." She clutched the pages until they creased. "I need your help, Captain Hallern. Britain needs your help."

It all rested with him, and he didn't seem happy about it. He glanced at his first mate. "I don't suppose the wireless is fixable."

"The machine is smashed," Suminwa said. "Outside my skills, alas."

"Well, you'll have to learn to fix a wireless for next time," Hallern said, and Suminwa chuckled, like this was an old joke between them.

"It's just as well we can't send a message," Mrs. Monroe said. "To any outside observers, we've vanished. No one will discover where we are until it's too late." She had a gleam in her eye, like a hunter on a scent.

Ava's parents would be expecting a telegram when she reached Nassau, to let them know she'd arrived safely. Now, it seemed she was not going to arrive safely. At least not to her planned destination. This had suddenly gotten much bigger than a bacteriological study. To hear Mrs. Monroe talk, the fate of the world—or at least part of it—might hang in the balance. Then again, Ava might like to see Cape Colony. The huge animals of the savanna, the treasures sought by big game hunters, elephants and lions, gazelles, and wildebeests traveling in great noisy herds of thousands. Her parents had never been to Cape Colony, and wouldn't they be jealous—

"Miss Stanley. Ava, dear."

Ava started awake with a gasp. Mrs. Monroe was standing over her, her hand gently resting on her shoulder. Mrs. Bell was nearby, and she seemed amused rather than concerned. Mrs. Bell, who'd killed her husband, and Ava didn't know a polite way to ask her about it. The men had all left.

"What—"

"I think you fell asleep," Mrs. Monroe said, smiling kindly.

Well, wasn't that embarrassing? She rubbed her head and sighed, frustrated. She wondered what she'd missed. She had been up all night, using more Arcanism at once than she ever had before in her life. Multiple *practica*, one right after the other, with barely time to think of it. No wonder she was exhausted.

"You had a busy night," Mrs. Bell said. "I don't know anything about Arcane Taxonomy, but it seems to have taken something out of you."

"Yes, it usually does," she said.

"Come along. Let's get you to your cabin."

Being escorted by the two older women made her feel like a child, but she was grateful for the company. Her mind was still fuzzy, and the ship somehow looked different than it had the day before. More dangerous, more ominous. The decks and ladders felt like mazes. At least the ocean was the same, an endless expanse of potential. Ava paused to look out at it. The sun was up. In the still-early morning, it was rising, on the left, to port. Which meant they traveled south.

"You convinced him to go to Cape Town," Ava said.

"I think he made the choice he needed to," Mrs. Monroe said diplomatically, and Mrs. Bell snorted a little. A cynic, like Captain Hallern.

"What about Nassau?" Ava said. Her voice sounded small. She felt small. A parasite riding along on some much larger creature who didn't even notice it. A barnacle stuck to a whale.

"Nassau will still be there when this is all over."

When they got to her cabin, she remembered what she'd done to the door to escape. Mrs. Bell traced the splintered wood around the missing handle. More rotten pieces fell from it. "That's impressive," she said.

Ava just stared. She couldn't think of a solution to the broken door at the moment.

Mrs. Monroe could. Of course she could. "I'll ask Mr. Suminwa to send someone to make repairs. Or move you to a different cabin. Meanwhile, perhaps you can prop it closed with a chair?"

"Yeah. All right." She rubbed her eyes, which felt like sandpaper. "Thank you both. You're very kind."

Except for the murdering part. Ava and Mrs. Bell, both of them murderers. And she wondered about Mrs. Monroe.

Ava convinced them that she didn't need any more chaperoning, and they departed. She got the door propped shut as Mrs. Monroe had suggested, and managed to at least get her boots off before she collapsed into bed. She didn't move again for a good long time.

NINE

Yersinia pestis

Ava woke up still feeling a thrum under her skin, like warning of an approaching lightning strike. She rubbed her arms, which were covered in goose bumps, though she wasn't cold. She'd never gathered and used so many *practica* at once. She had never been in battle. It had exhausted her.

She began to see the attraction of the dime novels, as opposed to an actual adventure: The stakes in a novel were clear cut, the heroes and villains straightforward. Also, she could flip to the end of the book and see how it all turned out. Now that she had a moment to think, the uncertainty of what might happen next was almost worse than the terror of confronting people who were trying to kill her. Then, her choices were clear, and only one real path lay before her. What clarity! But this wasn't a story, and the clear answers she wanted might not be possible.

She immediately sat up, racked with urgency. How long had she slept? What was happening? She must find out. She found her pocket watch—morning, all over again. She'd slept all day and another night on top of it. No wonder she was so out of sorts.

The door to her cabin had been replaced, the handle and lock secure again. She'd slept right through the repairs. She hadn't changed clothes, and her hair was a mess. She hardly knew where to start in putting herself back together. Well, as with anything, one step at a time. She changed into a fresh dress, poured water in the basin to wash her face, and combed and pinned up her hair. The mirror told her she looked presentable; she had to trust it because she didn't really feel it.

Outside her cabin, she paused, taking in the sun. The weather was calm, the sky clear, which felt confusing after the uproar of the other night. There should have been a storm. Passengers had been released from their rooms. Some of them walked up and down the decks or sat in deck chairs reading books and newspapers. Did they even know what had happened? How much danger they'd been in, and that people had died?

She turned a corner to the stairs that would take her up to the dining room and salons, and hesitated. This spot of the deck looked like any other, teak boards under her feet, whitewashed wall on one side, wood panels and polished railing on her other side. But she knew this spot. Edging to the rail, she chanced a look over, her heart clenching at the long drop to the deck below.

There, a crewman was on his hands and knees, a wash bucket beside him, scrubbing a particular spot. Mrs. Brannock was no longer there, and the last traces of her blood were being washed away.

Ava quickly pulled back from the railing.

A few dozen yards down the deck, toward the stern, Mr. Marchand leaned on the railing, smoking a cigarette. Suddenly, he stamped the cigarette underfoot and turned to walk away. Just a man out enjoying the morning. He might not even have seen her, though she couldn't help but feel he'd been watching her. Surely that was paranoia. Lingering nerves. She thought of calling after him, just to confirm that he was real, or that she was.

She hurried up the stairs to the salon. Mrs. Monroe and Mrs. Bell were there. They'd changed clothes. Mrs. Monroe wore a dark-blue walking dress with gloves and a simple hat, and Mrs. Bell was dressed in somber gray. They both looked much better than Ava felt. Without a word, Mrs. Bell got up and poured a cup of tea, which she offered to Ava. Ava accepted it gratefully.

"You poor dear, you slept the whole day through! You must have been exhausted," Mrs. Monroe said. "Are you feeling better?"

Honestly, Ava wasn't sure how she was feeling. She gripped the hot cup, trying to assess. "I'm still a little overwhelmed, I think."

"Very understandable," Mrs. Monroe said.

"What's happened? What have we found out about the Brannocks? What are they doing about the saboteurs?"

"All in good time," Mrs. Monroe said. "Sit, drink your tea, catch your breath."

Next to the tea service was a platter full of sticky buns and pastries. Ava took one. Bit into it, chewed slowly, and made herself finish. The second bite came more easily.

"Now, what have I missed?" Ava asked.

"Not much, I should think. Captain Hallern seems to have everything well in hand. A good man." Maddening. The ship might be wrecked and sinking, and she would remain calm.

"Was there anything in the Brannocks' cabin? Any other clues about what they were trying to do with this . . . what do we even call it? Mutiny? Piracy?"

"Piracy, I should think," Mrs. Monroe said. "We'll simply have to be patient. We might not have all the answers until we reach Cape Town."

Mrs. Bell flinched a little at the mention of Cape Town and only offered the hint of a smile. "I can't say I'm exactly looking forward to that."

"Oh, my dear, no one is going to arrest you. I'll see to it. It wasn't even murder, not legally."

"Well, not this one, at least." Her gaze dropped to the cup of tea resting on her lap. "None of you have looked at me the same since I mentioned my husband. You're shocked."

Ava glanced away, because yes, she no longer saw Mrs. Bell as the quiet woman who'd come on board at the start of the trip.

"It was . . . unexpected," Ava said, and Mrs. Bell stifled a laugh.

"There's no denying you saved the day," Mrs. Monroe said matter-of-factly. Maintaining a normal demeanor. "But I confess to feeling a good deal of curiosity about you."

"You are too polite to ask directly." Mrs. Bell's smile grew, but it was sad. Pensive. Despite her curiosity, Ava was almost afraid to hear the story. "Well, I've never told anyone. Maybe I should." Mrs. Bell's grip on the teacup tightened. She didn't look up. "It's why I left England. There'd be no defense for killing my husband, not really. So I ran. I suppose that makes me coldhearted."

"But you must have a good defense," Ava said.

"I'll let you be the judge," Mrs. Bell said. "I was young when we married, foolish. He wasn't a good man. He got involved in scheme after scheme. Business ventures, he said. Extortion and embezzlement, more like. Finally falling down into outright theft. And I put up with it. He was my husband. What else was I supposed to do? It's just like you said—isn't a wife meant to help her husband in his work? We had a little place in the East End, and I kept it up as best I could. I would have stuck it out, stood by him. But he got my brother involved. And you see, Dave wasn't . . ." She closed her eyes and hesitated.

"Dave was simple. A good boy, but he was never going to be able to care for himself. He was so eager to please, though, and when you gave him a job, he'd put his head down and do it. Hauling crates, loading wagons. I told Ed not to bring Davey along on his work. I begged him. Dave didn't understand what he was doing. He just wanted to make Ed happy.

"They, these blokes Ed was stealing from, they beat Davey to death. Ed ran instead of helping him. The damned coward. Too much a coward to tell me what happened. I only found out when the police came to tell me. They were looking for Ed, but I didn't know where he'd gone to until I found him hiding in the back alley. He didn't even say he was sorry, just made excuses, said it was Davey's fault for not running. And I . . . I'd been chopping potatoes. Still had the knife in my hand. Didn't even think of it. Suddenly he was on the ground, bleeding. With the most surprised look on his face." She was staring into the middle distance, as if the memory was still right in front of her. She shook herself back to the moment. "And then I ran. What could I do but run? Just like Ed did. But I don't want to hang for killing the bastard."

Mrs. Monroe put her hand on Mrs. Bell's arm. "You had no one to help you. No one to confide in. Oh, you poor thing."

"Don't pity me," Mrs. Bell said with forced brightness. "I'm as free now as I've ever been in my life."

"I assume Mrs. Bell isn't really your name," Mrs. Monroe said.

"No. But Gilda is. Please call me Gilda."

"And you must call me Diane."

"Well, Miss Stanley?" Mrs. Bell asked. "Are you horrified by me?" Her narrowed gaze suggested she didn't much care one way or the other.

Ava didn't know what to make of it, except that for all her travels, she really knew so little of the world. "I'm thinking . . . that I would kill to defend my brothers. Absolutely. And please, call me Ava."

"Ava, more tea?" Mrs. Bell—Gilda—asked, with forced politeness.

"Oh, yes please." Ava reached for a second bun as well. And was unaccountably thrilled to find a spot of green on the bottom.

Diane hissed reprovingly. "Oh, those must be left over from yesterday. I don't suppose I can fault the kitchen after recent events, but really, I expect better."

She reached to take the bun away—to get rid of the offending object. But Ava held it close. "I'm keeping it—not to eat, of course!" she said quickly to Diane's offended glare. "The mold. I can take a sample. It's probably *Rhizopus stolonifer*, but I won't know until I have a look under the microscope." Just to make it seem a little more decorous, she wrapped the bun up in a napkin and tried to look earnest, as if this was perfectly normal.

The two other women devolved into the sort of commonplace conversation Ava had always associated with tea and parlors, the weather and headaches and what was being served for supper. She didn't know how they did it.

She'd finished her second cup of tea when the salon door opened. Mr. Suminwa came in, giving a little bow to the women. He'd also managed to get himself polished, freshly shaved, his jacket and trousers clean and pressed, his hat and scarf arranged neatly. But his eyes were tinged red, swollen with exhaustion. He and the captain must have had a time of it, getting the crew sorted out.

But he smiled kindly at her. "Ah. Miss Stanley, you're awake. Are you well?"

She wasn't exactly sure, but right this moment, she supposed she was. "Yes, I think so."

"Good. I could use your help on the upper deck, if you have a moment, please."

"I have all day, apparently."

"Perhaps we'll all have time to walk on the deck later," Diane said. "I know the sea air has done me good after all the excitement."

As she left, Ava dropped a little curtsy in spite of herself, like she was a little girl approaching the elderly Sir Archibald. Diane inspired such gestures.

Suminwa stepped aside to let her go ahead, up the stairs and around to the wheelhouse. He was quite tall, loose limbed. He touched the railing every third stride or so, not because he needed balance but to make contact with the ship. He constantly looked out over the waves. It put her in mind of an old pirate captain, searching for the next target.

"How's the ship?" she asked.

"A bit rattled, I think," he said. She couldn't tell if he smiled or was just squinting into the sun. "A crew should trust each other when we have so many lives under our care. Hard to get that back when it's gone."

"I'm sorry."

"I think I would rather sail through a hurricane than a mutiny."

"Have you sailed through a hurricane?"

"I have." Now, that was definitely a smile, and his dark eyes turned to her. "The trick is to keep moving, yes? I think this will be the same."

"You and Captain Hallern have worked together a long time," she said.

Suminwa nodded. "Some years ago, we piloted a riverboat on the Congo together."

And what an adventure that must have been. "A rough part of the world."

"Eh, to me it's just home. But then I hear stories of your Wild West, and that seems very dangerous. Gunfights, Indian attacks, tornados?" He shook his head in apparent disbelief.

She started to deny it. Then again, she'd seen Buffalo Bill's Wild West show. If that was all you knew about the prairie and Indians and bison and the rest, what else could you possibly think? "That's all just stories, you know."

He raised a knowing brow and turned his hand up. "Just so."

"Mr. Suminwa . . . may I ask an awkward question?"

His smile was broad, full of amusement. He might have anticipated her. "After these last two days, I think you have earned some awkward questions."

"Captain Hallern relies on you a lot. Almost as if . . . well. He called you *sir* last night. Which of you is really the captain of the *Penelope*?"

He ducked his gaze and chuckled a little. "Charlie would tell you . . . he would flatter me by saying I am the better seaman. I could tell you we work well together and leave it at that."

She had avoided considering one of the obvious reasons behind such an arrangement. But she had brought up the question. Why stop now? "The shipping company would never hire a Black man to be captain. So Hallern is the captain, and you run the ship."

He only shrugged, leaving the question open.

She continued, "My stepfather is Black. His mother was Bahamian."

"Yes, I know. Charlie is a great fan of your stepfather."

They arrived at the wheelhouse. Suminwa knocked on the door and didn't wait for an answer before pushing inside. "Charlie?"

Another crewman was at the wheel while Hallern stood at the table, consulting charts and making marks in a logbook. His prosthetic left arm was back in place, cleaned up, resting on the table. Like the rest of them, Hallern seemed tired, pale, his hair mussed under his cap. Then again, his hair always looked mussed. Now he moved with urgency.

"Ah, Miss Stanley. Thank you for coming. We could use your help."

"For what?"

He marched past them, out of the wheelhouse to the storeroom next door, the very same one where they'd been locked up the other night. Hallern swung open the door and let the sunlight stream in. A young man sitting against the opposite wall squinted against it, pulling up his knees defensively.

It was Jones, hands and ankles tied, cringing.

"For an interrogation," Hallern said.

TEN

Komagataeibacter xylinus

Well, at least Jones hadn't been thrown over the side during the late disaster.

"I don't know anything about interrogations," she said coldly, backing away. "Well, except for my younger brothers when they filched cake, but that's not exactly the same thing, now, is it?"

"Just talk to him. See if you can get anything out of him."

"I already told you everything!" Jones pleaded.

Hallern chuckled darkly. "I don't believe you." When he spoke to Ava, his tone turned soft. A condescending patience. "I've heard that Arcane Taxonomists can change people's minds. Influence their moods. If you could just try—"

"I think you deeply misunderstand what Arcane Taxonomy can do," Ava declared. "I can't even light a candle!"

Jones stared at her, trembling. "You're an Arcanist? Oh God!" He struggled harder against the bindings, wrenching as if he could break free through sheer willpower. Which was ironic, since breaking the ropes was something she could actually do.

"Really, Jones, settle down," Hallern ordered.

"That's how you all got away, then," Jones said. "God, the Brannocks must have been so surprised. I'm serious, Captain, I was coming to set you free, but I got here and you'd already broken out, and—that was you?"

She'd had enough, but Hallern stepped in front of her, blocking her escape. "To read Brandon West's accounts, Arcanists can do nearly anything," he said.

"Well, unfortunately, I'm nothing like my father," she declared, then shut her mouth. She hadn't meant to say that. The bitterness of her own words surprised her. She had thought she didn't care, being nothing like Bran West.

Hallern was studying her even more closely now. He'd had all week to study her, and he knew Anton was her stepfather. Surely he could have guessed. She refused to be shamed by the confession and matched his glare.

"All right, yes, I did it!" Jones burst out suddenly. "I let the Brannocks into the engine room. They had guns, they were going to start shooting people—what was I supposed to do!" Sweat had broken out at his hairline and stained his shirt. He looked at Ava wide eyed, as if he really was afraid, and she wasn't sure how to feel about that. She wasn't dangerous; what did he think she was going to do to him?

"How much did they pay you?" Suminwa said calmly.

Jones looked away.

"God Almighty, you really are a coward," Hallern said, disgusted.

Jones insisted on making the situation worse by continuing to talk. "I only told them I'd help to try to get more information from them. I was going to learn their plan and then come tell you. I swear!"

Suminwa shook his head sadly. "Do you know what the worst of it is? We gave you a chance when no one else would hire you. After that business out of Mumbai, you'd never have worked on a ship again. But I thought, He's young. We are all young once. Give him a chance. And now here you are."

"I'm sorry," Jones said through gritted teeth. "I'm sorry for all of it!"

Jones had been so quiet. Nice, even. She didn't want to believe his treachery. And yet here he was, representing another story full of dark secrets. She was starting to get the feeling she'd gotten on the wrong ship at Southampton.

"Well," she said to Hallern. "You didn't need me at all, did you?"

"Oh no, I think you worked very well," Hallern said. "If it wasn't Arcane Taxonomy that made him talk, maybe all he needed was a pretty girl to motivate him." He gave her a lopsided smile.

Somehow, that was even worse. Nothing more than a pretty girl, after all she'd done.

"*Really*," she huffed, and made to storm out.

And was once again stopped when Suminwa put out his arm across the door. "We also need to know where they planned to take the ship. Jones?"

"I don't know anything," he said, slumping against his bonds. "They didn't tell me anything!"

He'd likely been in on it from the start, playacting all this time. Still playacting. Could they believe anything he said? What did he think he was accomplishing here?

She hesitated, turning toward the prisoner. Glaring at him, she raised her hand and rubbed her fingers together. Like the West character in the dime novels. "*De finibus bonorem et malorum*," she murmured, just loud enough for them all to hear.

Jones cried out, pulling his knees up to shield himself. "Swakopmund!" he said. "Swakopmund, it's Swakopmund!"

The word seemed like nonsense, but Hallern straightened, and Suminwa stepped closer. She raised a brow, and Suminwa explained. "The port city in German South West Africa. Right to the heart of it."

"Swakopmund was where they were trying to take the ship," Jones said. "But I don't see that it matters now that they're dead and you're going somewhere else." His brow furrowed. "Where are we going, anyway?"

"Oh no, I don't think so. You're staying here for the duration." Hallern marched out of the storeroom.

Jones tried to catch Ava's gaze, but she had no interest in being caught and followed Hallern out. Suminwa also exited, shutting the door behind him.

Hallern cornered Ava. "You could do it all along!" he said excitedly. "Use Arcanism for an interrogation—"

"That was Cicero," she said. "'On the ends of good and evil.' I told you before, *Mr.* Hallern, Arcane Taxonomy is nothing like it is in the stories. And to think I was really starting to like you." She hadn't meant to say that either. Flustered, her cheeks hot, she didn't dare look at Hallern's expression. "If you'll excuse me. Captain Suminwa." Suminwa tipped his cap at her.

She walked down the deck and away.

She hid away in her cabin to stew in her anger, to let it burn itself out. Work would distract her, so she got out slides and set up the microscope.

The difficulty was you couldn't judge bacteria by what you saw of them. You could see that an arctic tern was built to cross miles of open ocean. A hummingbird was built to hover. Moles were built to dig, the cheetah built to run down prey. With the usual collection of flora and fauna, you could see how form followed function, how they had evolved certain traits, certain abilities. Birds could fly, fish could swim. Sometimes, it was as simple as that.

But bacteria . . . They were small, a mere collection of biological material adhering to a certain structure, no matter what they did. They were built for pure survival, and little else. What traits did they have; what were their abilities? To infect, to destroy. Except the destruction was merely a byproduct of their actual intention, which was to reproduce themselves. To survive whatever conditions they'd evolved in and reproduce.

Their traits were secondary, unintentional. A body developed a fever in an effort to fight off infection, not because the bacteria caused fever. They aided in fermentation because of the chemicals their biological functions produced. Nothing in nature was intentional; it merely *was*. Attributing volition to evolution was a mistake. Darwin himself had emphasized that.

All bacteria shared this one trait: survival. Other traits they might produce required more study to discover. This was the scientific method, wasn't it?

A light knock rattled the door. She straightened in her chair. "Yes?"

Hallern opened the door. He didn't cross the threshold and left the door standing open, all very polite for a man dealing with a young woman. There was nothing at all improper about this. She was still angry with him. With the door open, she'd be less likely to yell.

He pulled off his cap and left it hanging on his prosthetic hook. What an absurd gesture, but one he must have made all the time, it was so unselfconscious.

"I owe you an apology," he said.

She set down the pencil on her open notebook. "You do, don't you?"

There was that slouching shrug of his. "I'm sorry. I should not have brought you into that situation without warning. I should not have made assumptions."

He'd been desperate, angry, tired. He would have tried anything to learn what he could. She ought to stay angry at him, but anger was exhausting. "Apology accepted," she said. "You know, I can read German. I'd probably be more help translating the documents you found."

"Ah, yes. Probably." He lingered.

"Is there something else?" She had a feeling she knew what else he wanted.

"May I be very forward?"

"Why stop now?"

His smile turned crooked, conceding the point. "Your last name is Stanley, not West."

"Yes. My mother's first husband's name."

"But your mother's first husband was not your father."

"No. He died before I was born."

"He could still be—"

"Fourteen months before I was born."

"Ah. And Anton Torrance . . ."

"She married him after I was born. She is not married to my natural father. Does that bother you?"

"Pardon me for being so presumptuous. I'm only trying to understand. Is it a secret? That Brandon West is your father?"

How did she explain? She never had to explain because most people were too polite to ask. "Not really. But we don't talk about it."

"And you have brothers. Are they . . ."

"Here, it's easier to show you."

She drew another journal from the stack of books on the desk. Her private journal, not her research book with all her scientific notes and drawings. The one where she shoved the letters she'd been writing to Harry and Archie until she could reach a post office. Tucked in the back, she kept a photograph, the most recent one of the whole family, the last time they were all together in London, right before Ava had started at the New Hospital.

It became clear when you saw them all lined up together. In the picture, Beth was seated in the middle, wearing a gentle smile, a pleased matriarch at the center of the family. Her gown was simple, well fitting and trimmed with velvet at the collar and sleeves. At her right shoulder stood Anton Torrance, possessing an elegance that matched hers, wearing a tailored suit, charcoal colored, not a crease out of place. He had one hand on the back of the chair and another on the cane with the walrus-tusk handle that was something of his trademark.

Behind the chair and to her left were the children—not so much children anymore. Archie, looking dapper, his chin tipped up, full of himself. The picture captured his attitude in his rather arrogant stance. Ava next to him, looking very much like her mother but with darker hair and a more serious expression. Her face was young, but her mouth had a worried tightness to it. Ava didn't much like the way she looked in pictures. She had her hand tucked in the crook of Harry's elbow. At Mother's insistence, Harry had taken his glasses off, and while his eyes seemed heavy lidded, you wouldn't know he was blind just from looking at him. He'd been trying to grow a mustache, and the brush of hair around his mouth made him seem studious. He'd shaved it off shortly after.

And to his left, with his hand on Harry's shoulder, was Bran West. The good family friend. Harry looked very much like him, his skin pale, his facial hair rough and uneven. On the other hand, Archie shared Anton's brown skin and dark eyes. Both boys had Beth's round face and graceful build.

Hallern studied the photograph, his brow furrowed. "It's an unusual arrangement," he said diplomatically.

"I think the most unusual thing about it is that they've never tried to hide it. They also don't speak of it openly. Bran and Anton both raised us as a father would." How strange it would be, to only have one father, or none at all.

"I'm a bit envious," he said. "They're heroes, you know. Great men."

She scoffed. "Anton Torrance snores. Did you know that?"

"No, I don't believe it. Not the great Torrance!"

"It's true. And Bran West is forgetful. Coats, gloves, hats. Always forgetting them."

Hallern laughed. "That never seems to make it into the memoirs, does it?"

"No, it doesn't," she said. "I have to tell you, it's a little odd how interested you are in my stepfather and his best friend."

His expression turned closed in, defensive. His arms crossed, his hat squishing against his elbow. "Is it? I simply think they're interesting people."

"Your ship is *full* of interesting people, in case you hadn't noticed. There's more to it."

He nodded, appearing suddenly young, bashful. He might have been a cynic, but he still sought out stories of adventure. Still seemed to believe in adventure. "I went to a lecture of theirs when I was younger. Maybe fourteen? In London. The one on Inuit culture. They told the polar bear story. I was entirely taken in. Filled my head with such . . . wonders. They seemed like characters out of Jules Verne. I thought I might follow in their footsteps, captaining a ship through the Northwest Passage, succeeding where Franklin failed. Then this happened." He held up his left arm, the hook reflecting the light. "Then I wasn't sure what I could do."

"I'm sorry," she said. "If it means anything, you seem to manage very well on the *Penelope*."

"Practice," he said. "Stubbornness. Mr. Suminwa picking up the slack."

She ought to tell him about Harry and how he managed much the same. Practice, stubbornness, and the help of friends.

"Let me know if you'd like me to take a crack at translating those documents," she said.

He smiled. "They'll be in the wheelhouse, waiting for you. Good afternoon, Miss Stanley." He pulled his cap back on and ducked out, shutting the door behind him.

"Good afternoon—" He was already gone and likely didn't hear her.

Sighing, she sat back. She'd completely lost track of what she'd been looking at on the slide under the clips. Maybe she ought to take a break. Read a little instead.

Torrance and West and the Terror of the Zambezi

If the explorers had seen these creatures in a more natural setting, at peace in a jungle perhaps, or deftly climbing trees with their natural agility, they would have said they were gorillas, hulking figures covered in blackish-gray fur, broad shoulders and swinging arms, small eyes peering out from heavy brows. But these beings walked upright, arms at their sides, and they wore scuffed bronze breastplates—armor. Evidence of civilization in such an unlikely setting: a wide staircase leading to an entrance carved into the living rock of the cliff face. Ornate columns and friezes, partly overgrown with vines and moss, revealing an ancient temple that no outsider had seen in generations.

The simian guards had a purpose about them that might even have been intelligence when they surrounded Torrance and West and prodded them up the steps. Two guards flanked them, and two others followed behind. When Torrance attempted to step out of place, one of these hefted a rock, threatening. While it was not a purpose-made weapon, the stone would easily crack a man's skull. The ape guards grunted menacingly, and Torrance relented, keeping his place, a prisoner of these strange creatures. The ape beside him pointed into the dark maw of the palace entrance.

"By all means, lead on," Torrance murmured, exchanging a glance with West, who remained stoic, his expression unchanging.

The guards clambered up the stone steps, setting knuckles down every third step or so and glancing over their shoulders to be sure the human men followed. The darkness swallowed them.

But not for long. Soon, a soft blue glow punctuated spaces on the walls and ceiling until the light grew constant, bright enough to see by, though still strange, unreal. They all appeared something like ghosts in the monochromatic light, more shadows than men.

West had taken on a familiar, studious expression, narrowing his gaze at the walls.

"A natural phosphorescence," West said. "*Lampyris noctiluca.* Glowworms."

The passage went on for perhaps fifty yards and then opened into a chamber, and the blue glow gave way to bright golden light, strong enough to make them wince.

When their vision cleared, they saw that this wasn't a cave but rather a room that had been carved into the rock, the walls polished smooth until they gleamed, reflecting the light of a dozen torches burning in sconces.

The ape guards stood aside and bowed reverently toward the back of the chamber. Torrance and West inevitably turned to see what held their awe.

There stood a dais holding a throne made of the same polished stone–carved in place, emerging from the rock wall. A woman reclined in the throne, perfectly at ease, a wonder to behold. As perfect in form as a Greek statue, with graceful curves, her dark hair elegantly looped and braided around a most alluring face, eyes gleaming with self-assurance. She wore a gown that seemed richer than silk, clinging to her in soft folds, shining with light as if it were made from spun diamonds. Her bare arms were bedecked with bracelets of gold and jewels. So brightly did she shine, she was difficult to look at.

This, then, was the treasure spoken of in the marketplaces, rumors and wonders passed down for generations, luring men to the heart of the jungle and to their doom. The Deathless Queen of the Hidden Temple of Rala'Shi.

She flicked a hand, and the guards stepped away at her command. Sitting up, she leaned forward to study her new prizes.

"Come closer, gentlemen, so that I may look upon you." She spoke some unknown language, words that might have once been heard on the lost island of Atlantis. And yet her speech reached them as proper English, and they understood her.

The two men's hearts raced, sweat breaking out all over as they were drawn toward the queen, trembling with terror at her. If she commanded them to die for her, they would. And yet some small part of them recognized the danger and held their ground.

"West," Torrance stammered. "What is happening?"

"Some kind of mesmerism. Fight it, man!"

"I'm trying . . ." But his will might not be enough. His knees buckled, forcing him to kneel before her.

West began to murmur under his breath. Latinate words, the scientific names identifying living beings of the earth that had existed for longer than even the Deathless Queen. He hoped, prayed even, that the living world held more power than she did . . .

ELEVEN

Listeria monocytogenes

Ava got permission to bring the materials collected from the Brannocks to the salon, where she spread them out on a desk and got to work over the next several days. According to various letters and permits of transit, their true surname was Baumbach. They appeared to actually be married. Ava wasn't sure why this surprised her. So much else about them had been lies; that seemed another obvious one.

The materials included letters, sailing schedules, rail timetables. Dossiers on their targets, including Diane and Frederick Monroe. Ava learned that Mr. Monroe had worked his way up in the Foreign Service at colonial offices in India and Hong Kong. A photograph revealed him to be a striking white man of middle age, with a mustache of steel gray and a strong square jaw. He seemed the kind of man who'd played cricket at Oxford or Cambridge. There was a disturbing account of Mrs. Monroe's typical schedule in London. What restaurants she visited, meetings she attended, societies she was a member of, and so on. They seemed to have been following her for some time. Mrs. Monroe betrayed no obvious response to this information.

While the rest of them didn't have official dossiers among the papers, a sheet of quickly scribbled handwritten notes was included in the packet, describing each of them in a couple of sentences, with a memo to forward them on for further information. The pair hadn't counted on facing any opposition to their takeover of the ship and had been surprised by the group that had ultimately defeated them.

Ava lined up several sets of timetables, explaining to the others who were gathered around. Diane Monroe, Gilda Bell, Marchand, Hallern. "Here, shipping schedules and lists of docking companies, not just in London and Nassau but also in Lisbon, São Paulo, Marseille. I think they were ready for you to sail out of anywhere. I'm not sure going to Nassau first would have distracted them at all. Cape Town's on the list too. If they couldn't divert you, they'd find you there." She pointed to the relevant page, a list of ships with Cape Town on their routes. "What I can't find are contacts. Who else they were working with. Who their contact in Cape Town might be, if there is one."

Diane beamed at her like a proud teacher. "Well done, Ava. You could work for Scotland Yard. I'm sure they could use an Arcane Taxonomist."

Ava entertained the notion for a brief, very brief second. Wouldn't it be exciting? Think of all the mysteries she could solve . . . No. She already had plenty of mysteries. "I'm sure they've got several. And really, I already have too many jobs."

Diane compiled the information into a report she could pass on to her husband and the Foreign Office. Hallern sat at another table, working on what appeared to be a logbook. Compiling the same information, one assumed. Early afternoon, someone from the kitchen brought a tea service. Gilda poured cups for everyone.

Mr. Marchand was reclined on the sofa, reading a book. Ava had been so involved in examining the papers and translating German she hadn't noticed what he was reading until now. On second glance, she recognized the cover: *Torrance and West and the Fires of Mount Erebus.*

She must have made some noise of exasperation, because he chuckled. "I thought I would try the book about your stepfather. It's very exciting!"

"There isn't anything about my stepfather in that book," she said.

"But he is an explorer, yes? He went to Antarctica?"

She couldn't deny it. "The Antarctica in that story bears no resemblance to the real thing. Those books are all lies."

Hallern glanced up. "They're not *all* lies," he insisted. "More like . . . inspired interpretations?"

"But there's no cave at the base of Mount Erebus that gives secret access to an underground world where the dinosaurs survived!" Ava said.

"Ah," Hallern said, brow lifted. "So you have read it."

Well yes, of course, she'd read them all. She had to know what she was up against. She let out a huff.

Diane tsked. "Dear, the more annoyed you get, the more they'll poke at you."

"My mother always said to ignore my brothers' teasing, but it never, ever worked. You know what worked? Popping them in the nose." Ava gestured with her fist.

"Your parents must have the patience of saints," Gilda said wryly.

Beth always said they'd stopped at three children so the adults wouldn't be outnumbered.

Marchand tapped the page open before him. "They are just about to pull the ancient treasure from the rock. If they can do it before the Tyrannosaurus attacks them. The roaring is getting closer."

Needless to say, the adventurers survived, since they starred in several more novels.

"The closest Anton Torrance ever got to a Tyrannosaurus in Antarctica was a fossil crinoid."

"Not nearly as dramatic, I think," Hallern said.

Ava wasn't going to win this. But she tried. "What I don't understand is why anyone needs to make up such outrageous things when the truth is already so interesting."

"Human nature," Diane said. "We always want more than what we have."

Before the argument, or polite discussion—whichever side of that line they were on—could continue, the door opened and Mr. Suminwa came in, nodding a greeting.

"Tea, Mr. Suminwa?" Mrs. Monroe offered.

"No, thank you," he said. "I'm only here to let you all know—we are officially overdue at Nassau."

Hallern sighed and tapped the pencil against the book. "Well, there it is, then. The clock starts ticking."

"What does that mean, officially overdue?" Gilda asked.

"It means the shipping company starts looking for us," Suminwa said. "Perhaps even the navy."

"If Mrs. Monroe wants to remain unnoticed, she's going to have a difficult time of it very soon," Hallern said.

"That's not all," Ava said, thinking of the pages before her. The dates and numbers were starting to blur together. "When will the Brannocks be overdue at Swakopmund? Your company might not be the only ones looking for us." The thought hadn't seemed so ominous when she was only thinking it. Speaking it out loud—it definitely sounded like a threat.

Marchand said, "The Brannocks, whoever they work for—you think they will send a ship after us? A hunt?"

"They might," Suminwa said.

"How long until we reach Cape Town?" Diane asked.

"Six more days, I think, assuming all goes well."

"Well then. Once we reach Cape Town and I meet Frederick, he'll report to the Foreign Office, and all will finally be well. We must do all we can to avoid being found before then. Can you do that, Captain Hallern? Mr. Suminwa?"

"We will certainly try, ma'am," Suminwa said.

"Very good."

In a strange way, she seemed pleased. She had to be pleased that the Brannocks hadn't succeeded in their mission to capture her documents.

But more than that, the pursuit seemed to excite her. A whole spy network centered on her. Who wouldn't be flattered?

The *Penelope* crossed the equator. Gilda was the only one of them who hadn't crossed before. Hallern insisted on enacting a line-crossing ceremony. This seemed ominous; Ava had heard stories of such rituals getting out of hand on navy and merchant ships. But Hallern only meant a bit of fun, and after declaring himself a representative of King Neptune, he summoned blessings of safe travels over Gilda and doused her with a pan of seawater Mr. Suminwa had pulled up over the side. Rather than taking offense, Gilda laughed, wearing the most earnest smile she'd had the whole journey. She almost seemed happy.

Six days until they reached Cape Town, before Ava got to see how this all played out. Met Frederick Monroe and found out what all this looked like from his side, assuming the Foreign Office didn't keep quiet and swear them all to secrecy. Ava needed to distract herself for almost a week, so she studied, sketched the miniature monsters she observed under the microscope, made notes. Wrote rambling letters to Harry and Archie that probably wouldn't make any sense when they read them, if they read them. She might decide not to mail them at all. If they knew what had been happening to her, they'd only worry.

When her eyes ached from staring through the microscope eyepiece, she retreated to the deck and fresh air, bringing along a couple of newer journals with articles by Professor Koch, the famous bacteriologist. Her intention had been to claim a deck chair and catch up on reading, but the sun and sea air were so soothing, so comfortable, she just sat and watched the waves. The other passengers seemed to have taken the change in course well enough, and carried on as they would have, walking the decks, admiring the view. They smiled at Ava as they passed, and she smiled vaguely back.

She might have been drifting off to sleep when the cry of a bird roused her.

A flutter of gracefully sloped wings brought a bird in to land on the railing. Gull-like, it was streamlined, with a stylish black cap and an orange bill shaped like a dagger. A tern. Maybe an arctic tern? Beth and Bran would know.

She set her book aside and stared at it. The tern stared right back, unbothered by her. Very unbirdlike behavior.

"Mother?"

The bird tilted its head, and the breeze ruffled its feathers.

Definitely an arctic tern. *Sterna paradisaea.* Beth Torrance had become the first woman to be granted a rank in Arcane Taxonomy on the strength of her *practicum* drawn from the arctic tern. Second Rank—the officials of the Treasury Department couldn't bring themselves to grant her a First, which was both predictable and ridiculous. At the time Beth had said something about choosing one's battles. Ava had been younger and hadn't understood. She understood better now.

The arctic tern was best known for its incredible migration pattern, traveling between both poles, a round-trip journey of some twenty thousand miles. From the north to the south in the winter, and back again in the spring. Through its migration it encompassed the world, in a sense. It traveled everywhere, saw everything. Beth and Bran had tapped into that trait.

It wasn't perfect, Beth explained. She could only follow where the birds went, take advantage of where they traveled. But once she found them, she could travel with them. See what they saw. Learn about them, and the world around them.

While Beth claimed she couldn't control them, this individual bird was certainly taking an interest in this particular spot. If Beth could do more than she claimed, Ava wouldn't be surprised.

"Can I assume you've gotten the news, then? That we aren't in Nassau?"

The bird adjusted its feet, getting a better grip on the rail, and shook out its wings. On a whim, Ava tore a blank sheet out of the back of one of the journals and used her pencil to write out words in big block letters: **CAPE TOWN**. She held it up, feeling silly. Birds couldn't read. Even if her mother was contacting this bird's senses, the details wouldn't be clear.

The tern suddenly took off. A crewman came down the deck on some errand or another, walking with purpose, and tipped his cap to Ava. The tern had been startled away. Or maybe the message worked. Ava lost sight of it quickly, its white shape disappearing into the sky and clouds.

Maybe Beth Torrance really had found her. If so, Ava would be rescued. Her parents, all three of them, wouldn't let anything happen to her.

This was a child's thought. Rationally, how could they possibly help her when they were thousands of miles away? Even with Arcane Taxonomy at their command. Ava would have to hope that she would not need help at all. The Brannocks and their plot had been thwarted. The ship would reach Cape Town, Mrs. Monroe would accomplish what she needed to, and Ava could go her own way. All would be well.

Belatedly, she thought that Mrs. Monroe wouldn't appreciate Ava giving away their destination. Not that she'd really delivered a message, and not that they would believe it if she had.

She folded up the sheet with the message and stuffed it in the back of the journal.

What would it be like, to try to see the world through the senses of protozoa, bacteria, or some other microscopic creatures the way her mother could use *Sterna paradisaea*? A ridiculous notion—bacteria didn't have eyes. So. Think. If she wanted to deliver a message across the world, what would she try? Did any insect migrate so far? Disease-bearing bacteria had certainly traveled around the world, carried by animals and people. If she had samples of tuberculosis, of bubonic plague, from London, and from Nassau, or wherever she ended up on this errant journey, could she connect them? *Was* there a connection between them? Could she travel the currents of the world through the countless plankton that called those currents home?

She considered the fundamental difference between Arcane Taxonomy based on specimens you could hold in your hand and study, and that based on creatures you couldn't even see. Maybe her mother and other bacteriologists were right. It couldn't be done.

But it was all life. Therefore, according to Darwin and other naturalists, it had power.

She was developing a headache.

Ava put out her sieve a couple of times, fishing for plankton, but in the warmer region of the tropics she didn't pull up much. The water was clear, underpopulated. The *Penelope* steamed on, puffing coal smoke, cutting through chop.

A more interesting experiment struck her. With swabs and a stack of petri dishes from her lab kit in hand, she went around the ship collecting samples. She swabbed the handrail on the stairway to the dining room. The teapot in the salon—the one they'd been pouring tea from for the last two weeks. She very kindly asked the head cook if she could swab his hands, and he was skeptical but indulged her. Rails, doorknobs, the handles of mops the crew used to clean the decks, the mop heads themselves. She swabbed the wheel in the wheelhouse after promising Suminwa that she'd let him see the results.

And what fascinating results they were.

Ava nurtured the little colonies of bacteria. Within only a day or two, a dozen petri dishes held multicolored blooms in expanding circles and dotted puffs. She found examples from the *Staphylococcus* genus. Diphtheroids, *Streptococcus, Neisseria, Bordetella.* Several strains she couldn't identify at all and might never have been categorized. Fascinated, she sketched, made notes, compared results to those in journals and catalogs she'd brought with her, and made identifications when she could. The ship was inhabited by a jungle of microorganisms. The chief cook would be horrified to see what colonies grew from organisms taken from his skin. (She lectured him on the power of handwashing and sterilization, the greatest actions that could promote public health.) She showed the dish sprouting spots and swirls of microorganisms from the wheel to Hallern and Suminwa, and they both turned a bit ashen. "Maybe just clean the wheel a bit at the end of the day," she suggested, with a thin smile. The germs were everywhere; they had to learn to live with them.

Some of these species traveled to places they might never have reached without oceangoing ships, without people carrying them from port to port. No one could stop these migrations. A country might be able to stop people at its borders, but plagues would pass through via air and water with no one the wiser. The most powerful, omnipotent creatures on earth, and no one could see them. There must be some power in that, even if it was only the knowledge that human beings were powerless in the face of the measles or bubonic plague.

In spite of the work, her mind turned to the journey ahead and what awaited them at the end. If Diane Monroe's dire predictions had any merit to them, the port would be swarming with spies, villains like the Brannocks waiting to ambush them. In spite of herself, Ava felt a little thrilled at the possibility. A kind of latent memory of that night's fear and uncertainty.

So she also worked on Arcanist *practica*, anything that might be useful in a fight, anything she might be able to use if she faced another adversary like the Brannocks. She wanted to be prepared.

Meanwhile, the ocean had its own sense of predictability in its constancy, the regularity of its tides, the names of the creatures that lived within it. The sun would always rise and set, as it had done for hundreds of millions of years. Life had burgeoned and evolved under that sun. There ought to be some comfort in that.

The surge and ebb of waves lulled her, and her thoughts drifted further, into dreams of microscopic cilia rippling with the rhythm of water, the medium of travel for so many creatures, from diatoms to whales and everything in between, and how small the *Penelope* was compared to that great tapestry, the ocean currents circling the world.

An interruption. In a sense, every steamship, dinghy, sailing yacht, and canoe was an interruption of currents that had flowed for millions of years until humanity evolved the capacity to build vessels and take to the water. They made their own roads, shipping lanes, routes drawn on charts—

—coming right toward them.

Ava started awake, and the book that had been balancing on her lap fell to the floor, and her chair scraped back as she stood from her desk in shock. For a moment she was sure she could feel the ocean currents under her, the way they sloshed against the hull, curling back as part of the wake. The dream, what dream had she been having . . . Something important crashing on her, revealing itself to her . . . She closed her eyes and struggled to put her mind back in that place, that feeling of expansiveness, where she wasn't just aware of the current but was part of it.

Another ship, where one wasn't expected. Where it shouldn't be. Like finding a trilobite fossil on a mountaintop. A sense of foreboding lodged in her gut. She might be sick over the railing from it. So irrational, and yet she couldn't ignore it.

The *Penelope* was being hunted.

She raced to the upper deck, to the railing at the bow, shading her eyes to study the surrounding waters. The day was partly cloudy, with sun and thin clouds. She pushed wind-tossed strands of hair away from her face and squinted against the glare. A telescope would be better for this, but she'd only brought the microscope. She was so much more used to focusing inward rather than out to the horizon. Every bit of sea-foam and chop caught her attention. She wasn't even sure what she was looking for.

There . . . there it was. A break in the pattern, an incongruous detail that didn't belong. A puff of smoke, darker than the surrounding mist and haze, rose up, no wider than a strand of yarn, far enough away that little else of the ship was visible.

"Miss Stanley?" Suminwa came up the deck from the wheelhouse, Hallern at his heels. "What have you found?"

They would think her mad. After all the time she'd spent telling them Arcanism wasn't magic, wasn't anything like the stories, was she supposed to tell them she'd had a vision? Gained some kind of clairvoyance?

"I'm not sure," she said. She pointed at the smudge of smoke toward the southeastern horizon. "Is that a ship out there?"

Suminwa had brought a spyglass with him and used it now. The lines at both men's eyes, the evidence of years of staring out at bright seascapes like this, deepened. The smoke left a trail, and then they glimpsed the ship itself, a sliver of a shape. Impossible to tell details at this distance. But Ava *knew*.

"It's them, isn't it?" she said. "A ship out of Swakopmund. Whoever is working with the Brannocks." Even to herself, her voice sounded haunted, still caught in whatever spell had overcome her.

"Is that a guess, or clairvoyance?" Hallern asked.

Ava shook her head. She didn't know.

"Hard to say from this far out," Suminwa said, handing the spyglass to Hallern. It should have been awkward, the way he held the instrument in his right hand, balanced with the hook on his left, but he seemed quite comfortable.

"What'll happen when they learn the Brannocks aren't here?" she asked.

Suminwa grinned. "No need to let them find out. A little game of cat and mouse, yes?"

"You'll let us know if you somehow gain any other extraordinary insights?" Hallern asked, brow raised.

"Only if you don't tease me about it," she muttered in response.

"Right. Sorry. I suppose we could ask Jones if he suddenly remembers anything else, eh?" He added a bitter chuckle.

"No," Suminwa said. "We keep the boy locked up. Don't let him think we still need him."

It seemed harsh. Jones's remorse had seemed real. "What did Jones do before?" Ava dared to ask. "Mr. Suminwa, you said this was his second chance. What did he do?"

The two men glanced at one another. An unspoken question—they both knew, but neither of them wanted to answer.

She shifted nervously, ready to excuse herself. "If it's too awful to tell me—"

"He was a junior officer on a passenger ship out of Mumbai," Suminwa said. "They ran into trouble. Damage to the engine, a crack in the hull. Started sinking. Taking on water, nothing to be done. Middle of the night. Captain ordered the lifeboats put out."

"That sounds reasonable," she said.

"There weren't enough lifeboats. So the crew used them and left the passengers behind."

Ava had thought that whatever he'd done couldn't be so awful, but it turned out to be worse. Unthinkable, even.

"We were there at the inquiry," Hallern said, nodding at Suminwa. "We heard the whole thing. What a bloody mess."

"Then how is Jones not in prison?" Ava said, disbelieving. "Shouldn't they all be in prison?"

"He was 'following orders, sir.' That's what he said to the judge."

"He was young," Suminwa said, as if that was any better of a defense.

"And when does he stop being too young to know better?" Hallern countered. "At any rate, it isn't worth speaking of any further, is it?"

"I'm sorry," she said softly. "It's awful."

"The whole world is awful, isn't it?" Hallern said bitterly.

Hallern and Suminwa went back to watching for the ghost of smoke identifying another ship on the horizon. Feeling the dismissal, she fled.

Amazing that anything at all could find anything else in the vast ocean, but millions of creatures found food, mates, homes. A million others were invisible, camouflaged, to avoid predators and stay safe. Another ship with ill intentions might very well be looking for the *Penelope*, and it didn't want to be found.

Ava could attempt a disguise. There was a thought. She knew ways of turning attention from herself. Could she expand that to the whole ship, simply from proximity? A whole category of Arcane *practica* made use of camouflage and stealth. The silence of a stalking tiger, the ability of a chameleon to perfectly blend in with the rocks around it. The fundamental characteristic of bacteria was that they remained unseen. They impacted the world in ways that far exceeded their size.

She would not know if such a *practicum* worked any more than she could tell just by looking at a sample of water if *Vibrio cholerae* infected it. Her head ached thinking of it.

She took her journal and pencil to the bow of the ship, the foremost part she could reach, the leading point where she felt the mist rising up. Here, she had an unbroken view to the horizon, and she wrote. She listed names of waterborne organisms, their characteristics, the effects they evoked. Testing herself, convincing herself she knew anything at all, organizing the list in a way that made sense to her. Naming the scientists who had discovered them, and where she had first encountered them. Most of them, she'd actually seen under the microscope herself, and that seemed to have some power to it.

The writing was a way to classify her own thoughts, which at the moment seemed as much a tangle as the plankton in a drop of seawater. Making sense of the world took patience and the will to organize. The willingness to embark on a task that would never be finished.

She hoped the task would carry her to her destination.

Torrance and West and the Fires of Mount Erebus

You, reader, safe in your comfortable parlor in the dead of winter, snugged in front of a fireplace while the snow falls outside, may think you have been cold. You have been caught outside on a winter's night without your hat and gloves and felt the bite on your skin, the stinging that seems like fire until it sinks to your bones, numbing your extremities, forcing you to hop around and flap your arms to put some heat back into yourself. Your breath fogs; ice forms on the tips of your mustaches or your scarves. Your eyes water; your cheeks chafe, roughened by cold borne on a chill wind.

This is nothing. No matter how cold you have ever been, it is nothing to the cold of the deepest south. Of Antarctica. In civilized lands you can retreat to your warm parlor and have a cup of steaming hot tea before the fireplace, a great woolen blanket over your lap. On the freezing expanse of the southern continent, you have no retreat, no shelter, no reprieve. Nothing but an icy wind and temperatures plunging ever lower. During the winter, you have no daylight at all for months on end. Never-ending cold, never-ending dark.

What man could ever conquer that realm? And what might he find if he succeeded?

If any man could triumph in the quest, it would be Anton Torrance, with the able assistance of his trusted companion, Brandon West.

From the indomitable tribes of the Far North, Torrance learned to construct snowshoes out of leather and sinew. He learned to build shelters of ice and snow itself, to keep alive during the fiercest storms. He could hunt seal, use the blubber of walrus to fuel lanterns to light his way during the winters, when the sun sank below the horizon and would not rise again for months.

And West—West had mastered that most elusive of sciences, Arcane Taxonomy, that gave him mastery of the natural world, an affinity with those wild laws of tooth and claw. He could take on the hunting instincts of the great orcas, the wolves of the ocean. The ability of the emperor penguin to survive in the cold. The eyesight of the skua that scanned the frozen coastline for its prey.

Torrance and West sailed to the frozen continent of Antarctica and the far edges of human frontiers, sure they had the knowledge and experience to conquer that land, to uncover all its secrets.

But the secrets they found were more wondrous, and more terrible, than even they could imagine.

"You have a weakness, my friend," West informed Torrance as they stood on the broken-up ice fields of the glacier. They had hoped to cross the ice sheet and make camp some dozen kilometers ahead. But the sight before them had arrested their progress. Torrance was enraptured.

A mountain stood before them, a towering cone capped with shining ice. No, not a mountain, for a tower of smoke and steam rose up, a writhing thread climbing into the heavens. Not a mountain—a volcano.

"Weakness? No, never," Torrance insisted. "An obsession, perhaps."

"Fine, all right, an obsession."

When Torrance saw a mountain, a stark peak rising up like a flag planted on new territory, he felt an undeniable urge to climb it. To scale its treacherous heights. To reach the summit.

Particularly if no one had ever done so before. And as of the year 18–, no one ever had.

West knew without asking where their expedition was now headed.

TWELVE

Latilactobacillus sakei

Meals grew a bit sparse. The ship had been scheduled to resupply in Nassau, and now the cooks were having to make do with tinned meats and bread made from the last sacks of flour. Not quite having to ration, but nothing close to the elegant dining advertised on more high-end ocean voyages. Ava gathered that Hallern was receiving complaints from other passengers.

They approached Cape Town with a sense of growing urgency. Each day brought them closer to . . . something. Either resolution and relief or an as-yet-unknown danger.

Two days before they were due in port, supper was potatoes and tinned beef. Barracks fare. Hallern had come up with a bottle of wine to help wash it down. Ava maybe had a bit too much of the wine and should have been paying attention when half the others refused any wine at all. But it dampened the spirals her mind had been caught in, the currents of flagellate protists traveling the world and taking her with them.

In a lull, amid an ordinary conversation about the weather and food in Cape Town, she asked the question that had been gnawing at her. "Mr. Suminwa, any word on the ship we spotted?"

Forks paused over plates. "A ship?" Diane asked.

Ava hesitated; she had assumed everyone knew, that Hallern and Suminwa had told them. Apparently not. She had to consider that she wasn't very good at keeping secrets. She might make a decent detective but wouldn't make a very good spy.

Suminwa finally answered. "Yes. Miss Stanley spotted a ship, possibly out of Swakopmund. We were concerned that it was watching us, but we have not seen it since yesterday." He gave a fatalistic shrug.

Coincidence, surely. Ava couldn't take credit for disguising their passage. Not without more evidence and repeatable methods.

"They were watching for us," Diane said evenly.

"Perhaps," Hallern said, grinning. "We didn't stop to ask."

Diane merely nodded, accepting this new wrinkle with little emotion. She'd seemed to anticipate everything that had happened.

"Mr. Marchand, I understand you're a good hand with a pistol," Gilda said, gaze lowered to her plate.

"I am," he said, straightforward, without modesty.

"Will you teach me to shoot?"

He hesitated, but only for a moment. "Yes. If you'd like."

None of them tried to argue that they wouldn't need an extra hand with a pistol before this was done.

Seabirds were few and far between on the open ocean. Ava didn't have to argue with Marchand about shooting albatross or terns or the like. Her mother had passed on an aversion to shooting birds for anything but food. Not a single hat sported a single feather in their house.

Suminwa assigned a deckhand to toss bottles off the stern, while Marchand coached Gilda on sighting down the barrel and pressing the trigger of his pistol in a way that maximized her chances of striking her target.

She was a quick study. Soon, shattered glass was raining into the water on a regular basis. The noise, the repetitive blasts of small explosions as Gilda went through the chambers of the revolver, then again after Marchand taught her to reload, was too much for Ava. The bangs rattled her spine and seemed an ominous tolling for whatever awaited them when they reached port.

"Miss Ava. Would you like to learn?" Marchand asked, holding up his pistol like it was something to be admired.

"No, thank you," she said, hugging her journal to her chest, preparing to flee the noise.

"Eh, then again, why would you?" he said, shrugging. "You are an Arcanist! You can do anything!"

The others' knowledge of Arcane Taxonomy bore as much resemblance to the real thing as the dime novel characters Torrance and West did to their inspirations. Which was to say, none at all.

Ava's first glimpse of Cape Colony resembled the approaching views of a dozen other coastlines. A line marked the edge of the gray and rippling sea. Land, identifiable mostly in that it was static, a haze, a bit of yellow contrast. Cliffs and beach. The presence of fishing boats, small craft with single masts that never left sight of shore. A sudden proliferation of birds, shorebirds and gulls and such that lingered near land. She wasn't the only passenger leaning on the rail, watching the scene slide past.

Empty coastline, a countryside made up of grassland, some trees, an occasional house, and isolated estates, gave way to congestion. Villages, then towns, then a city crammed with buildings. A series of striking, mountainous ridges rose up behind the city and seemed to hem civilization in, crowding it between land and sea. The waterway thronged. Fishing vessels, cargo ships traveling in and out of port, occasional patrols. The Union Jack flew from dozens of masts, in case anyone doubted who ruled here. A few other flags made a showing, including the Stars and Stripes, but not enough to give a sign that this was any other place than Britain. The empire.

Diane seemed sanguine, watching the approach to the city. “Once I contact Mr. Monroe, all will be well. My only task is to pass this on to the governor’s office.”

Ava hoped for a chance to meet Mr. Monroe, this man who had Diane’s complete loyalty. Not to mention a chance to see how this all played out. For her part, as soon as she disembarked, she’d need to send a telegram to her family to assure them she was well. Then she supposed she’d need to decide whether to stay in Cape Town or book passage to Nassau, where she belonged. She was almost sorry it was over. Like coming to the last few pages of an enthralling novel.

The four passengers had gathered at the prow in front of the wheelhouse to watch their arrival. Through the glass of the wheelhouse, Hallern and Suminwa seemed intent on their work. The harbor was busy. This was a crossroads, trade from two different oceans, two different parts of the world, coming together at the Cape of Good Hope.

Quickly enough, the harbor seemed crowded indeed. A sloop flying a Royal Navy flag paralleled them, flashing a signal lantern. Suminwa came out to the rail and flashed a lantern back. The signals went by too quickly for Ava to tell what they said. Anton would have known.

When Suminwa returned to the wheelhouse, Diane Monroe stalked after him, uncaring if she got in their way. Ava followed her example and tagged along. How else was she going to find out what was happening? Gilda and Marchand were right behind her.

“Captain, I don’t suppose there’s a way for us to reach port without drawing so much attention?” Diane asked in the same tone in which she might have requested more sugar for her tea.

“I beg your pardon, madam, but we are four hundred feet stem to stern and six thousand gross tons, so no, there is no way for us to enter the harbor without drawing attention.”

“Not to mention the name of the ship is painted on the hull,” Ava observed.

“Hm, we should have waited for nightfall.”

Hallern stepped away from the helm. "Would you like to be the captain?"

"Oh good heavens, of course not. Carry on."

Returning to land should have been a relief after the days at sea. The ship had begun to give Ava a sense of being trapped. Diane seemed to see enemies everywhere, and her outlook was contagious, spreading through proximity. As if delivered by airborne microbes.

The navy sloop escorted them to a slip a little ways out from the main passenger piers. The street along the pier had fewer shops and more warehouses. A few wagons and horses hauling cargo passed by. Rough-looking dock workers, both Black and white, paused to watch the *Penelope*'s approach.

The crew worked efficiently, tossing lines to men on the pier, who secured them to great steel cleats. Just a handful of them managed to bring the enormous craft home. The ship's engines stilled to a distant thrum, and the smoke from the funnel thinned to a gray line.

A dizzying moment of hesitation, a still breath. They were neither on land nor at sea, waiting for the next step. Next, the ship's crew worked with dock workers to get the gangplank in place. Passengers were already starting to gather, eager to be off. Meanwhile, on the pier below, carriages were arriving, and a crowd was gathering.

From shore, a dozen men crowded toward the gangplank, most in military uniforms, a few in suits with packets tucked under their arms. Port officials, in coats with brass buttons, surrounded by dock workers. A pair of the uniformed men stood guard at the base of the gangplank, but they were implacable in the face of the unexpected and unwelcome commotion.

Ava put on a hat and ran down to the main deck to find out when they'd be allowed to leave. Hallern was already there, explaining to passengers that they wouldn't be leaving the ship, not just yet. Some harsh words were exchanged, some passengers making threats, declaring how their schedules had been disrupted. They were on the other side of the world, and what did he have to say for himself? Hallern calmly explained they would have to take it up with the Royal Navy and the shipping company he worked for.

"What's this?" Marchand asked as he came up behind Ava. Diane and Gilda weren't far behind.

"We can't disembark," Ava said.

"There's certainly no sneaking out of this," Mrs. Monroe said.

"Ah, you can always jump over the side and swim," Marchand said merrily.

"Spoken like a man who has done exactly that, hm?" she answered, and Marchand laughed. Oh, the untold stories.

"This isn't normal?" Gilda asked. She'd never left England. For all she knew, uniformed soldiers always stood watch at gangplanks.

"The portmaster coming aboard to see the manifest is," Suminwa said. "The soldiers, not so much."

Hallern straightened his collar and tugged his cap more firmly on his head. It somehow made his hair look even rougher. "I'll clear this up."

A short time later, the gangplank was secured, and Captain Hallern marched down with his logbooks in hand.

They were close enough to hear some of the conversation between him, the portmaster, and the man who turned out to be a lieutenant of the local army garrison, in charge of security at the port.

"Your ship was reported missing some days ago," the lieutenant said.

"And I'll tell you all about it if you'll give me a moment."

"I've been directed by the admiralty to conduct a full investigation."

"At least may my passengers disembark? We're nearly out of provisions."

"I'm afraid that won't be possible, Captain."

Gilda shifted nervously, and Marchand straightened, on alert.

"Here's your investigation—the perpetrators of our change in schedule are dead."

"All the more reason for an investigation, don't you think?" The lieutenant seemed young, but his gaze was hard, his expression impassive.

"I don't want to talk to him," Gilda said. "I can't talk to him."

"You won't, dear," Diane said. "Mr. Suminwa, we can dispense with all this nonsense if I could simply deliver a message to my husband at the Foreign Office."

"That simple, eh?" Suminwa said. "Well, let's go hand off that message."

While Hallern, the lieutenant, and the portmaster continued discussing what should happen to the *Penelope* and its passengers, another man in a smart suit pressed in from the back, raising a folded paper over his head.

"I have a telegram!" he announced. "Urgent telegram to deliver!"

The lieutenant scowled. "What's this?"

"Telegram for Miss Stanley, Miss Ava Stanley!"

Suminwa, Diane, Marchand, Gilda—all looked at her, curious, maybe even dismayed. Ava blushed.

Marchand asked, "Who knew to send a telegram to you here?"

She knew exactly who. Whether or not they'd understand if she tried to explain was another question. Well, it wasn't like she had any other excuse. "My mother."

"How?" Diane asked urgently.

"She's an Arcane Taxonomist," Ava said, as if that explained everything.

Marchand huffed. "Are we supposed to think it is magic?"

"It isn't magic," Ava said. "My mother tracked Anton Torrance all the way to Antarctica. She's famous among Arcanists for the *practicum*."

"And she tracked you just the same?" Diane asked.

"She's my *mother*." She couldn't hide the edge of frustration. Imagine, not being able to go anywhere in the world without your mother knowing about it.

"Who else would your mother have told?" Diane asked. This was an interrogation.

"Mr. Torrance. Mr. West. That's all."

"They're safe? You trust them?"

"Of course I do!"

Diane didn't seem convinced, narrowing her gaze at Ava, who recognized the expression: *You young, naive child.* "Anyone at the telegraph office on either end would know. They could have sold the information."

Gilda said, "I thought telegraph offices were secure."

"Money will always buy information."

"Look," Suminwa said.

On the gangplank, Hallern was shifting his cap on his head, the gesture curt and frustrated. He turned and marched back up to the ship while the lieutenant and a couple of his soldiers followed. The rest were stationed at the bottom of the gangplank.

Gilda turned and fled toward the cabins. Diane followed.

"Ladies, gentlemen," Suminwa said and went to the stairs up to the wheelhouse.

"What's it mean?" Ava asked.

"One step at a time, mademoiselle," Marchand said. Then he left as well.

All Ava knew was she had a telegram waiting for her. She charged toward the gangplank, pausing only when she met Captain Hallern and the lieutenant blocking the way. The soldiers barred the messenger at the other end.

"Captain?" she asked worriedly.

"Lieutenant Claremont, this is Miss Stanley," he said.

Lieutenant Claremont studied her. He was tall, intimidating, and not just because of the red coat, helmet, and gleaming brass buttons. A hint of blond hair peeked out from under the helmet, running into well-trimmed sideburns. His forehead sported a permanent furrow, and his frown seemed constant.

"Hello, sir," she said lamely. "Apparently, I have a telegram?"

Claremont looked at Hallern and somehow frowned even more deeply. "She's American?"

Like he'd found some vermin stowed away. She bristled, and said with exaggerated politeness, "Yes, sir."

"Who knew to send you a telegram here?"

Hallern answered for her. "Her family is full of Arcane Taxonomists. I blame prognostication."

"Is that so?" Claremont finally sounded interested rather than offended.

Ava was getting tired of this. "May I collect my message?"

He considered her request for a drawn-out moment, and she was about to find some other way of asking, such as suggesting that one of the soldiers bring it to her, when he relented.

"Yes. But don't leave the gangplank if you please, miss," the lieutenant said, stiffly polite.

"Yes, sir."

She signed for the telegram while standing at the bottom of the gangplank, and the man from the telegraph office never left the pier, all under the supervision of the soldiers on guard. All very proper. She ran back up and found a deck chair to settle into.

The message was simple. *Ava dear. Send word. Confirm status with Foreign Office. Much love. A. Torrance.*

So. Anton had pulled strings and status to get news through the Foreign Office. She might very well have been the reason everyone knew about what had happened to the *Penelope*. Until the last week she would have never thought there was anything politically fraught in such a communication. What a mess.

While she sat with the paper half crumpled in her lap, an insect buzzed past her face. She swiped at it, then stilled, and the creature came to rest on the polished arm of the chair.

Six long, graceful legs as fine as threads, with relatively small wings attached to a bulbous thorax. The abdomen was thin, the head round. The long, needlelike proboscis gave the family away, if not any finer classification: Culicidae. She wasn't familiar with the various genera of mosquitoes found in South Africa. She would have to learn.

The common impulse was to squash the thing, to keep it from biting, to win one small battle in the war between species. It was only possible to win a small battle, an individual *Homo sapiens* squashing one small member of Culicidae. In terms of sheer numbers, however, the mosquito might very well defeat the superior intelligence of humanity.

Ava let the mosquito fly away.

It took less than a day for the situation to get worse.

THIRTEEN

Bacillus anthracis

Lieutenant Claremont and his men spent that day prowling through the ship, poking into every cabin, demanding to see weapons and asking everyone on board the reason for their travels. Most of the passengers were just trying to get to Nassau for business or to see family. Marchand produced his pistol, which the soldiers confiscated. The Frenchman was so unbothered by this, Ava was sure he'd hidden another pistol or two somewhere they couldn't find.

They spent extra time in Ava's cabin, studying her scientific equipment with apparent bafflement. They knew very well what it all was, the microscope and slides, bottles of solvents and dyes. They just didn't seem to understand why a young American woman would possess such things.

Hallern and Suminwa took turns standing watch by the gangplank as the lieutenant and his soldiers trekked between deck and shore. By the afternoon, Claremont was back on the pier, receiving and sending messengers, while Hallern and Suminwa waited for news at the top of the gangplank, shading their eyes to look over the pier. Marchand was strolling down the deck toward them as Ava ran down the stairs to learn any new information. Surely they'd be allowed to get messages out today, if not disembark entirely. Even send a note to the Foreign Office, as Anton had all but commanded her. While she hoped her own ability would get her through this situation on her own, she would pull the strings of influence that led back to her stepfather if she had to.

Diane and Gilda had been making a leisurely circuit around the main deck and paused at the railing toward the stern, looking to shore, as many passengers were doing. Ava thought about going to meet them, to see if they'd had any news. But halfway down the stairs she hesitated and watched an odd set of motions. Diane drew a pair of opera glasses from her clutch. Reflexively, Ava nearly looked for the bird she'd spotted. When her mother used opera glasses, she was almost always looking at some bird or other.

Diane seemed to be studying the comings and goings on the pier. Meanwhile, Gilda shifted, turning her body to block the view of anyone watching her from the deck. From the stairs, Ava could see Diane focus in on a target—a man on the shore. An ordinary-looking young man in a suit, maybe a clerk. A junior administrator from some government office. The Foreign Office, perhaps? He caught Diane's gaze and touched his temple, an innocuous salute. She tapped her white-gloved hand on the rail. There was a pattern to it. A mix of taps and pauses Ava couldn't follow. Morse code?

Then the man was gone, and the two women turned from the railing. Ava hardly knew what she'd seen. She didn't dare ask.

Marchand was already speaking with Hallern when Ava arrived. "Will we be let off the ship today, do you think?"

"There's the man to ask." Hallern pointed his hooked hand up the pier, where Lieutenant Claremont was striding purposefully toward the gangplank. The pair of soldiers at the base saluted him smartly as he went to board the ship.

"Sir, might my passengers be allowed to disembark now?" Hallern asked.

"I'm afraid not, Captain," Claremont replied, not bothering to hide his smugness. "We still have more questions than answers. The admiralty has decided to impound the ship."

Hallern usually took things in stride, but now he gaped. "I beg your pardon?"

"This is the site of international espionage. The Foreign Office takes this matter very seriously and is impounding the *Penelope* for further investigation."

"The company might have something to say about that."

"I'm sure they will."

"I'm just supposed to dump my passengers on the other side of the ocean from where they're meant to be? What are they supposed to do?"

Claremont turned a hooded gaze on him, shadowed by the brim of his helmet. "Not my concern, happily."

With impeccable timing, Diane and Gilda strolled up to join them and heard the exchange. "What's this about not being allowed to leave the ship?" Diane asked. "Lieutenant, I assure you, if I may be allowed to deliver a message to my husband, Mr. Frederick Monroe—"

"Madam, it's out of both our hands now. I must ask all passengers to stay in their cabins."

Meanwhile, Marchand was looking elsewhere. Across the stern, to the southern part of the harbor. "Captain? Do you know that ship?"

A sloop under full sail was crossing the harbor straight toward them. It seemed intent on ramming the *Penelope*, which was ludicrous—the sloop was a quarter of the size of the steamer; it would shatter against its hull. But at the last moment it tacked, veering around the stern of the ship where it jutted out past the pier. Diane and Gilda were in plain view of it.

The next few moments happened in a blur, very quickly, perceived by Ava's instincts rather than any rational analysis. She was moving before she realized it. She acted without knowing why, or even what she was doing.

She ran toward the stern, where the sloop was coming about; Marchand was a stride ahead of her, pistol in hand. So he *did* have other weapons that he hadn't turned over. They'd both seen the man at the starboard side of the sloop, holding a rifle aimed at the women lingering near the *Penelope*'s stern.

Ava knew better than to get between Marchand and his target. Besides, her senses were elsewhere. The sloop's sails collapsed as the craft paused, bobbing in the water. A shot rang out, and Ava couldn't tell which gun had fired.

Sudden insight overwhelmed her. The sloop had followed a route through the harbor, cutting a path through microscopic creatures: bacteria, larvae, diatoms, protists that made the surface of the water their home, an unseen trail leading back to where the sloop had sailed from, the other side of the harbor, a pier and series of warehouses—Ava could picture them, though she had never seen them. She had never been to Cape Town, but a map of the harbor presented itself to her: where the mosquito had flown, where plankton had traveled, riding on the barnacles on the sloop's hull, the algae lodged in the fibers of the lines of its anchor, all the nooks and crannies of civilization that harbored unseen life; it all painted a picture, and for just a moment Ava could see it all—

"Miss Stanley! Miss Stanley, I know you're in there."

Then she was sprawled across Mr. Suminwa's lap, and he was tapping her cheek lightly. Captain Hallern knelt next to him, holding her hand with his good one. She was embarrassed that they were cradling her like a child, looking on her with such concern. She had the distinct feeling she had missed something important.

"What happened?" Sitting up, she pulled away from them. She was almost sorry, because free of their touch, she felt rootless, floating on the harbor's waves. She didn't know where she was until she felt the deck under her and saw the white-painted sides of the *Penelope*. Saw the sky overhead and breathed a lungful of smoky, salty harbor air.

"You fainted," Suminwa said.

"The sloop! The guns!" The ship was at dock, but her head swam and swooned, as if the ship pitched on stormy waves.

"Miss Stanley, calm yourself!"

"I'm calm," she argued. "What happened?"

Suminwa sighed deeply with an air of fatalism or frustration, as if commenting on a storm that still pummeled his ship. "Two men on the sloop apparently had designs on Mrs. Monroe. Mr. Marchand prevented their actions by shooting one. Both went overboard; neither has been found. The sloop is currently being examined by Lieutenant Claremont and his men. This has done nothing to make him reconsider impounding the *Penelope*."

Ava spoke quickly, needing to get it all out before the image faded. "The sloop came from a set of warehouses on the west end of the harbor. Three big brown buildings, with a water tower at one end, with a big letter painted on it? Which letter . . . I can't see it. Does this mean anything to you?"

Suminwa and Hallern exchanged a glance. They knew the place she had described. Hallern stared at her, his brow furrowed. "How do you know this?"

She blinked stupidly. It was like a dream, scattering in daylight. But the memory of it was so clear. "I don't know," she said. "Diane—"

"We could use your help in the salon," Suminwa said.

Ava's head ached. She was still trying to make sense of what she had seen. "The warehouses. You'll find out who they are there."

"Come on, Miss Ava. Let's get you out of the sun."

Hallern and Suminwa got her upright, and though her head swam, she managed to not topple over. By the time they reached the salon, she didn't need to lean on them anymore. Her head had mostly stopped spinning.

Outside the door, Marchand stood guard, arms crossed, the pistol in his right hand resting on his left forearm. All his former good cheer had vanished, and he now gave the impression of a statue. His dark eyes scanned the pier, and even gazed upward, as if an enemy might swoop from above.

"Miss Stanley, you are well?"

"What happened?"

"Inside." Hallern opened the door and steered her in.

Diane had lost her hat, and her hair was coming loose, a roan lock curling past her shoulder. Dust smudged her gown, and the skirt was torn. She was so uncharacteristically disheveled that Ava was astonished. The earth might as well have tilted off its axis.

But worse was Gilda Bell, sitting beside Diane on the sofa, her face pale and jaw locked with pain. The right sleeve of her gown was torn off, and blood soaked the square of linen—a napkin from a dinner service, it seemed—Diane was holding in place on a wound on her biceps.

This, no one had to explain.

Ava shrugged off her jacket and rolled up the sleeves of her blouse. "Will someone please get the kit from my cabin? It's the small bag at the foot of the bed." Suminwa charged out.

The tea service was still set up on the sideboard. But where was the kettle, the stove—

"You need boiling water," Diane said, getting up.

It hadn't even occurred to Ava to ask the elegant woman to boil water. But Diane was off and ringing for the galley.

Ava peeled back the bandage to reveal the angry chunk torn out of Gilda's upper arm. "You've been shot."

"Just grazed."

"Well, 'just grazed' is more than enough, I think."

Hallern brought over a glass of brandy, and Ava was about to admonish him that it wasn't necessary, but her patient had already drunk it down before she could say anything. Gilda sighed and closed her eyes.

This was a concrete problem that Ava felt confident in her ability to solve. The rest of the intrigue could take care of itself. Suminwa returned with her bag, Diane with a kettle of hot water. Ava scrubbed her hands clean, got out her bottle of antiseptic to sterilize the needle, and yes, she had a packet of silk sutures. The complicated work was cleaning out the wound, pulling out fibers of shirt, searching for shrapnel, investigating the damage. The wound didn't reach the bone. The amount of blood was impressive, but Gilda was right—the damage was superficial. When she was satisfied, Ava stitched closed the gaping skin. The simple work of a first-year medical student. Nice, being useful.

"She saved my life," Diane said, watching Ava work. "The shot struck her when she pushed me out of the way."

"Very heroic," Ava said. She tied off the last suture and wiped the incision with antiseptic. Gilda hissed in pain and accepted another glass of brandy from the captain. "You'll want to keep your arm in a sling for a time. You'll have a scar. I'm sorry, I can't do much about that."

"Badge of honor," Gilda said. "Thank you, Dr. Stanley."

"I'm not really . . ." She ducked her gaze. "You're welcome."

"And what happened to you?" Diane asked.

"She fainted at the sound of gunfire," Marchand said.

"I did not!" Ava declared. "You think I've never heard a gun go off before? Really! I . . ." But it felt like it had happened a million years ago. She couldn't explain. "I just thought I saw something."

Ava cleaned up and repacked her kit while trying to ignore the ominous feeling that she was going to need it again soon. Hallern and Suminwa left again on ship business. A steward brought supper. Marchand had to be persuaded to rest. Gilda took his place, standing guard with the pistol despite her injured arm, secured in a scarf turned into a sling.

"Gilda, you're in no fit state to stand guard," Ava said, exasperated.

"She's perfectly capable," Diane said firmly. "I trust Gilda. Ava, you've had a difficult day. Perhaps you should go to your cabin and get some rest?"

They called her a doctor in one breath and treated her like a child in the next. "I'm not leaving until I find out what happened, who those assassins were. This is a bigger tangle than you've been letting on, isn't it?"

Diane drew back, and for once didn't have a calm and easy response.

Hallern, looking even more annoyed than usual, if possible, returned just then, with Lieutenant Claremont in tow. Ava was really beginning to loathe every time the officer appeared. If his expression had been cheerful, if he'd given off any sense of bringing them good news, she might have felt differently. But he had the air of a man getting ready to command a firing squad.

Mrs. Monroe smiled at the officer. "Lieutenant Claremont, good afternoon. May I offer you some tea?" She gestured toward the tea service on the sideboard as if this were her parlor, as if she were the one in charge here.

Claremont's jaw tightened. He seemed taken aback. "No, thank you. I'm here on business."

"Oh, indeed?" Diane said.

"I need to ask some questions." The lieutenant turned to Ava.

Embarrassingly, Ava's heart started racing with nerves. She dreaded what was coming, and wondered how she might escape. Bran West had an Arcane *practicum* that stopped time, briefly. The way he explained it, it wasn't so much that time stopped. More that perception slowed, the way a hunting raptor might see its prey the moment before it struck. The very idea offered astonishing possibilities. Alas, Bran was a First Rank Arcanist. Ava ought to learn to light a candle before trying to manipulate the fundamental workings of the universe.

But if she could freeze time, she could escape without anyone noticing.

"Miss Stanley, is it? I must ask how you knew the origin of the sloop and what your connection is to the Trans-Southern Merchandise warehouses?"

"The what?" Ava said dumbly.

"Also, tell me again—who sent you the telegraph when the ship arrived in port?"

"That was my stepfather. Anton Torrance. You might have heard of him."

If Claremont had heard of him, he gave no sign. "You seem to be in possession of a great deal of information that you have no explicable reason to have. One of the crewmen says you speak German. Is this true?"

Now she started getting angry. All this had reasonable explanations. Well, no, Arcane Taxonomy wasn't always reasonable, and that was the problem, wasn't it? "Lots of people speak German!"

At the same time, Hallern stepped in. "What crewman told you that? Have you been questioning my men behind my back?"

Claremont paused, then spoke. "A man by the name of Jones. Very helpful fellow. Not sure why you were keeping him under lock. I've encouraged him to lodge a complaint."

Hallern cursed, and Suminwa chuckled darkly. "Protecting himself," Suminwa said. "Can hardly blame him."

Jones had switched loyalties again. Whatever came next, he'd side with Claremont. Suminwa was right; in hindsight it hardly seemed like a surprise.

"Let me be blunt, Miss Stanley," Claremont said. "First, you are in contact with persons who knew your location despite the ship being declared missing for a number of days. Second, you're aware of the origin of an assassination attempt. How am I to explain this?"

What could she do but tell the truth? "Honestly, I have no idea how to explain it to you."

"She was right?" Hallern said. "About the warehouses?"

"Yes," Claremont said.

Hallern grinned at her. "And you say it isn't magic."

"Lieutenant Claremont, what exactly did you find?" Mrs. Monroe asked.

"Shipping schedules. The *Penelope*'s route for the last three months. Letters stolen from Frederick Monroe. All of it connecting the Brannocks with a plot to capture you, Mrs. Monroe. So again, Miss Stanley. How?"

"*Calanus finmarchicus*. An Arcane *practicum*. I've been imagining how such ubiquitous life creates networks, patterns, and . . . and I just saw. My mother does something like it with *Sterna paradisaea*."

"And what in God's name is *Sterna paradisaea*?" Propriety before the women seemed to be the only thing holding back his frustration. Ava found herself wondering how Claremont would treat Bran in such a situation. But ah, Claremont would take Bran seriously and not question his abilities.

"Arctic tern," she said, knowing the name would mean nothing to him. He was like most people, to whom all birds seemed the same and all insects were simply bugs.

"Whatever it means, however you came by it, your knowledge of these affairs is very suspicious."

Mrs. Monroe said, "Surely you saw in the captain's account that Mrs. Brannock tried to kill Miss Stanley. And Miss Stanley defended herself."

"Or prevented Mrs. Brannock from revealing sensitive information?"

Ava was almost flattered, given the complex strategizing he was accusing her of. Made her seem much smarter than she was feeling. She was wondering if she should try to flee out another door before he tried to take her to the stockade. And would anything look more suspicious than that?

A knock came at the door, and one of the soldiers entered the salon and saluted precisely. He carried a folded letter.

"Ah," Claremont said. "The inventory from the warehouse—"

"No, sir. This is for Mrs. Monroe, sir."

While the lieutenant was gaping, Diane rose from the settee and granted the young soldier a beatific smile. "Thank you, Corporal."

The poor young man blushed.

They waited, but instead of reading the letter she tucked it in some secret pocket and regarded them coolly.

Claremont had finally had enough. "You should all consider yourselves restricted to your cabins until I have word what is to be done with you."

"Doesn't that seem extreme?" Hallern said.

"Protest to the courts, Captain. Good evening." In a modified salute, Claremont gave the brim of his hat a particularly vigorous tap and spun out the door. His footsteps on the deck were audible for some time after.

"Well. That's certainly something." Hallern crossed his arms, hook resting on right elbow, and paced along the back of the salon.

Calmly, Diane withdrew and opened the letter she'd received. She held the page out, indicating a need for reading glasses, but this probably wasn't a good time to make such a suggestion. Diane's gaze narrowed, and her face paled. If Ava hadn't known better, she'd have said Diane was worried. Finally, something had surprised her.

"Well?" Hallern asked.

The moment of uncertainty passed in a flash, and Diane recovered herself, as self-possessed as ever. "Mr. Monroe is not in Cape Town."

The solution Diane Monroe had been relying on was no longer available.

Gilda reached over and clasped Diane's hand with her uninjured one. The two women exchanged a glance of comfort, of solidarity, that Ava couldn't interpret.

"Then there's no one here to help us," Ava said.

"We will have to help ourselves," Diane said, quickly regaining her resolve. "My husband has gone to Kimberley, so I must follow."

Ava tried to recall the map of Cape Colony. Kimberley was inland, almost a thousand kilometers by train, near the border of what had once been Boer territory. Yet another long journey.

"Lieutenant Claremont will never let you leave Cape Town," Hallern said.

Mrs. Monroe regarded them all. She had steel in her shoulders, flint in her eyes. "Then we will not ask permission, will we?" She turned to Marchand. While he seemed unconcerned, even amused, judging by the curl to his lip and mustache, he was in fact standing guard, leaning against the wall with ready access to the door and a view of the windows. The gun was on casual display.

"Mr. Marchand, you are clearly an able soldier. Might I prevail on you to continue on with me, as a sort of guard? I can offer a retainer."

"I have a confession, madam. Your husband already hired me to look after you. Back in London. I will continue to do so." He chuckled. "In fact, I think we must find him if I am to get the rest of my payment."

So much became clear then. He'd had no reason to be so interested in recent events, and every reason to stay far away, to not get drawn in. Even if he was curious or had a strange sense of adventure—like Ava, for example—he'd put himself in danger. He was a mercenary.

"Ah," Diane breathed, a sigh of understanding. "Dear Frederick. Always so thoughtful."

"Of course I'm going with you as well," Gilda said. "But how are we to get off the ship?"

Hallern scratched his chin, lips pursed. "I might have an idea about that."

FOURTEEN

Lactobacillus helveticus

Ava was in this way over her head, a jellyfish in the current.

They retired to their cabins as the lieutenant requested. After dark, they left again, as he had specifically ordered them not to.

They set off in the dead of night, when the world seemed preternaturally still. Even the water slopping against the hull of the ship sounded muted, muffled, as if the harbor were filled with tar instead of water. Perversely, their footsteps on the deck echoed.

On the pier, lantern light expanded, drawing attention to the soldiers patrolling, to prevent exactly the escape they were attempting. Surely any movement on the deck of the *Penelope* at this hour must be obvious, like a flag snapping in a breeze.

One by one, they gathered on the starboard side, opposite the pier, and worked in darkness. Hallern and Suminwa had already lowered one of the lifeboats. It jostled gently on the water below. The ladder Suminwa secured to cleats and unfurled over the side barely credited the name. Made of rope, it was knotted to offer the barest footholds as one climbed into the dinghy tied off below. Unsteady, it twisted unpredictably at every step, every shift in weight. Ava had climbed rope ladders like this before. When she and her brothers were kids, they'd spend whole afternoons climbing up and down, jumping into the sea when they anchored in warm waters while their parents embarked on some zoological study or other. The ladder didn't frighten her. However, the stealth, the threat surrounding them, and all the nerves? She was forgetting where to put her feet.

She'd brought along her microscope, lab supplies, and medical kit. It didn't seem like much to her, a box with a handle, along with her valise. All together, they were no more than the valises the others were bringing. But Hallern raised his brow.

"What good will this do you?" he asked stiffly. His frustration likely had more to do with the situation than with her specifically.

"I need it." This was her greatest tool, her access to the world, the answers to questions. Any power she had, scientific or Arcanist, was here, in this box. "I can carry it myself. I don't need help."

She was sure he was going to keep arguing, and she hugged the box just in case he was thinking of grabbing it and throwing it overboard. She tried not to bristle back at him, and wondered if she would ever see him again.

He pulled something from his coat pocket. A small notebook, clothbound and worn. "Here. Don't look at it until you're well away from here."

"What is it?"

"Well, if I told you, you wouldn't need to look, would you?" He tucked the book in her valise and snapped shut the closure before she could argue further. "You'll understand."

She hoped so, because she certainly didn't now. "Thanks. I think."

A voice from the pier called out, and they all froze. Just one soldier hailing another. The night soon fell still again.

"Are you sure you both won't come with us?" Diane asked the two seamen in a whisper. "You're good in a crisis, and we might need that."

"I hope you don't, madam," Suminwa said. "Besides, I will not set foot in this country. It isn't kind to men like me."

"Sailors?" Diane asked, sounding both curious and confused.

"Black men, madam." He touched his cap in a wry salute.

"We must stay with our ship, I think," Hallern said. "Cover your escape."

"What will you tell the lieutenant?" Ava asked.

"I'll express outrage that one of the lifeboats is missing," Hallern answered with a crooked smile. "Don't worry about us—we're already skunked on this trip. No sense in you lingering over it."

"Very well." She nodded once.

Marchand went first, carefully stepping down the ladder, making an effort to maintain silence. Suminwa handed down the luggage to him—except for the microscope box, because Ava insisted on looking after it herself. Gilda was next, managing well enough with her injured arm bound in the sling. She tried to reach with it once, then hissed in pain. Then was Diane. The two of them already in the boat reached up for her and guided her down, like footmen easing a grand lady into a carriage. That left Ava for last.

"Miss Ava," Suminwa said, stopping her while she had one leg swung over the railing, her skirt fanning out. "If anything goes wrong, if you need help—send word. Yes?"

The words were a lifeline. They might have been rowing off into a dark harbor, but someone was looking out for them. The intent look in his eyes eased something in her.

"Yes, of course. Thank you." She squeezed his arm, and turned to Hallern, lingering for one more farewell. "Mr. Hallern—"

"Charlie," he said. "Call me Charlie."

He took hold of her hand, suddenly, impulsively, and brought it to his lips. Only a quick kiss, and she was wearing gloves, so she only felt it as pressure. She wanted to squeeze his hand, lean in, call him Charlie as he'd asked—but he'd already let go, stepping away. Looking over the side to straighten a line, preparing to set the lifeboat free.

She glanced at Suminwa, as if he'd have some explanation. He merely shrugged, but his eyes were laughing.

Sighing, she stepped onto the ladder. The old skills came back, and she managed to climb down, even holding the microscope case in one hand.

Marchand took the microscope case from her and stashed it with the rest of the luggage. He picked up one oar. Gilda reached for the other, but Ava pointedly took it from her. Gilda might have been stronger, but Ava wasn't about to let her patient exert herself. Again, a childhood spent with explorers and brothers, crossing Seneca Lake by canoe, even punting in Cambridge, had prepared her for this. She glared at Marchand, who didn't try to argue again.

Up at the rail, Hallern and Suminwa watched them go. No one waved, no one spoke. The only noise was water rippling, splashing. That seemed loud enough. All the soldiers must be looking at them. They'd be waiting at the dock where the lifeboat came ashore, unless she and her companions could pass unseen in the darkness.

Ava rowed hard, aware that Marchand was slowing his own rhythm to keep pace with her. He didn't complain or chide her. Least she could do was keep up her end of the work, even when her hands and shoulders began to ache. The slipping of water against wood lulled her, soothed her. So much possibility lay in water.

Obfuscation. Water clouded by algae. That time in the summer hills when pollen blew from the pine trees in yellowish clouds. The mist spewing from a whale's blowhole, though that was more her father's *practicum* than her own. They could have an argument about it, whether megafauna gave one greater access to taxonomic powers, or if the immense trees and forests offered just as much, if not more. Or did the sheer number of insects, bacteria, the biology of the microscopic world, hold its own power? Her parents were skeptical, but they'd spent very little time looking through microscopes.

The number of species in the microscopic world far outstripped the number of visible species. This was a hard thing to imagine, and yet it was true. Where did the power lie? Bacteria had killed far more people than tigers or sharks. The difference was, did bacteria even realize what they'd done?

Cloudiness was a sign that microorganisms populated the water. Algae blooms, cyanobacteria, *Aphanizomenon*, which she'd first identified in stagnant ponds in the Colorado prairie. So simple, and yet the thickest blooms of algae prevented one from seeing through a body of water and could be toxic.

"Is it getting colder?" Gilda asked. She shivered. Diane hugged her coat close.

"Hush," Marchand urged them, but he looked out over the water, brow furrowed, his expression uncertain.

The region was entering the summer season, but the night was still cool, humid. Gilda was right, though; the temperature was dropping. Earlier, the sky had been cloudless, the stars overhead visible, blazing. Now, a fog shrouded them, a mist rolling over the water. The lights on the pier on the other side of the *Penelope* were no brighter than indistinct glows, vague and otherworldly. If they could barely see the pier now, then surely no one on the pier would see them. They rowed carefully, barely making a sound.

They reached the other side of the harbor before dawn, that moment when the stars faded, when the shadows of the world around them, buildings and trees, the shapes of the docks and piers, became visible. They were shivering, stiff from spending time in the open water. Ava had been sweating with effort, but now her damp clothes brought on a chill that sank into her bones, and Ava wished she had a *practicum* for fire, or any way to get warm. But they couldn't risk the light.

As they approached the dock, Marchand whispered quiet instructions, and Ava let him take the other oar and guide them in. When the wood hull of the dinghy hit the post of the dock with a soft thunk, they shook themselves awake and got to work. Marchand tied off the line, securing them to the dock, and the women handed their luggage and each other up to solid footing. They shook out their coats, straightened their hats, and set off in search of a carriage. Hallern had done some reconnaissance for them and directed them to this part of the harbor, quiet and away from more official quarters, the port agents and military. This was a dock where local fishermen tied up their smaller boats. At this hour, the place was starting to come to life, fishermen coming out to fold nets and check lines. Their little lifeboat drew some attention, but no one approached as they gathered their bags and crossed the dock. The resourceful Mrs. Monroe asked one of the gray-coated, wary fishermen where she might find a cab. The bemused man pointed off to the workshops at the end of the pier and the street beyond. She thanked him kindly.

They ended up having to walk nearly half a mile, a tiring trek after being awake all night. At a ferry depot, from which ships carried passengers to local destinations around the coast, they found a cab stand. Carriages let off passengers, and Ava and the others were able to lose themselves in the rush of people.

By the time they hired a cab to take them to the train station, the sun was edging over the horizon. Ava looked back, hoping to see the *Penelope* across the bay, but she'd lost all sense of direction. That part of the journey was over. Right about now, Lieutenant Claremont was probably discovering that his prime suspects had fled. She hoped Hallern and Suminwa wouldn't get in too much trouble.

Once they were settled in the carriage, which trundled off into the heart of the city, Diane narrowed her gaze at Ava. "Was that you? That very convenient fog hiding our path?"

"Maybe a little. It helps if the atmospheric conditions are just right."

"Hm. You keep revealing talents."

"I'm not that talented—"

"You must stop speaking of yourself that way. You're in danger of believing it."

Ava shut her mouth and felt rather stupid. Marchand had on his watchful, amused grin, and Gilda gazed out the window, cradling her injured arm. It must have ached terribly, but she didn't complain.

When they arrived at the station, Ava half expected a squadron of soldiers to be waiting for them, to drag them off to the fort and add accusations of attempted flight to the rest of the suspicions around them. But the only soldiers were a pair of guards walking a circuit along the platform.

The station had the same design and decoration as dozens of train stations all over the world, all built by the British. Sloping roof, white plank walls, twisting ironwork struts, boards showing train schedules, all in English. Ava could hardly believe they were in Africa at all. But the place names were not English: Bloemfontein. Durban. Johannesburg.

Diane knew just what to say to the ticket agent to arrange their travel. The trip had the feeling of a very slow chase—they must get on board and on their way before Claremont could find them. And yet they had to wait.

Ava watched the people—again, all somehow familiar, well-dressed gentlemen and ladies, working men and women in more rugged clothes, families with children who ran and shouted until called back by their parents. There were more Black faces here, reminding her of the Caribbean. She must take notes, to write about this to Harry and Archie.

"I wish I could get a telegram off to my family," Ava said with a sigh. "They must be worried about me."

"You mustn't," Diane said. "I know they don't intend ill, but they might cause ill anyway."

"That could be said of so many things," Ava murmured.

Trains were familiar, at least. It came time to board. They settled into their private compartment and were finally able to rest.

When the train steamed away, Ava regretted that the only time she'd spent in Cape Town was leaving it. The train picked up speed along tracks that curved around the mountains, which cut off her view of the city. Soon after, they were traveling into the countryside, past farms and villages. Pastures and orchards stretched out under wide skies, rolling hills visible in the distance. She wished the circumstances were different; she'd have thought this was lovely.

At last, she had time to dig into her valise and look at the book Hallern had given her. The cover was plain, scuffed. When it was new, the pages would have been blank, but flipping through, she found they were full of writing, a quick but careful hand. Words crossed out, revisions marked in tiny writing between the lines. She recognized Captain Hallern's writing from the logbooks and notes he had written over the course of the voyage.

Turning to the front of the book, she found a title written on the first page: *Torrance and West and the Pirates of Tenerife.*

This was not one of the published adventures she was familiar with.

She read on.

There are ceremonies, rituals that must be performed when one crosses the Equator by ship for the first time. The great sea-god Neptune must be appeased, an acknowledgment made that it is his realm where those who sail have cast their fate.

Torrance and West had crossed that line many times. They had already undergone the ceremonies, which they remembered fondly. After so many years of travel they were well aware of the dangers and allure of Neptune's realm.

And yet for all their experience, they could still be surprised. Even on those well-traversed latitudes of the Atlantic, they could meet a challenge.

Ava was enthralled in spite of herself, picking out the author's handwriting, reading around the revisions, thrilled that she was reading a manuscript, a story that no one else in the world had read. She turned the page and read about the pair sleeping in a lifeboat set drifting on the ocean, and Bran West poking Anton Torrance to get him to turn over, to keep from snoring, and realized . . .

Charlie Hallern had written the novels of Conrad Zane.

Torrance and West and the Fires of Mount Erebus

"Here, old chap," Torrance called. "Take a look at this."

West clambered up the broken ice field, where Torrance was chipping away at an object frozen in place. It seemed to be a long length of wood, polished smooth, with a primitive blade of some kind lashed to one end with sinew. Together, using pickaxes, they pried the weapon from its icy bed.

West raised the sharpened point to the diffuse Antarctic sunlight, turning it this way and that. "What is that, bone? Ivory? Walrus tusk, maybe?"

"There are two problems with that suggestion," Torrance replied.

"There are no walrus found in the Antarctic," West said. "Look here, see these carvings? These designs?" A row of lines and hatch marks had been scratched into one side, regular enough to be a pattern. Writing. Runes? "Is this an Inuit spear?"

"Which points to the second problem, doesn't it?"

"No Inuit in Antarctica either. So where did this come from?"

The obvious assumption would be a prank, that some recent explorer had planted an Inuit spear here in order to confound anyone following in his footsteps. The most obvious difficulty with that explanation was, of course, that no one had traveled this ground before Torrance and West.

"Give me a moment, and I'll see what I can find out."

Despite the bone-chilling cold, West pulled off his goggles and gloves so that he was holding the spear with his bare hands. No matter that the wind bit into him, that his skin was soon touched with the white of incipient frostbite. He needed only a moment, his eyes half lidded, his lips murmuring one of the strange spells of Arcane Taxonomy that gave him access to unseen knowledge, to the powers of the natural world—a spell that would give him the information he sought. How this impossible spear could have possibly arrived at this impossible location.

His breath blew out in a white fog, and he quickly tucked the spear under his arm so he could restore his thick, fur-lined gloves to his hands, rubbing them together to stave off the cold.

Torrance knew better than to rush West when he was in the throes of one of his Arcane spells, but this was one case where he simply couldn't wait. "Well, old boy?"

West held the spear out horizontal to the ground, and slowly turned, sweeping it around, tracing a line to the horizon. And then—the carved spear head began to glow, a faint yellow light shining gold in contrast to the silver-and-sapphire ice all around them.

"There," West said. "The spear came from there."

The peak of the steaming mountain of Erebus was lost in a fog of cold and mist, an ominous portent, as if the boiler of some great engine rumbled within. Here at the base, though, a cracked and tortured landscape revealed its details: crevasses, fissures, shattered rock and uplifted sheets of ancient, solidified lava.

In the direction the spear pointed, they could now make out a new feature, a crack in the stone that had been lost amid all the other broken rock. On closer inspection, this one ran wider, deeper, starting some dozen feet above the ground and widening at the base. Inside, it was full of shadows, somehow even darker and more ominous than the rock around it.

This was an entrance to a cave. A tunnel. Who knew how far it went?

Torrance and West exchanged no words. They didn't need to. A mere glance between them was all they needed to agree to the next step on their journey. Torrance offered an eager grin, and West gladly answered it.

The pair set off, stomping and scraping until they reached the cave entrance, and went in.

FIFTEEN

Shigella dysenteriae

November 1902
Kimberley
Cape Colony

No wonder Hallern hadn't explained in person; he must have known she'd be furious. That she'd have questions he wouldn't want to answer. At the same time, she felt the immense trust he'd placed in her. He likely didn't have another copy of this new Torrance and West adventure, and she could easily decide to toss it in the fire.

She hoped she would see him again so she could give the manuscript back to him. She'd try not to be furious.

After tucking the new Zane novel in a safe place in her valise, she started a letter to Harry and Archie. She recorded events out of habit rather than out of desire. Keeping a record was the best way of remembering, but she was overwhelmed by feelings rather than details. Useless woolgathering. Or was she leaving concrete evidence that would reveal all to an enemy if her letter fell into the wrong hands?

She wasn't entirely sure which hands were wrong. She would probably never send the letters anyway.

Marchand settled into the corner of the seat, pulled his hat low over his eyes, and slept, no matter how the train rocked and rattled. It should have been a sign that the train was safe, if he didn't feel a need to be vigilant.

Gilda maintained vigilance for all of them. She didn't seem to need sleep. She never dozed, never so much as let her eyelids droop. She'd glance at Mrs. Monroe now and then before turning to the window, expressionless, serene. Her arm seemed to bother her less, at least. Ava had changed her bandage and looked at the wound, which appeared to be healing well enough. As soon as any sort of service was available, Mrs. Monroe ordered tea. Ava accepted a cup, along with scones and jam and a serving of cold cuts, the first food she'd had since the previous day. She didn't realize she was ravenous until it was all placed in front of her. After eating, she fell asleep.

She awoke with a crick in her neck and a distinct impression that the ground under her was rocking, like the deck of a ship in a storm. It was merely the train, rattling on its tracks. She wanted a bath and clean change of clothes. She had thought she would get these in Cape Town at a nice hotel. Surely she could get a bath in Kimberley, but she didn't know anything about the town.

Every step of this journey had resulted in some shock or catastrophe. Her expectation—her scientific conclusion based on past observation—was that this would continue as the peril surrounding Mrs. Monroe and her quest continued. Ava had no idea how to prepare. The heroes of the Torrance and West adventures would—they would laugh in the face of danger. That seemed not just unrealistic but also unwise.

Later, Diane slept, resting on Gilda's shoulder. Awake in turn, Marchand sat by the door of the compartment, hand resting near a pocket of his jacket.

Ava turned to the window and took in whatever she could.

The landscape had its own vast beauty, wide plains cut with hills and mesas—though they probably called them something different here, *mesas* being a Spanish word, and she wondered about the vocabulary used to describe this territory. *Veld* rather than *prairie. Bush*, *savanna*, something else. For a taxonomist, vocabulary was everything, and her ignorance felt like weakness. This place was familiar and yet so different, all at the same time. Periodically, the train stopped at towns. The engine smoked, and passengers came on and off; cargo was loaded and unloaded. British soldiers patrolled at every stop. Ava reassured herself that they weren't looking for her.

Much of the landscape reminded her of the American West, where she'd grown up, with its small patched-together towns scattered across wide, expansive country. Then she'd encounter an utterly new sight, like the dark-skinned herdsmen wearing tunics draped over their shoulders, using sticks to guide small herds of rangy-looking horned cattle. She thought she might see lions and elephants, tribes of Zulu warriors, a dozen other exotic scenes she'd read about in books. Books like the Torrance and West adventures? And what stories did people tell about the American West that had nothing to do with reality? Shoot-outs between gunslingers, Indian raids?

She had traveled between well-established cities along the Rocky Mountains, like Colorado Springs, Denver, and even Laramie to the north and Albuquerque to the south. All had universities, clubs, and institutions where her parents had lectured. They had stayed in hotels, traveled in clean carriages on paved roads. The days of stagecoaches and Indian attacks were well in the past. Even the gunmen and outlaws existed only in stories. But those stories were all some people knew of her home. All she knew of Cape Colony was stories, and what she'd read in papers.

They steamed into Kimberley, which it turned out was a well-established city. Its train station was expansive, its streets paved and busy with traffic. Cape Town had been insulated, the only evidence of recent war with the Boers being a greater concentration of soldiers than one might expect. But Kimberley had been under siege at the start of the war and still showed signs of it. Bunkers, trenches, craters from mortar fire, the sides of buildings scarred with bullet holes. And tents.

Acres of round tents pitched on the southern approach into the city, arranged in haphazard rows, as if they'd sprouted up like mushrooms, appearing spontaneously rather than planned. A few quickly built plank structures marked the outskirts. Barracks or administrative buildings, maybe. Fences with barbed wire strung around them. In many places the wire had been pulled from fence posts and coiled to the side, where it lay tangled and rusting. Not a camp, then, but a prison, though in the process of being dismantled.

The aisles between canvas were filled with people, a great temporary city. The war might have ended months ago, but a sense of exhaustion still lay over the area. The town was wounded, as clear as a bloody scrape on a knee. It might be scabbed over, but there would be a scar.

However much Ava had traveled, wherever her parents had taken them, they had stayed away from war and its aftermath. For all the knowledge their parents had poured into them, they had avoided certain difficulties.

Ava did the math—this many tents per row, this many rows—and came up with hundreds. All the faces looking back at her as the train passed were white. Then another camp came into view, another set of tents, more families clustered around campfires, their gazes vague and lost, as if they had been through too much and couldn't face any more, and these faces were all brown. The same clothes, cotton dresses, shirts and trousers, hair trimmed close or tied back with kerchiefs.

Ava wondered: Where was the drainage? How was sewage managed? Was there any clean water?

"*Shigella*," Ava murmured.

"I beg your pardon?" Diane replied.

"*Shigella*. It's a genus of bacteria that causes dysentery. This many people in this small a space—I'll bet you they've had dysentery." Disease followed war, like scavengers followed the hunt.

"Can you cure it?" Diane asked.

The short answer was yes. If she were omnipotent. If she could somehow wave her hand and grant this camp clean water, good drainage, and waste disposal. Keep those already infected well hydrated and clean. Frustrating, that the solution was evident. She wondered if any of these hundreds of people had doctors on hand.

The train slowed and rolled toward an imposing brick building alongside a neat platform with a trim roof and decorated pillars. Very British. She had seen architecture just like this all over the world. A wide street outside was full of carriages, wagons, and pedestrians striding along on urgent business. They might have been in any town in England—until the differences emerged. The desert dust in the air, the palm trees outside some buildings, and an unidentifiable scent in the air, dry and earthy. Many signs were in Dutch as well as English. A half dozen other languages were being spoken within earshot. The diamond mines here had made this city cosmopolitan. There were electric lights on the street outside.

This was a mining town, and Ava recognized the signs from time she'd spent in Cripple Creek and Virginia City. An air of grimy effort hung over the place, as men both Black and white in sweat-stained clothes trekked on a street that led to a hillside covered in scaffolding, with black smoke billowing from some engine or other. An industrial fog hung over the place. The sun was high and burned hot. Their wool coats would be too much here.

They gathered their bags and disembarked. Ava and Gilda lingered, gawping. Diane and Marchand knew better than to muddle around like tourists. They steered them all through the station to the walkway by the street outside.

"Where to, madam?" Marchand was looking all around, assessing, analyzing.

Diane Monroe focused straight ahead, intent on her goal and determined to move ever forward. "Wait here," she said, then marched to a porter stand by the station entrance.

The others dutifully obeyed. When she returned a few moments later, she had the address of a respectable guesthouse and a cab on call for them. The woman was astonishingly efficient.

On the way to the guesthouse, she ordered the cab to stop at the post office. No messages had been left for her. Ava wondered what she expected—no one was supposed to know she was here. As long as they stopped, Ava could find the telegraph office, which ought to be nearby, and get a message to her family . . .

"No," Diane ordered her. "Let's just wait a few more days."

A few more days while their whereabouts were still unknown. Ava understood, but she didn't like it. "I really need to tell my family I'm all right."

"A few more days. Please."

Ava relented, though the delay was wearing on her. She felt some panic when they arrived and found that the guesthouse was near army headquarters. Surely Lieutenant Claremont had discovered their escape by now and sent word. The whole country must be looking for them.

Diane must have a reason for bringing them here and risking discovery.

"You think the army knows where your husband is," Ava observed.

"I think the men who've been fighting and patrolling this part of the country for the last few years know many useful things," Diane said. Spoken with a confident air that of course those men would gladly tell her these many useful things.

Ava's parents taught that you must observe the world as it was and learn from it. You couldn't guess how a mystery would unfold; you must wait for the right clues, the right information, to reveal the truth.

Ava had a thought: that Diane Monroe expected the world to bend to her will. To her, there were no mysteries. Only problems that must be gotten rid of.

The matron of the boardinghouse welcomed them, especially after Diane brought out her checkbook. Diane refused the others' offers of payment for the train tickets, cab fares, and this. She simply paid for it all, sweeping them along with her.

Across the street and the next block down, the army headquarters was a colonial-looking building standing behind a wall. The flag of

Cape Colony draped from a pole out front, glaring in the sun: the Union Jack in the upper left corner of a blue field, with the colony's coat of arms in the middle. Diane eyed it appraisingly, then stepped into the road with the intention of crossing over to it.

"Now?" Marchand demanded. "Perhaps it may be wise to rest first? Have supper?"

"The sooner the better, I should think," Diane answered, tossing the words over her shoulder. She didn't slow down.

With their bags stashed in the guesthouse's vestibule, they hurried after her, caught up in her wake.

At the front gate, a soldier in a khaki uniform stood guard, rifle over his shoulder. Up a short walkway past the gate stood the headquarters itself—two stories, frame and planks put up in a hurry—which still had a decorous coat of pale-yellow paint and a couple of scraggly trees out front in an attempt at a garden. Diane strode right toward the guard despite Marchand's sigh of consternation and mild cursing in French. But Diane was on a mission.

"Good afternoon, Corporal. Could I trouble you to deliver this to your commander as soon as possible?" Diane produced a letter from her purse. Who knew when she'd written it, or if she always carried around letters that might be useful when she was approaching colonial outposts.

The soldier was young, couldn't have been much older than Ava, but he had a heaviness to him. He regarded the group of them flatly, like nothing could surprise him. "Ma'am, I'm afraid I can't leave my post."

"This is a serious matter, I assure you."

He was tough enough not to be intimidated by her, and professional enough not to appear annoyed. Calmly, he set the butt of his rifle on the ground and reached back to ring a brass bell hanging inside the gate.

They waited. Which gave Ava time to realize that she was hungry, thirsty, and tired and wanted nothing more than to sleep in an actual bed. Her body was still swaying, from the movement of either the ship or the train. Or maybe both. Her brain seemed to be rattling inside her skull. Several birds in a tree across the street were squawking up a racket.

She could see movement in the foliage, but the birds maddeningly didn't reveal themselves. This was the problem with birds. So many times, they'd had to stand in place for an hour while Beth and Bran waited for their quarry to emerge so they could identify it. Bacteria, once they'd been stained and smeared on a slide, stayed put.

Still, she wanted to get a look at the birds, to let her parents know what she'd seen.

When the door of the building opened, Ava nearly jumped. She hadn't been paying any attention, and wasn't that exactly the wrong kind of behavior in someone who was supposed to be on the run? Survival of the fittest indeed. Marchand lifted an eyebrow, smirking. Ah. So he'd noticed.

Another man in a uniform—this one a sergeant—emerged from the house and joined the young corporal. Before he could even ask what the matter was, Diane handed him her letter. The sergeant's mustache frowned; the corporal blandly refused to meet his questioning gaze. When the sergeant opened the page, Ava couldn't hope to catch a glimpse of the writing, but the letterhead showed the arms of the Foreign Office. Of course.

Any of them might have been forgiven for wondering which of them was really the spy, Mr. or Mrs. Monroe.

The sergeant nodded. "Very good, Corporal. Keep to your post. Madam, if you'll come inside."

They followed him up to the building and inside, where they were shown to a perfectly normal parlor, plush chairs and sofas arranged for conversation, patterned paper on the walls, along with a smattering of military-themed art, including a painting of Wellington riding off to battle on a crazed-looking horse, neat red-coated regiments marching along. The sergeant sent a servant for tea. The servant was a brown-skinned man in white—from India, Ava thought. Another corner of the empire. Infecting every part of the world, though that observation wouldn't go over well here.

Marchand refused a cup of tea, and refused to sit, instead pacing around the room, glancing out windows, regarding the closed door on the other side of the room. He was looking for lines of sight, for escape routes.

Placidly, as if this were her own parlor, Diane stirred a teaspoon of sugar into her cup.

A clock sitting on the mantel told them they waited for forty minutes.

During that time, Ava took her own turn around the room. One window looked out over a dusty stretch of land, sunbaked prairie. Or what would have been sunbaked prairie back home. The plot was marked by a fence strung with barbed wire. Beyond that, a few dozen tents glared in the sun.

This was the edge of the camp she'd seen from the train. She might have miscounted—the camp must have contained hundreds of tents. Thousands of people. A couple of gray, weathered buildings, hastily built, little more than sheds, stood near the fence and a gap in the wire. An entrance or checkpoint. Here, she recognized familiar signs: nurses in white aprons and caps hurrying back and forth with bundles of bandages; fires under great steaming kettles, boiling water; a lump of bloodstained, soiled sheets sitting isolated, waiting to be burned.

However temporary, however makeshift, this was a hospital.

When the sergeant opened the door, Ava flinched, startled; the others did not. He invited them inside the next room: an office, properly military. Not nearly as comfortable as the parlor.

The man behind the desk stood to greet them. A red-coated officer, colonel by the rank. Experienced, judging by his gray hair and the long-suffering pull to his wrinkles. Sweat matted his hairline in the heat.

Only one chair was available, and of course Diane took it, perching elegantly. The colonel acknowledged her with a surprisingly respectful nod. He might have been acknowledging a fellow officer.

"Mrs. Diane Monroe? I am Colonel Harcourt. But I suspect you already know that."

"A pleasure, Colonel."

God, who was actually in charge here?

Marchand stood by the door, arms crossed, glaring. He wouldn't be intimidated. Gilda was nearby, making herself unobtrusive. Ava hardly knew what to do with herself. She set herself to studying yet another painting, this one of a group of cavalry charging into a swarm of dust meant to represent a battle. These horses seemed even more crazed than the previous one, eyes rolled back in their heads and nostrils flaring red, in a way she'd never seen a horse look in real life.

Disconcertingly, Colonel Harcourt took his time considering them all. It made Ava feel like a child who'd stolen sweets.

"I've got a message from Cape Town about you four," he said finally with false cheer, waving a telegram at them. Telegrams traveled faster than trains. A simple matter of physics. "Something about suspicious activities and being wanted for questioning in relation to an act of sabotage aboard a passenger ship?"

Ava's stomach churned, but Diane glanced ceilingward and scoffed. "Oh really, that's all a willful misunderstanding of the situation on the part of Lieutenant Claremont."

So much relied upon the stories one told about a particular situation. Whose version would win out, and be elevated to the truth that Colonel Harcourt acted on?

The colonel studied her. "You think I should listen to you rather than to one of His Majesty's trusted officers?"

"You have my letter. You may decide for yourself whom to trust."

The colonel put his hand on a second piece of paper, Diane's letter, sitting next to the telegram on his desk. They were only two out of whole stacks of papers, records, dispatches, files, and ledgers, cluttered along with inkwells and pens and random splashes of ink. A visual representation of the problems before him.

Ava hadn't read the contents of the letter, but she could guess: It bestowed some kind of authority on Mrs. Monroe, on behalf of the Foreign Office. Which left the colonel in the position of deciding whether he should recognize that authority, and no doubt speculating on the consequences if he guessed wrong. Ava wondered if either of them had ever played poker.

The colonel gave way first. "Then I suppose my only question for you is, What favor are you going to ask of me?"

"An answer to a simple question. Have you seen my husband, Mr. Frederick Monroe?"

Ava tried to read the officer's expression. All she could conclude was that he was working very hard not to have any expression at all, which meant he knew something.

Ostentatiously, he flicked the telegram again and raised a gray eyebrow at the rest of them. "Now, let's see . . . You are Mr. Luis Marchand, some kind of French adventurer. And you—Lieutenant Claremont said your name is Gilda Bell. He had nothing to say against you except that you were associating with this lot. I see you've been injured. Do you need medical attention?"

"No, thank you," Gilda said softly.

The colonel shrugged. "That leaves you, Miss Ava Stanley?"

"Yes, sir."

"And it's true, that you speak German and were somehow in the middle of this plot?"

She could probably drop her stepfather's name and get this all cleared up right now. Or . . . get Anton implicated.

"A lot of people speak German," she said. Mostly German people, she reflected glumly—not so many Americans. About the only thing she could do to deflect suspicion was play up just how entirely inexperienced and naive she was. "And I'd say the plot sprang up around me before I realized what was happening."

The colonel graced her with a thin smile.

Diane stepped in. "Miss Stanley was instrumental in recovering control of the *Penelope*. Lieutenant Claremont wasn't there, and he doesn't know."

Harcourt looked Ava over, clearly skeptical that this earnest young woman could play an instrumental role in much of anything. "Well, I suppose there's no harm in telling you that Frederick Monroe left Kimberley almost a fortnight ago."

Ava counted back—that would have been about the time the Brannocks sprang their plot on board the ship.

"Did he leave a message for Mrs. Monroe?" Gilda asked.

Diane shook her head. "He wouldn't have. I'm supposed to be in Nassau, remember? Colonel, might I ask for your assistance in searching for him? You must know where he went, and when. It should take little effort to go after him. I only need a guide, I think. Perhaps a willing soldier or two."

"You might ask, Mrs. Monroe. And I'm afraid I will have to decline. You see, he insisted on heading toward the German colony. The border there is currently unsettled, and I can't have ordinary citizens plunging into it causing trouble. That's how the last uproar started, you understand. I'm happy to offer you quarters here at the fort—"

"Where he can keep his eye on us," Marchand put in.

"No, thank you. We're quite well looked after," Diane said evenly. She wasn't going to put herself under anyone's thumb.

"Ah, well then, I really think you'd be better off staying in Kimberley. It's quite a nice town, once you get used to it. As soon as I get any word from Mr. Monroe, you'll be the first to know."

Ava expected Diane to argue. To fight back. To offer some wily excuse and persuade the colonel to see things her way. Shockingly, she relented.

"Of course, Colonel. Thank you so much for your assistance." Her voice was so smooth, it was almost a purr.

That was it? What was next for them, then? More waiting. Ava had done enough of that. As the others turned to the door, she stepped forward.

"Colonel, I noticed the nurses outside in the camp," she said. "I have medical training, and I'd like to help if I can. Make myself useful and such."

"You're a nurse?" he asked.

She'd almost said yes, to save long explanations, when Diane answered for her. "She's a doctor."

Ava almost gave the reflexive amendment: *almost a doctor, not quite a doctor*. But she couldn't contradict Diane. "I trained at the New Hospital for Women in London."

"And she's an Arcane Taxonomist," Diane added.

The captain raised a brow. "Really?"

His tone was curious rather than skeptical. Ava could have handled skeptical rather than curious. Curious meant he'd have expectations. Easier to confront skepticism.

"Fourth Rank," she said. "US Department of the Treasury. If you want to see my badge."

"Oh no, that's not necessary. If you really want to help, I'll turn you over to Captain Boyd and his miscreants."

She supposed she'd find out soon enough what that meant. "Thank you, sir."

"And in case I wasn't clear—I must insist that you all remain in town for the time being. Until we get this business with Mr. Monroe cleared up, hm?"

"Of course," Diane said sweetly.

Ava knew right then that Diane Monroe was planning to leave town at the first opportunity.

SIXTEEN

Frankia alni

The matron of the guesthouse, Mrs. de Haas, spoke with a thick Dutch accent. Not Dutch, Ava learned—Afrikaans, a language near Dutch but not quite, spoken by the Boers, descendants of the region's early Dutch settlers. Ava could almost understand it, but precise meanings slipped away from her. Mrs. de Haas prepared a supper for them, then showed them to a smallish bathroom. Ava nearly cried with relief. After a thorough scrubbing, she slept well for the first time in days.

The next day, she was the last one to wake up, and by the time she went down to breakfast, the others had already gone. Mrs. de Haas had two letters waiting for her by her setting at the breakfast table. One, an official-looking letter from Colonel Harcourt. The other, a simple folded sheet of paper from Diane Monroe. Harcourt's letter was an introduction to the army physician who ran the infirmary at the nearby camp, Captain Boyd. Diane had penned an elegant note explaining that she and the others had gone to take in the sights of town, and would she like to join them for tea later at a café that had been recommended to her? Time and address enclosed.

Diane had a way of writing such a request to make it sound . . . well, not quite like a command. But Ava felt inexplicably guilty at the thought of declining the invitation and disappointing her. She was sure there was more to the invitation—Diane had gotten new information, or had set up a meeting with a secret contact. This was the next step on her mission, and she had to be clandestine about it.

Rather than generating excitement, this thought exhausted Ava. No more. She needed to be someplace she could actually do some good. Or at least have a better chance of doing good. She tucked Mrs. Monroe's note away, collected her kit and microscope case, and headed out to find this infirmary.

Close up, the encampment seemed disturbingly permanent. The tents were worn, the canvas stained and sagging, and the pathways between rows were trodden down with the passage of many feet over many days and weeks. The war had nominally been over for months, but the camp was still here. On the porch of one of the buildings, children were gathered, sitting on the floor while a teacher spoke, presenting chalk writing on a small slate. A school, of sorts.

A makeshift courtyard formed a space in front of a simple square block of a house. Here, steam rose up from an oven and basin where water boiled, tended by young women assistants in skirts and aprons. Barrels were lined up; the boiling must have been a constant task. A difficult one, in the heat—midmorning, the sun already beat down uncomfortably. The assistants confirmed that the building was the infirmary. The front door stood open.

"Hello?" Ava asked as she entered, knocking cautiously.

The interior made a good show of looking something like a doctor's front vestibule, a kind of shabby parlor with a faded rug on the floor, a couple of chairs next to a table holding an oil lamp, a couple of cabinets in the back and a desk in the middle, where a fortyish-year-old man was bent over notes. He was clean shaven, frowning, reddish with what seemed to be a permanent sunburn. Round, wire-rimmed glasses were set on his nose. His red uniform jacket was hanging over the back of his chair.

"What is it?" He glanced up, studying her through his glasses, furrowing his brow at her.

She had to clear her throat a little. "Captain Boyd? Colonel Harcourt said I should come meet you."

"Ah. Yes. He sent over a note. An American lady doctor, are you?"

"Close enough to it."

"Dalrymple!" he called over his shoulder to another room.

A younger, bearded man slipped in through the doorway. He must have been in his mid-twenties and also went without a jacket, shirtsleeves rolled up to his elbows. He was drying his hands with a grubby-looking towel.

"What, sir?" He sounded brusque, almost surly, as if annoyed at the interruption. But he seemed full of energy. Not yet worn down.

Boyd waved at him. "This is my assistant, the Egregious Dalrymple."

"I'm not familiar with that rank," Ava said blandly.

"Lieutenant," Dalrymple said, glaring, curling a smile.

"Harcourt says you're an Arcane Taxonomist?" Boyd pronounced this with a theatrical air that somehow endeared him to her. They both seemed entirely unconcerned with formalities.

She nodded. "Fourth Rank, US Treasury—"

Boyd gave a dismissive snort. "That bloody American system. Meaningless. Who trained you? What's your lineage?"

"With all due respect," she said, determined. "The American system is more empirical than relying on vague academic networks."

He turned a withering stare on her. She swallowed a lump in her throat, offering a token. He might know the names. He might not. "I started at Radcliffe with Mrs. Agassiz. My parents are Elizabeth Torrance and Brandon West."

Boyd raised a brow, and Dalrymple whistled low. So yes, they knew the names.

"Well, that's certainly a lineage. You inherited their feel for the Arcane?"

"I wouldn't go that far," she said. By his thin smile, she guessed that endeared her to him.

Dalrymple hitched a thumb at his superior officer. "The captain here started with Wallace and Huxley. My lineage isn't nearly so impressive."

"You'll have to name *me* in your lineage, boy," Boyd said cheerfully. "Poor sot."

She gaped. "Alfred Russel Wallace? *Really?*" Wallace, friend and rival to Charles Darwin himself, who helped establish the theory of evolution as a basis for modern Arcane Taxonomy. The closest Ava had ever come to such an esteemed figure was meeting the American botanist and Arcanist Asa Gray, but she'd only been four years old and didn't remember it.

They were both Arcanists. Harcourt should have warned her.

"Here," Boyd said, and did the inevitable: He turned to one of the cabinets, drew out a beeswax candle in a brass holder, and set it on the desk between them. "Go on, then. Show us."

How could she ever explain? "Um. I can't."

"Oh, come on. Everyone can light a bloody candle."

As annoyed as she was at this, his forthrightness was somehow comforting. He had no ulterior motives. She suspected he didn't like *anyone*. Dalrymple stood with his hand over his mouth, hiding his expression.

Well. She wouldn't lose anything by trying.

Nothing she had tried so far had worked, so she went far afield, outside the usual *practica* that started fires. No bright reds, no natural forms of light. Rather, think of the chemical nature of fire, of exothermic reactions. Oxidization, the breaking of chemical bonds that in turn caused heat and light. That was the scale where microscopic beings worked. Decay caused heat. The heat of a compost pile, a nest of mushrooms in a damp forest. Such as *Thermoascus aurantiacus*.

The wax began to sweat, and Ava was sure she had simply repeated the *practicum* she had found back in England with her mother, a kind of humidity, moisture dripping down the wax. But this was more. The wax itself sagged, overcome with heat, melting. She pushed the power, weirdly satisfied to be accomplishing something, anything. This was the effect of flame, if not the flame itself, and the candle turned to liquid, sinking and slumping into an undistinguished mass of wax over the candleholder.

"Well, it's not nothing," Dalrymple said.

Boyd raised a brow. "Is your doctoring as unpredictable?"

"I suppose you can set me loose and see if I kill anyone." They both gave her a look, and she winced. "That was a joke."

"Good God," he muttered. "Miss Stanley, this isn't your nice upstanding London hospital. We have very few beds, no real roofs. We don't have enough medicines and bandages; we have diseases we can't treat, wounds from the bush that have been left to fester. God help us if war breaks out again."

Ava was alarmed. "Is that likely?"

At this, he slumped. Tired, like a man who'd been through quite enough war. "A few mad Boers are still up in the hills looking for revenge. Some bands of Zulus out for a fight. Though you're American, you know all about that sort of native scuffle, with Indian attacks and such."

"I can honestly say I've never been attacked by Indians," she replied.

"Really? Well then. Just be warned. If you really want to work here, you'll *work*."

"That's all I'm asking, sir."

"Dalrymple. Show her around. Report back. Good morning, Dr. Stanley."

She felt like she was back on the ship, the deck swaying underneath her. It was rather exciting. "Is there someplace I can set up my microscope? I can run samples for you, if you like."

Boyd sighed. "Dalrymple?"

"Yes, sir." Dalrymple waved her through the back of the room. She dutifully followed.

This appeared to be a laboratory and storeroom, and Boyd hadn't been lying. The room was full of rickety shelves obviously built from spare lumber. The shelves themselves were sparse. At first glance they contained just about everything a roughshod infirmary would need. Bottles, boxes, stacks of folded clothes, tins of instruments. But . . . they didn't contain very much of it. On the other side of the room was a desk of sorts, and a small cupboard holding bottles of solvents and chemicals. Dalrymple indicated she should set her microscope here. This was the lab, then.

"So. Why can't you light a candle?" Dalrymple asked. "Everybody can light a candle."

"Why is that the *practicum* that everyone decided defines an Arcanist? Why this and not something else?" she countered.

"It was Linnaeus's original *practicum. Linnaea borealis*. Light in the darkness."

"But he didn't light a candle. He generated light, yes, but not flame. Phosphorescence, like that of Lampyridae. Who was the first Arcanist to light an actual flame?"

"You know, I'm not sure."

She'd be interested in finding out.

Dalrymple brought over a candle, something that could be used to bring light to a microscope mirror. Without any apparent thought, he passed his hand over the wick, which flared into a merry yellow flame. She tried not to be jealous. It wouldn't have bothered her so much if this didn't seem to come so easily to other Arcanists.

"What do you use?" she asked.

He hesitated, as if the answer were some great secret. Many Arcanists felt that way about their personal *practica*. "*Electrophorus electricus*," he finally revealed.

She had to think a moment, but this was a case where the scientific name actually did give a clue about the namesake. "Electric eel?"

"Just so."

"Nice. A little obvious."

"Perhaps. But I don't believe there's any advantage to be had in being mysterious or metaphorical."

Dalrymple steered her out a back door to a smaller building containing a rather minimal surgical theater in one room and a recovery ward in the other. It wasn't much, but it would do in the absence of anything else.

They left the surgery and started down the aisle along the first row of tents. They spent the next half hour walking up and down the lanes between tents. Most of the residents of the camp seemed to be women and children, and a cloud of despair hung over the place, as if this were the end of a long road, and the hundreds of people had settled right where they stopped, full of resignation.

"What's the story here?" she asked Dalrymple.

"They're Boer," he said. "The army burned the territory during the war. Farms, houses, crops, everything. The people who lived there lost everything and didn't have anywhere else to go, so we put them here."

Put them. Did the people have a choice about staying here, or not? "One can't help but notice the coils of barbed wire on the outside boundaries. Is this a refugee camp or a prison?"

Dalrymple's shoulders slumped. "Depends on who you ask," he said tiredly.

"You were here for it? The war?"

"I was," he said, politely dispassionate. "An idealistic young surgeon, fighting for king and country. Well, it was queen and country when we started. You know."

She wasn't sure she did. "Did the army—did you—really have to burn everything?"

"They were sheltering the enemy. Refusing to surrender. How else were we going to win the war?" This seemed so matter of fact to him. No alternative offered.

"What were you fighting for?"

She wasn't sure she expected an answer. But he glanced at her and said, "You know, the usual. To protect subjects of the Crown."

"And the diamond mines?"

He stifled a chuckle. "And the diamond mines. Yes, I suppose."

They walked on, reaching a wider lane, enough room for a couple of wagons to pass one another. More tents lined the other side, and Ava started to cross over to them.

"Wait. Stop," Dalrymple said. He reached, almost taking her arm, pulling back at the last moment.

"What's wrong?"

Shifting uncomfortably, he looked away. "We don't allow white nurses into the Black part of the camp. I must assume that rule applies to you as well."

"But I'm not—" She wasn't a nurse. But she was white, and a woman, and she suspected this was where the heart of the rule lay. Ava could see a cluster of children in shirts and trousers, barefoot, playing a game with glass marbles on the ground. A woman walked up the aisle with a baby on her hip. "There's as much illness and injury there as there is here. Bacterial infection isn't going to care how wide the road is or what the rules are. Please tell me that *someone* is there looking after people."

"Yes, some missionaries."

Ava crossed the road and went into the next camp to have a look, rules be damned. How would they stop her? She sensed Dalrymple sputtering and fuming behind her, but he inevitably followed.

The children talked at each other, over each other. She didn't recognize the language—it wasn't Afrikaans—and wondered if she could get them to teach her a few words.

"Hello?" she said, aware that she was looming over them. They fell silent and stared at her. She hoped her smile was friendly, at least. "Can you tell me about your game? What are you playing?"

Dalrymple came up beside her and spoke a few words in their language. One of the kids laughed, and they held up their marbles to show him before plunging back in as if he wasn't even there.

"What did you say to them?"

"Oh, nothing in particular."

"I don't believe you."

"Perhaps just something about how Americans are often very forward."

They smirked at one another amiably.

The woman with the baby eyed them warily as they passed. The tents in this part of the camp were just as run down as in the other, and they were just as overcrowded, but at least there seemed to be good drainage, and something resembling sanitation, pit latrines a good distance away. At the end of one row, she smelled telltale scents of antiseptic, alcohol, acrid and sour—illness and medicines battling with one another. Inside the tent, a dozen patients lay on bedding. Not even cots—they were right on the ground. A white man in a dark suit was working at a table full of jars and basins, assisted by a Black woman in a nurse's gown and apron.

The man looked up. "Ah. Lieutenant Dalrymple, what brings you over to this side?" He had a Scottish accent and gray in his beard. He handed a brown glass bottle to the nurse, who nodded and took it away to another table, where she worked mixing the contents with water. A round of medication, then.

"Hullo, Macintosh," Dalrymple said. "Just showing around a visitor."

"Ava Stanley, hello," Ava said, before Dalrymple called her a doctor and she had to explain again. She reached her hand out for shaking.

"Ah, American? Very good." He nodded and smiled as if pleased at the information. "And how are you liking Kimberley?"

"I haven't seen much of it yet," she confessed. "But it's a little overwhelming. Do you need any help here? I've had some medical training."

"Here now, you promised to help us," Dalrymple said.

"Can't I help you both?"

The two men exchanged glances, losing their previous jovial manner. Dalrymple raised a brow, apparently sending the signal to Macintosh to explain.

"The two camps don't cross over that much," Macintosh said. "Really rather a surprise to see any whites here at all, apart from us missionaries." He said this with a finality that suggested she would do well not to ask further.

"Oh, I see. Well, maybe I can come visit again. I'd like to help."

The two men talked over each other then, Macintosh brightening as he said, "That's very kind of you—" and Dalrymple insisting, "You really shouldn't—"

She glared at the lieutenant, and he broke off.

"Nice meeting you, Mr. Macintosh," she said, before leaving with Dalrymple to continue the circuit of the camp.

They went several dozen paces before she could think of what to say, and finally just came right out with it. "My stepfather is Black," she felt the need to explain. "It seems wrong, having two different camps when we all need the same things."

She couldn't read Dalrymple. She'd only just met the man and couldn't tell if his lack of expression was studied. Did he not care, or was he suppressing opinions he didn't dare express? And what were those opinions anyway? She was preparing to be angry.

"While I might agree, the reality is that we must make concessions. To some definition of propriety, to local customs—"

"Must we? Must we really?" she asked.

"I think we should be getting back to the infirmary."

When they circled back to the infirmary at the main camp, she attempted an observation. Just to see if he would listen or scoff. "You need more wash stations. Antiseptic washes at every doorway. Oh lord, please tell me you wash before and after surgeries."

"Of course—we aren't *barbaric*. But we've mentioned the supply issue? We need peroxide, alcohol, and we have so little to spare. Clean water is at a premium. Please don't look so dismayed," Dalrymple said.

"This really is better than it was. We haven't had a case of cholera in months."

Back in the supply room, she took stock of what was on hand and got to work. A tin basin sat on a stand, clearly intended to be used as a wash station. A pitcher nearby held water, which she was sure ought to be boiled for a good long time. But she could do more with it. She skimmed her fingertips on the surface.

Fermentation was a biological process as well as a chemical process. She could replicate the effects, *Saccharomyces cerevisiae*, brewer's yeast. Concentrated, impurities bubbling away into the air until all that was left was the ethanol. The air took on a rich, yeasty scent, dissipating into the heat and dust.

This might very well be the most impressive *practicum* she knew.

Dalrymple frowned. "Did you really . . ." He touched the surface and tasted his finger. He grimaced. "It's alcohol. How?"

"*Saccharomyces cerevisiae.*"

"Fermenting yeast. Of course." And wasn't that a thrill, that he understood without her explaining? "Well, I hesitate to think too deeply about the theological implications."

Transforming water into alcohol, if not specifically wine? She'd never thought of it like that, but she considered the idea now and found she wasn't bothered.

"I think the implications are obvious," she said. "Clearly Jesus was an Arcane Taxonomist."

SEVENTEEN

Streptococcus pneumoniae

Ava thought she might have time to collect and culture samples. Her Nassau collecting project, transplanted, to make the best of the situation.

But she didn't have time; there was too much work to do at the infirmary. Children were malnourished, feverish, and displayed the general catalog of childhood illnesses. On a regular basis, soldiers came in with injuries. Broken bones, cuts and gashes, mishaps with rifles, falls and fights. The first time a soldier with a sliced arm came in, Boyd watched her clean and suture the wound. Apparently, he was satisfied with her work and happy enough to let her deal with the camp's women and children, which was who lady doctors usually treated.

Evenings, after washing up, she went back to the guesthouse. When Mrs. de Haas learned she was helping in the camp, she fussed happily over Ava, urging her to sit, bringing her tea and meals, asking if she needed anything, anything at all. Apparently, Ava's work was a great boon. Word about it got around fast. The response left Ava a bit baffled.

Diane didn't say a word about Ava declining to join her and the others on their treks through the town. Ava had lined up her defenses, the argument that she was doing good work, that the infirmary needed her more than Diane and her mission did. Clearly, Diane didn't need Ava at all—and in spite of herself, Ava felt a bit of a pang at that. She wouldn't get to see how the quest for Mr. Monroe turned out. Not until later, anyway.

The work at the infirmary was more important.

The others didn't talk much about how they spent their days. They explored the town, met the mayor, and learned all sorts of gossip. Marchand called it gathering intelligence. Pursuing their mission, whatever they were doing to track down Mr. Monroe. Ava almost expected the man to turn up on their doorstep one of these mornings. The matter of the mining survey, the border, and who belonged where would all be cleared up. Gilda stopped using the sling and insisted the wound was healing well. She didn't seem to be in much pain, at least. She got a job in the army barracks kitchen. Like Ava, she wanted to keep busy.

However she spent the days, Diane maintained an air of anxiety, and Marchand always seemed to be looking over his shoulder.

Ava finally got a chance to start some cultures, and within a few days had a dozen petri dishes full of thriving bacterial colonies to compare to reference drawings. This was both thrilling and dismaying—to think, all this growth happening around them all the time, invisible to their eyes. She'd swabbed samples and stained slides and was just about ready to put the first of them under her microscope when a voice interrupted.

"Miss Stanley? Ava?"

Gilda Bell stood at the door of the supply room, looking around with some suspicion at the unfamiliar territory. "Those strange officers out front told me you'd be here."

"Yes! One minute." She had just gotten the lens focused on this slide, the stained cells coming into bright definition. They looked like rivers of tiny seed, bunched together. She eased away from the desk. "Gilda, here, sit down. I'm afraid we're not civilized enough to offer tea."

"As long as you're not serving up whatever's in those." She nodded at the row of dishes sprouting puffy growths of white and yellow.

"Of course not. Those are my babies."

Gilda raised a brow in lieu of displaying actual disgust. She sat at the edge of the room's other wooden chair. "Can you do something for me?"

"Of course." Even after the last weeks she couldn't guess what Gilda was thinking, what she was planning. This woman who was capable of murder. But Gilda had had a good reason for every murder she'd committed.

"Can you cut my hair?" She touched the bun at the base of her neck tentatively, like she wasn't sure Ava would ever agree to such an odd request.

"It's long past the time when surgeons were also barbers," Ava said wryly.

"I know you'll be careful," Gilda said.

In fact, she was flattered that the cautious Gilda would trust her with such a task. Ava was on the verge of asking why Gilda wanted her hair short. The heat was enough of an excuse—they were all sweating under their hats and jackets all the time. But in the end, it didn't matter.

"Come on, let's do this outside."

They found a spot behind the infirmary building in the open, not a place that Ava needed to keep clean. They brought along a chair, a linen towel, a comb, and a pair of sharp scissors that would usually be used to cut clothing from the injured.

"I'm not sure I know exactly what I'm doing," she said, unpinning Gilda's hair and combing it straight down her back. Black, silky, this was the kind of hair Ava had often envied, in contrast to her nondescript thin brown. Part of her thought it'd be a shame to cut it, but Gilda seemed determined.

"You have brothers, don't you? You ever watch them trim their hair?" She had. "Cut it like theirs."

"You want your hair to look like a man's?"

She nodded quickly. "Easier to take care of in the dust, I think."

Ava gathered the hair into a thick hank at the back of Gilda's head, letting it fall halfway down her back. This felt momentous, like crossing a boundary or boarding a ship on an ocean voyage. "You're sure?"

"Yes," Gilda answered, no hesitation.

Ava cut through the thickness at her neck, and was left with a handful of orphaned hair. She reached around and offered it to Gilda, who held the hank like she might a wounded kitten. Careful, uncertain.

"I've heard that some women sell their hair," Ava said. "You might ask Mrs. de Haas if anyone in Kimberley is buying." It could be made useful, valuable, not to be cast off.

"That's a good idea," she said, and tucked the hank of hair in her jacket pocket.

Gilda shook her head, and the remaining fringe swung around her neck and chin, loose and free, wild and unmanageable compared to the long length that could be braided and twisted and pinned into place.

"How does that feel?" Ava asked.

"Strange," Gilda said, after a pause. "My neck feels naked."

Ava drew out lengths and clipped them to get closer to a man's trimmed style. Gilda closed her eyes and seemed to relax into the attention.

If she could get close to Harry's wavy, tousled cut, Ava would call it a victory. She trimmed a little at a time, sculpting the hair into something else.

She also took the opportunity to fish a bit. "So what's Diane planning?"

"Why do you think she's planning anything?"

"She's always planning something."

Gilda chuckled. "She'll tell you herself, if she chooses to."

"But you'll follow her. Whatever she decides, you'll agree to it," Ava said.

Gilda's new hair was taking shape. Parted in the middle, swept to either side above her ears. Her face might have had fine cheekbones, soft eyes. But if she wore a suit and bowler cap, she would seem at first glance to be a young man.

"Do you know . . . those first couple of days on the ship, I didn't care where I was going. It didn't matter. Nothing mattered. I . . . was going to throw myself over. Jump the railing into the waves. What else was there for me? I was sure to be caught, hanged for murder. Better to erase myself from the world. Then I met Diane. She makes her own way. Sets her own rules. I thought . . . maybe I could do the same. Of course I'll follow her."

When Gilda turned and looked up at her, Ava saw someone else. Gilda wasn't Gilda anymore. She was making herself into someone new. Ava felt strange, being an instrument of her transformation.

Ava ran her hands through Gilda's hair, ruffling it into place, shaking out the last of the cut bits. "There we are. I don't have a mirror on hand to show you. I hope you like it."

Gilda's eyes were half lidded when she reached up and stroked her own head, combing her fingers through her newly trimmed locks. She smiled.

That evening at supper, the others got a look at her new style. Marchand huffed with indifference—women's hairstyles were all the same to him, apparently. Her lips pursed, gaze narrowed, Diane seemed to be restraining herself from commenting.

"Do you like it?" Gilda said, tilting her head, running her fingers through the short locks. She seemed so pleased.

"It's lovely," Diane finally said, and Ava sighed with relief that she wasn't going to be harsh. "It'll feel marvelous in the heat."

"Yes, I feel so much lighter. Mrs. de Haas?" The matron had come in with the soup for supper. "Do you know of any place in town that buys ladies' hair?"

"Oh, Gilda, if you needed money, you should have told me! You didn't have to cut your hair," Diane said.

"It isn't about the money," Gilda said with her usual calm, unflappable. "I hadn't thought of selling until Ava mentioned it. I just wanted short hair. Might as well make use of it, though, yes?"

"Well then," Diane said, nonplussed.

Telling, that the idea of selling one's hair for money seemed to horrify Diane Monroe. She'd been shot at, tied up, engaged in some brand of espionage or another, but she'd never wanted for money or the means to get it.

"Diane," Ava started when they'd settled and begun on the soup. "I wanted to ask if it's safe for me to send word to my parents." It had been a week since their arrival in Cape Town. Too much longer, and the whole family might just hop on a steamer to come looking for her themselves.

"Can you hold off just a bit longer? I'm sure I'll get word from Frederick any day now. Just until then."

Ava wondered if anyone had ever told Diane no. She never seemed to expect arguments. Ava marshaled herself.

"I wouldn't go into detail about what's happened. Just a quick telegram to let them know I'm all right," she said. "I really don't see what harm it can do."

"And that's the reason to refrain—it's the harm you don't see coming that does the most damage."

Mrs. de Haas returned with an address on a card for a wigmaker who might take Gilda's hair. The meal continued, with conversation that was never more serious than the hot weather and the fine food Mrs. de Haas made.

Ava had had no thought of trying to recreate what had happened on the ship. When she found, or thought she found, the unmarked ship following them. When she traced the assassins' sloop to the warehouses that she'd never seen before. When she passed out. When she saw . . . more. She wasn't sure she could replicate the process away from the ocean, that conduit of connection, of liquid information. But she started to wonder: What would happen if she accessed that flow with intention? With direction?

Diane didn't want her to send word to her parents until Mr. Monroe was found. Fine—then she would do what she could to help find him.

The world was *alive*. Any length of time studying microscopic life revealed that truth: Life existed everywhere, grew on nearly every surface, on every breath of wind. Some Arcanists said the power of the microscopic world was beyond access because one couldn't hold the species in one's hand, because discovery required the intervention of technology, of microscopes and specimen preparation rather than the naked senses. When really, the power was around her all the time. The difficulty wasn't isolating such forms of life, but rather understanding these species on their own terms.

The next day, alone in the infirmary's makeshift laboratory, Ava took a quiet moment for herself. She sat in a chair, closed her eyes, and imagined. This wasn't just eavesdropping, as with the earwig *practicum*. She needed more.

Genus *Dermatophagoides*. Dust mites. This country was awash in dust, and she imagined gathering information through the creatures' sensory organs, feelers, antennae, even the tiny hairs on their feet. Passing unnoticed by anything larger than the head of a pin. She could go anywhere, drift anywhere, settle anywhere. They had access to everything—ask any housewife in charge of keeping a room clean. Ask anyone who traveled across a sunbaked landscape and collected dust on their boots, on their clothes. Some of it was dirt and some of it was pollen, mites, insects, more.

Now, travel north and west to the border, where Frederick Monroe was said to be traveling. Much like trying to find a ship on the ocean, except . . . it wasn't working. On the *Penelope*, she could see in all directions, and she knew what the ocean looked like. Here . . . she might as well have been trying to imagine a scene from a story.

And where was Diane Monroe now? At the writing desk in the parlor of their guesthouse. Every letter Diane had written since arriving here had been done at that desk. The pages, the ink . . . now there was a trail. That was how *she* was trying to find her husband.

And then . . . was it a memory? A vision? Or merely a hunch? What was Ava looking at, or imagining she was looking at?

Two sets of paper. Two documents in that precious packet the Brannocks had so desperately wanted. Diane had revealed one but not the other. The public one, the talisman to pave her way through Cape Colony, to win allies. The other, a secret. They were related. In keeping one hidden, she hadn't lied, per se. The one set of papers was exactly what she had claimed: a mining survey, a map of disputed territory and the means to gain control of it.

But what was the other? The power of the modern world, the empire, lay in paper. In maps, bank ledgers, government decrees, and real estate titles. Not nearly as straightforward as the treasures Torrance and West sought from lost temples and mountaintops. But then what was the line from that first page of *The Terror of the Zambezi*? About more intangible treasures? Or maybe this was a traditional hunt for riches, conducted in terms that the modern empire understood.

The view was obscured. Ava didn't understand what she was seeing.

The picture expanded. From the precise lines of a survey map to the broad, expansive, and uncontainable landscape where a single grain of pollen might blow for miles, might cover the distance of an entire country, and what would it mean to see it all, to travel it all at once, to take it all in, and honestly, if she walked that country—or flew over it like a mite caught in the breeze—she couldn't tell where Cape Colony began and German South West Africa ended, or vice versa. They were lines on a map, not boundaries in life, and the mites didn't care about lines on a map. And while a dust mite could take it all in, her human mind that longed for organization, for classification—for damned taxonomy—couldn't, and to seek out one piece of information was to be willing to take in everything around it, and it was all too much, too overwhelming—

"Miss Stanley! Miss Ava!"

She opened her eyes to find herself sprawled on the floor and Lieutenant Dalrymple cradling her while a swimming feeling turned her mind upside down. She jerked, rolling over so she'd vomit on the floor and not all over Dalrymple's uniform. He patted her shoulder awkwardly as she heaved up bile.

She had been flying over the veld, the rugged hills and arid landscape of the territory along the border between two countries. Two colonies. Before the colonies this had all been one vast savanna. Ava would never be able to see it otherwise, after this. This vision, this . . . clairvoyance.

"Miss Stanley?" Dalrymple's expression was a little less panicked than it had been when Ava had first woken up. She'd fallen over. She must have fainted.

"Sorry, sorry," she said, putting her hand to her forehead. Of course she had a racking headache. It was the least that she deserved.

Only then did she notice Captain Boyd standing in the doorway, studying her warily.

She was grateful for Dalrymple's steadying touch even as she wanted to insist she didn't need it. She needed to be strong because they would think less of her if she wasn't.

"I'll be all right—I just need to sit a moment." Dalrymple handed Ava a canteen of water before she could ask. "Yes, a drink, thank you." Her stomach felt queasy, and her mind was still turning, trying to make sense of what she'd experienced. The world from the point of view of a dust mite—no, from the point of view of *all* dust mites.

"What *practicum* were you doing that got away from you?" Captain Boyd asked with the tone of a curious professor.

"I . . . I don't even know." She drank the rest of the canteen and sighed. "I was trying to find something. Someone."

"*Sterna paradisaea*," Boyd said, unexpectedly, incongruously.

Traveling, seeking. Yes. "You've read my mother's work?"

He tapped the pages of her notebook on the lab bench. "Write down whatever it is you did, then try to replicate it. But next time wait until someone's around to spot you, yes?"

"Yes, sir."

"And get up off the floor."

She wasn't too proud to take Dalrymple's offered hand; the lieutenant helped her back into the chair. Her breath still felt wobbly; her lungs felt like she'd been running. And her mind was . . . elsewhere. Expanded. Still tumbling over the landscape rather than nestled firmly in her own body. Meanwhile, Dalrymple brought over a candle in a brass holder and set it on the table in front of her.

Ava frowned. "I couldn't possibly."

"Just try," he said.

By now, she felt she'd exhausted every bit of taxonomic trivia she knew, every possible creature she might associate with heat, with red, with even a little sense of burning. Fire ants and jalapeño peppers, scarlet birds and orange butterflies. The blooms of lilies that might look like flames in red light. And now her mind was too muddled to focus on any one thing. It ran in circles.

Absently, she sighed. Offered up all those thoughts in the hope of emptying her mind.

A smell rose up. Sharp, volatile. A hint of burning, like a distant campfire. Smoke, there was smoke, a thin line of gray curling up from the wick. She leaned in, suddenly eager, her breathing catching. Almost there, almost—

The curling wisp snuffed out, diffusing into nothing, like a candle flame just blown out rather than just flaring to life. Sighing, she sat back and scrubbed the weariness from her eyes.

"Perhaps you need to be distracted for it to work. Try *less* hard." Dalrymple passed his finger over the wick, which obediently lit up, a warm and inviting flame. Comforting. Somehow, it settled her still-anxious mind.

Her head hurt. The flickering flame stabbed at her eyes. She closed them and rubbed her forehead. "I've no idea what I'm really supposed to be doing with myself. Am I a doctor, an Arcanist, a bacteriologist, an adventurer—"

"You're *young*," Boyd said. He'd taken off his glasses to clean them with a handkerchief. Without them, his expression seemed less severe, more wry. "You're not supposed to know what you're doing. Dalrymple's right—perhaps you should be trying less hard."

Dalrymple pulled over another stool, putting himself on a level with her. "If I may be so bold, you might just worry about being yourself. You very much seem to be on your own path."

Strange, that such a man should see her. Maybe even understand her. He was hardened by experience, yet earnest. He didn't smile much, but he didn't frown either.

She found herself staring at him. "Thank you," she murmured.

"Now, now," Boyd said. "Enough philosophy. Back to work, minions."

Torrance and West and the Karakoram Quest

The wind drove pellets of ice into the men, nearly blinding them. A thousand small bullets sought to break through their parkas, their coveralls, their skin. The summit beckoned, but right now the real prize was mere survival.

The avalanche that barricaded their path seemed supernatural, as if the mountain itself were determined to bar their progress. Great shards of ice rained down, heavy as boulders and sharp as blades. By huddling in a rocky notch on the face of the mountain, they avoided direct assault, but they could not fully withstand the frozen fury.

West was the first to slip, the spiked treads of his boots insufficient to keep his foothold on the icy path when the very rock under him was shaking, as if the world itself crumbled to pieces. He swung his axe to dig in an extra hold in the rock face—and lost his grip on the handle. The wood of the handle and his leather gloves were both made so slick with ice and cold, no one could have hoped to keep hold. He fell along with the rock and ice, plummeting through the thin air and mist. If the drop beneath them was not bottomless, it must surely have seemed so. The bottom was lost in mist, so far below that a fall surely meant his death.

And then he jerked to a sudden stop, left clinging to the rock with all his strength.

By good mountaineering practice, Torrance and West had lashed themselves to one another. A coil of rope and good strong knots connected them, for good or ill. When West fell, Torrance felt the tug and instinctively threw his weight back.

This left them caught. If Torrance moved, West would lose his grip, resuming his fall down the mountainside. If West fell, he must necessarily pull Torrance with him. If only West could stabilize the rocks and ice with his powers. If only Torrance could gain supernatural strength to lift them both to safety.

There was another solution.

"Cut the line!" West shouted. If they separated, Torrance could save himself.

"Never!" Torrance called back.

The avalanche had ceased, and the air held a strange, sparkling stillness, as if they could hear the final drift of miniature ice crystals ringing, bell-like, as they settled in the aftermath. The rock under them shuddered but slid no farther. As suddenly as the carnage began, the air cleared. This left them suspended, quite literally. They had enough time to consider their predicament.

They would both prevail, or they would both fall.

"I'll pull you!" Torrance called. But when he hauled back on the rope, attempting to anchor himself on the razor-thin edge of rock, the ice glacier under him cracked with the sound of a gunshot. He froze, the grace of quick thinking and perfect balance preventing him from losing his footing and sending them both over the precipice.

When West tried to secure his own footing, to find notches and grips in the rock he could use to pull himself up, he faced the same problem—the rock was fragile, made impassable with ice and frost, with all the hazards of these dangerous elevations.

Both of them were gasping in the thin air. Both trembled from the exertion of the climb, from the stress of surviving this latest cataclysm. But neither shied away from the problem at hand.

"Well," Torrance said. "At least the view is lovely."

A typical British understatement. The view was spectacular, otherworldly. They were at the top of the world, hundreds of miles of land spread around them, and all of it mountainous, titanic. Sculptures of white-capped rock jutted up, a tangled chaos of mountains and valleys. The sky was a deep blue, as if they could climb into the heavens themselves. A shade impossible to capture in paint. They clung to the precipice of what was possible. They might have been on a world made of mountains, without another soul.

They could die here and be satisfied. But they would not. They could not.

If they seemed to exist in their own world here, then perhaps West could change the laws of this world, the very laws of physics. He must increase friction, reduce the pull of gravity upon them. He must stop the winds, remove the danger of the cold. Give them strength beyond what they believed they possessed. The strength of eagles, soaring above all.

West felt lighter. If his Arcane skills did nothing else, they gave him hope.

"Try now!" he called to his friend.

For a moment, nothing happened. Then, the line pulled taut. West inched up, back to the safety of the ledge. The rock and ice held. Torrance cried out with effort. But they got their miracle. Torrance hauled with more strength than he knew; West climbed with more grace and lightness than he'd ever possessed, and the footing under them was solid just long enough for them both to get to safety.

Torrance reached, and West took his hand to pull him the rest of the way. There, safe on the ledge, they embraced out of sheer gratitude for survival. They would live to have another adventure.

EIGHTEEN

Streptomyces albus

That evening, Lieutenant Dalrymple insisted on walking her back to the guesthouse in case she fainted again or some nonsense.

Ava found she was reluctant to walk those last few steps to the front door. The writing desk. The survey maps. Whatever Diane wasn't telling them. Her friends waited inside, and she didn't want to face them.

Dalrymple must have thought she was still feeling ill. "You're sure you'll be all right?"

"Yes, of course. I'll see you tomorrow. And thank you again."

He tipped his head, an informal bow, and walked off, an upstanding officer.

Behind the house was a potting table, and she filled a washbasin there from the pump to get some of the day's grime off her face and hands, then shook the dust from her skirt and shoes before she went in. Things were quiet, but this wasn't a surprise. The others had made a habit of walking out during the day, checking at the telegraph office and post office for messages, catching up with local newspapers, and meeting with government officials. Colonel Harcourt and his wife had taken Diane in and introduced her to local society.

Now, Diane was sitting at the writing desk in the front room, signing a letter, the familiar survey charts open before her. Just as Ava had pictured her. Before Ava could say anything—not that she had any idea what she would say, either an innocent question or a mad accusation—voices approached on the front walk outside. Marchand laughing at something, and Gilda answering softly.

Diane quickly folded up the survey pages, blew on the letter to dry the ink faster, and slipped the pages together inside a book, which she put in a drawer. All of it done by the time the door opened.

"This town is full of pirates," Marchand said. He held a cloth shopping bag in one hand. Gilda held another. "The prices in the market—robbery."

"That's a mining town for you," Diane answered amiably. "Did you find what you needed?"

"I think so," Gilda said. "With Mr. Marchand's help."

"I like a challenge," he added.

Gilda pulled out items from one of the bags to show off. She was beaming, pleased with herself. "What do you think?" She held up a pair of trousers, plain and sturdy.

"They're for you?" Ava asked, trying not to sound startled.

"Yes. I'm getting tired of dragging my skirts in the muck."

"Very practical," Ava said neutrally.

"I quite like them," Diane announced. "They'll come in handy, I think."

Ava met Diane's gaze from across the room . . . and Diane's smile faltered, as if she was surprised to find Ava standing there. Ava ought to act as if all this were comfortable, as if she were among friends. The truth was, she hadn't been comfortable in days, weeks.

And then Diane was smiling again. "How was your day, Ava?"

Confusing. Exhilarating. Her brain felt bigger than her skull. "Tiring. Just . . . tiring." She excused herself and went to her room to write in her journal.

Mrs. de Haas served a simple but satisfying stew for supper. Hot food went a long way toward settling Ava's nerves. Now, if only she could sleep. But she was still writing, still thinking, still pondering. She shouldn't stay in Kimberley. She ought to go back to Cape Town and get a ship to Nassau, where she was supposed to be. Or even back home, to her brothers, her parents, to safety. That felt like running away. Fleeing whatever was happening here. Torrance and West wouldn't flee. Anton and Bran? They would want her to be safe.

They would also want to know what was really going on here.

After supper, Mrs. de Haas let Ava help clear away the dishes but stopped short of allowing her to help wash. She had a girl who helped with that, and Ava relented. That left the four of them alone in the parlor, sipping after-dinner sherry. Ava was about to excuse herself when Diane cleared her throat and folded her hands on the table before her.

"My friends, I must ask for your help again," Diane said.

"You are going after Mr. Monroe," Marchand said matter-of-factly, drawing a cigarette from his coat pocket and lighting it. "Riding north, into the veld. To see what trouble he's gotten into."

For once, Diane seemed surprised, at a loss for words.

Shrugging, the Frenchman leaned back in his chair and explained. "What else can you do? Everything depends on finding him, yes? Getting the papers to him."

"Yes. Just so."

"And my getting paid depends on finding him. Of course I will go with you."

"Thank you," Diane breathed, as if she hadn't been sure of his answer.

Ava suddenly realized she couldn't tell if the emotion was genuine, or if Diane Monroe was acting. Displaying the emotion that was expected of her, that would secure Marchand's cooperation. Not just his cooperation but also his loyalty.

Gilda's hands were folded on her lap. Her newly cut hair settled in wavy curls over her ears. "Diane, I will follow you anywhere. But why must you do this? Why must you put yourself in danger for this?"

The insight swarmed on Ava. She breathed it all in, the dust thickening, choking. Full of *Dermatophagoides*. She shivered, as if she could feel microscopic feet scurrying up her arms. She knew what the second set of documents meant. Her gaze lit up, meeting Diane's across the table.

"Because she has a personal stake," Ava said. "This isn't just about the fortunes of empire. It's about *her* fortunes. Somewhere in that pack of papers she has a deed to a mine made out to herself and her husband. She needs the British Empire to protect it." This wasn't about king and empire, or at least not just about king and empire. For Diane Monroe, this was personal. A path to riches, to power. She would chop up this land for her own benefit.

Diane didn't wilt at the accusation. Her back remained straight, her shoulders squared. As indomitable as ever.

"Is this true?" Marchand asked, knocking off ashes from the cigarette onto a tea saucer.

Ava held Diane's gaze. A silent debate, a duel. Diane seemed unaffected.

"What do you think the empire is?" Diane said finally. "What else is it, but the means of protecting commerce? Of protecting the wealthiest nation the world has ever seen?"

"The wealth of merchants," Ava said. "Of aristocrats."

"Of course." Diane raised her sherry glass and took a sip.

"You think to make yourself another Cecil Rhodes?" Marchand asked. "Eh, I cannot blame you."

Marchand and Gilda would follow Diane. And Ava . . . Ava felt the split, the rift. She'd been tied up with these people in the closet aboard the *Penelope*. Whatever bond that had created between them was fraying now. Fungus, eating away at it.

"I won't go you with you," Ava said, her voice cracking. She wanted to look away, to flee their scrutiny. But she stood her ground.

Diane's breath caught. Ava's declaration surprised her. "Ava. My dear. I need you. Your abilities—your wonderful talent. I have a premonition that I'll need your help in the days to come. I have no idea what we'll encounter, and it would give me such great comfort to have you with us."

"You don't need me." Ava was growing more certain of this. The families in the camp needed her. Diane's adventure might be exciting, but it wasn't necessary, not really.

"Why do you say that? I . . . we . . . have needed you every step of the way! We wouldn't have gotten past the Brannocks without you."

"Somehow I think you would have found a way." A couple of weeks ago, Ava would have let herself be persuaded. But not now, not with the grand, borderless insight hanging over her.

Gilda reached over and touched Ava's hand. "It wouldn't feel right, going on without you."

"Thank you. But I'm useful here," Ava said. "I'm needed here." Every day she'd been here, she'd treated illnesses and wounds, looking right in the eyes of the people she helped. Studied, gained knowledge, learned microscopic and Arcanist wonders. All this, versus allying with Diane and her quest for empire. Her own, the British, it hardly mattered.

Diane's lips pressed together. She was marshaling another argument, and Ava was thinking how she might counter it. If she had to, she could simply leave the room.

But Diane smiled. "The soldiers here are louts. They don't know how lucky they are to have you."

Ava rather thought they did. "It's getting late. I should get to bed. But . . . I wish you all well. Truly."

Ava retired for the evening and slept surprisingly well.

In the morning, Diane, Gilda, Marchand, and their valises were gone. They must have crept out very quietly, very early. Ava had no idea if they took a train to an even more remote location, if they traveled by carriages and road, or if they galloped away on horseback like cowboys. Diane would carve her own way in the world no matter what. Ava might never see her again, and might never learn if she found her husband and succeeded in securing the territory. The mystery might haunt her. But Ava was used to not finding answers to every question.

She had other frontiers to explore. Even if they were very small ones, under the microscope. She understood the round glass dishes and the world under the microscope lens better than Diane Monroe's world.

"Your friends, they left?" Mrs. de Haas asked her over breakfast. Her tone was chiding, offended on Ava's behalf.

"They have business elsewhere," Ava said blandly. "My business is here at the infirmary."

"Well, I am glad to keep you," she answered, and this warmed Ava.

The first thing she did that day, before going to work, was to stop by the telegraph office and send word to her family. *Am well. Working at infirmary at camp in Kimberley. Challenging, interesting. Miss you, love you, Ava Stanley.* Finally, that was done. Another weight lifted.

Ava arrived at the infirmary and got to work in her makeshift lab. Sun filtered through dusty windows. The voices of the camp traveled in their own patterns, mothers calling to children in a half-familiar language, a man shouting in surprise, a dog barking, an officer calling to a soldier. It all faded against the work in front of her, cultures and dyes, samples smeared on slides, and the world that expanded under the microscope's lens. A whole other realm, unseen, unless one knew how to look.

"They're gone."

"Sir!" Dalrymple stood from the other end of the table, where he was making notes on case studies, and saluted smartly.

Ava needed a moment to draw her attention away from swirls of stained cells on glass.

Colonel Harcourt stood, a picture of authority, stiff in his red uniform jacket, eyes glaring like iron. It was all bluster.

"Who?" Ava asked innocently.

"You bloody well know who."

"Language, sir," Dalrymple said.

"She's bloody well heard this language before. Bloody Americans."

Ava suppressed a smile.

"Where did they go?" Harcourt demanded.

"North, I expect. After Frederick Monroe."

"That woman didn't tell you anything?" As if he couldn't even say her name.

"No, sir. I didn't ask." Technically true. She wondered if Harcourt knew about the Monroes' personal stake. All those letters from the Foreign Office . . . Diane and her husband had to have official backing.

He closed his eyes a moment and took a deep breath. "You should have stopped them."

"How, sir?"

"You're an Arcanist, aren't you?"

"Nominally," she muttered.

"All due respect, Colonel Harcourt, is there anything we can help you with?" Dalrymple asked in an act of bureaucratic chivalry.

The lieutenant's official politeness finally stymied him. He gave one last humph. "If you get any word of them, anything at all, you're to come straight to me with it. Understood?"

Diane Monroe was much too savvy to reveal anything to Ava ever again. Not after this . . . *betrayal* was too strong a word. Ava hadn't betrayed anything. She hadn't broken any promises. She just hadn't acquiesced.

"Of course, sir," she said, contrite.

Harcourt nodded curtly, made a smart regimental turn, and marched out. Both Ava and Dalrymple sighed.

"I suppose he had to ask," Ava said.

"Well, I think it's rude."

"You're very kind, Lieutenant Dalrymple."

"Am I? Well, my mother will be happy to hear it."

After her fainting spell with the *Dermatophagoides*, Captain Boyd sat her and Dalrymple down every evening for what she thought of as a seminar. Practice sessions. The kind of thing she'd have been invited to if she'd been allowed into Arcanist studies at Oxford, that women were just starting to attend at Harvard, at least on an auxiliary basis. She was thrilled. Boyd would order tea and cakes, close the doors of his little office, and they'd talk, the kind of philosophical discussions Ava hadn't heard since she was a girl in her parents' house during gatherings of their colleagues. Their own personal naturalist society.

If she were a romantic, she might think that all the unlikely crooked paths of the journey had led her here, to people who were eager to work with her. With the officers, she'd never had to defend herself or her belief in the possibilities of using bacteria species in Arcane Taxonomy. She hadn't imagined what a relief that would be. Possibilities . . . expanded. She contemplated ideas that wouldn't have occurred to her back at the London hospital or under her parents' judgment. This evening, Dalrymple was getting heated. "We're back to the original problem: Can bacteria be used as a basis for Arcane *practica*? I fear you've spent so much time looking into a microscope your attention's gone . . . small." He screwed up his expression; that must not have been quite what he meant to say.

"What I did with the dust mites was anything but small," she said firmly.

"Don't call it a problem," Boyd said, tapping a finger on the page where they'd been writing out lists of taxonomic names, Latinate syllables streaming out. "Just because it hasn't been solved yet doesn't mean it can't be. Puzzle—let's call it a puzzle."

"My parents don't think it can be done," Ava said. "I've been arguing with them about it for years."

"But you're a capable Arcanist. They haven't discouraged you, have they?" Boyd asked.

"Not exactly. They're thrilled I have any ability at all. At least they've said they are. I just think . . ." She pondered, trying to find the words. "I think they wish I were more like them. And I'm simply not."

"I keep having to remind myself your parents are Elizabeth Torrance and Brandon West," Dalrymple said wonderingly. "The pressure! My father was a banking clerk. Nobody expected anything from me."

"Bacteria are life," Boyd said. "Just like all the rest of it, if harder to understand."

"Yes, exactly!" she said. "No matter how strange or difficult to study, it's all part of the tangle."

Dalrymple straightened. "All right, then. Disease-causing bacteria generate fevers, don't they?"

"No." Ava huffed a frustrated sigh. "Disease-causing bacteria don't create fever—the fever is caused by the body attempting to fight off the disease, the invasion of an incompatible life-form. It's the body's own defenses that create so much of the danger of fever."

"So what in the body creates the fever?" the lieutenant asked.

"You're on the wrong track," Boyd said. "Forget the body. Go back to the object. Dalrymple here says you used bacteria to turn water into wine."

"Ethanol," she said. "And technically *Saccharomyces cerevisiae* is a fungus. A yeast. Not a bacterium."

Dalrymple groaned and rubbed his face. "'To name a thing is to know a thing,'" he said, quoting the common paraphrase of Linnaeus. "I don't know a damned thing. I give up."

"But God, what a thing," Boyd said. "You nail this, your reputation would be made."

"I'm not trying to make my reputation. I just want to light a bloody candle," Ava said.

Boyd rapped the table with his knuckles. "Miss Ava, you've been spending too much time around soldiers, and your language is going to shit. I beg your pardon. Now get out of here. Get some sleep. We'll try again tomorrow."

Mrs. Harcourt had invited Ava to dine with the colonel and his family. Ava suspected this was another attempt to wheedle information from her, but she accepted anyway. They had a young daughter still at home. Their older son had gone back to England for university. The girl was quiet and wide eyed, regarding Ava as if she were some exotic creature. Ava didn't know if this was because she worked with the army surgeons, because she was an Arcanist, or simply because of her American accent.

When she arrived at their house after washing up, Mrs. Harcourt greeted her brightly. "There's a message here for you, dear. It came to the colonel's office. The telegraph people weren't sure where to find you."

"Oh?" Ava opened it and read.

The telegram was from Anton Torrance. *Ava dear. Gratitude for note, Mother was frantic. Send word if you need anything at all. Write soonest. Much love, Anton.*

Instantly, her eyes started leaking tears. She didn't expect it, didn't know it was going to happen until it did. Just like that, she was crying, scrambling for the handkerchief tucked in her skirt pocket.

"Ava, dear, whatever is the matter?"

She recovered quickly enough, sniffling like a child and mopping up tears. "Nothing, ma'am. I'm sorry. Just a little homesick."

"Oh, I do understand that." Mrs. Harcourt came over and put her hand on Ava's shoulder. Ava accepted the gesture of comfort that was intended, however much she wanted to hide away under a rock. "This country is so very different from what we're all used to, isn't it?"

It isn't the country, Ava thought. She'd seen the world and could be at home anywhere, with the right people.

Ava arrived for the next day's work to find a whole family waiting on the bench outside the shed that served as their examination room. A woman, presumably the mother, with a collection of children, roughly ages four through twelve. Ava paused in the aisle, bracing herself. It was awfully early in the morning for this.

The woman seemed young to have four children hanging off her. The oldest, a girl, held the hands of two younger boys, while the mother held the youngest child on her lap. The mother was frowning, her eyes half lidded, as if she was falling asleep right where she sat. The boys seemed uncharacteristically quiet for their age. They should have been yelling and fighting. All of them were flushed pink, spots on their cheeks, sweat at their brows. Ava could almost see the fever rising off them.

She put the back of her hand against the girl's forehead. She was burning.

"When did the fever start?" Ava asked the mother.

She shook her head and answered in Afrikaans. Ava only knew a few words of Dutch and tried those, saying "Pardon me" and "Please." "What else?" she asked, and the girl put a hand on her stomach and winced. Stomach pains, then. The boys squirmed, hunched in. The youngest snuggled into his mother's chest. The mother winced, as if the noise hurt her. They were all sick with the same thing, and Ava began to feel a sense of doom. If they were already this far along in symptoms, it was too late to stop the spread. The whole camp had likely been exposed.

Ava murmured what she hoped were soothing comforts while gesturing to the family to stay where they were. After scrubbing her hands in a basin of antiseptic, she charged to the surgery's recovery room, where Boyd was removing the stitches in the forearm of a khaki-dressed soldier who was grimacing, failing to keep his stiff upper lip.

"Stop squirming, man!" Boyd ordered.

"Yes, sir," the poor soldier muttered in reply, sweating and whimpering.

"Captain!" Ava called from the tent's entrance. Belatedly she took in the scene and wondered if maybe she should have waited until he was finished. But urgency drove her; this couldn't wait.

"What?" Boyd barked. The hapless soldier looked blearily back at her.

"Captain, I think we've got a typhoid outbreak."

Boyd stared at her, his expression freezing into what could only be despair, but that was gone in a flash. Ava expected him to deny it, or to march off to see the patients and make the diagnosis himself. But he surprised her, nodding, fatalistic but determined.

His patient was regarding them both with suddenly wide eyes. He'd probably not looked so frightened in the face of an onslaught of bullets. Boyd clapped him on the shoulder. "Get out of here, man. Wash your hands!"

"Yes, sir." He charged away and washed his hands in the basin, Ava was relieved to see. But how difficult was it to flee what you couldn't see?

Boyd got to work, calling out to the staff. "Right. All right. Nurse! Dalrymple!" Masie, the head nurse, came in from outside. Dalrymple emerged from the lab, startled at the commotion. "Nurse, clear out the shed on the southwest corner away from the others. That'll be our quarantine space. Bring the patients there. Let's see how far this has gotten. Dalrymple, inventory our supplies, collect what we'll need for fevers. Organize clean water. See how many face masks we have, or if we have any cloth to make more." Boyd turned to Ava and hesitated. "Miss Stanley, get out. I don't want you in the middle of this."

She was rather touched and suddenly sure that he had children back in England, and that he worried about them. "I'm already in the middle of this, sir. And I've been inoculated."

"You have? Oh, well done. Right, then. Mask up."

After their first pass through the camp, they discovered two dozen patients showing symptoms. Ava made a brief visit to Mr. Macintosh and his nurses in the Black section of the camp, to warn them what was coming. With this many affected, the disease was likely already raging, and the worst was yet to come.

Boyd was able to establish a ruthless quarantine with his military authority. A cordon around the camp, no one in or out, healthy camp residents recruited to boil water and deliver food throughout the camp. Ava shouldn't have been surprised at the directness of his response—he'd been dealing with armies and refugees for the last three years. This wasn't his first outbreak. In awe, she stepped back to learn from him. There was precious little they could do but treat the fevers and work to prevent the disease from spreading any further. Boil water. Burn bedding. Boyd wasn't ready to attempt inoculating the healthy; they didn't have the tools or expertise for such an undertaking. Ava reluctantly had to agree with him.

The next day the number of affected rose to thirty-four. The next day, fifty. Damp cloths on foreheads to cool fevers, gallons of broth to keep patients hydrated and nourished. Keeping them alive until the fevers broke was the best they could do. Ava took samples, grew cultures, and confirmed the diagnosis of typhoid. In the middle of an outbreak, that seemed a minuscule accomplishment. The resulting slides were only useful to bacteriologists, researchers, and statisticians studying disease. They didn't help her bring comfort to feverish children.

The first death was the young child of the first family she'd diagnosed. Already undernourished from his time in the camp and the aftermath of the war, he simply didn't have the strength to pull through. More deaths followed. The cholera outbreak she'd discovered in London seemed very far away, very long ago. She'd been separated from it, culturing bacteria samples rather than treating patients. How cowardly, shutting herself away in a lab, confronting disease in the abstract. She ought to be more forgiving of herself—she was doing the job she had been given. Useful work, certainly.

Here, she learned to look sick children in the eyes and know which ones would survive and which wouldn't. When a child went limp, pale, eyes clouded and breathing shallow—she knew. None of her classes had taught her about this.

They pressed on. It was all they could do.

NINETEEN

Salmonella typhi

Ava slept in the infirmary's front building. They all did, to try to limit the spread of the disease, working in shifts with the nurses to treat who they could, make comfortable who they couldn't. The army barracks' kitchen delivered meals outside the camp's front entrance. The stoves boiling water burned all night. Ava obsessively washed her hands until her skin cracked and her knuckles bled. She slathered ointment on them whenever she had a spare moment.

One had to consider how fortunate they were. A generation ago, fifty years ago, before germ theory was generally accepted, before antiseptic procedures were practiced, they'd have been counting the dead in the hundreds rather than the dozens. Dozens were bad enough. The bodies were laid out under drop cloths for a burial detail to carry to a nearby cemetery, which already seemed large from all the fatalities of the last few years. Over five hundred people from the camp had died since it opened in January 1901. Dalrymple told her that something like fifty thousand had died at all the camps throughout the colony during the war. "But why?" Ava had demanded, almost unable to comprehend. Intellectually she knew what happened when people crowded together in terrible conditions. Disease, starvation. But Dalrymple hadn't answered her. He must have seen it all.

On the sixth day of the outbreak, Ava, Boyd, and Dalrymple were all awake, unable to sleep in the hot, airless night. She complained of the heat once, and Boyd told her this was still just springtime and the worst was yet to come. The buzz of cicadas started up, a hypnotic thrum. For once, Ava didn't feel the urge to go hunt down the local noisy insects.

Boyd had managed to get a bottle of whiskey delivered. Ava had declined, but Boyd put a cup of the drink in front of her, and it seemed impolite to refuse. The whiskey seemed to encourage talk, and they needed to talk.

"It's egregious that we can't do more to stop this," Dalrymple said, drinking half his tumbler of whiskey in a go. "Arcanism is rooted in the power of life, and so is disease. All disease is the conflict between incompatible forms of life coming into contact. Isn't that so?"

"That's such a gross simplification as to be useless," Boyd replied.

"We've got to start somewhere," Dalrymple shot back.

"It's circular," Boyd countered. "You keep looking at the effects rather than the thing itself. Yes, of course, it's all rooted in life, but how many of life's effects are accidental, unintended? Evolution does not carry with it intent!"

Ava wished she were writing this down but couldn't remember where her pen and journal were. "Bacteriophage," Ava said. "Identify an appropriate bacteriophage, replicate its effects—"

"You think no one's tried that?"

"I'm not talking about Arcanism, I'm talking basic bacteriology." She pushed the whiskey away. Two sips were enough.

Dalrymple leaned forward. "All right, so we can't outright kill disease without unintended consequences."

He was referencing a cautionary tale, a series of experiments performed a decade before by researchers at the Pasteur Institute, including several medical Arcanists. They'd sought reliable *practica* to destroy, restrict, weaken, or somehow otherwise neutralize disease-causing bacteria. In one case, an attempt to remove harmful bacteria from an infected rat using Arcane Taxonomy resulted in the instant vivisection of the rat—all its body parts and organs separated from each other, right there on the lab bench. A disturbing photograph of the results had been published in the journals, an image Ava had never forgotten.

"So we work indirectly," Dalrymple continued. "Set up . . . I don't know, a bacteriological fence, some kind of boundary that the buggers can't cross. It might make maintaining a quarantine a little easier."

"Like an antiseptic barrier?" Boyd speculated. "It would need to be part of the air itself. How would you do that?"

"A cloud, or a fog," Ava said.

"You're back to the same problem," Dalrymple answered. "How do you attack the harmful organisms without damaging the ones you're trying to protect? It's easy enough to attack organisms if you don't care which ones you kill."

Ava pointed. "Life only cares about life—it doesn't care if it's human or something else. We're the only ones who make these classifications."

"Do you know . . ." Boyd hesitated. He took off his glasses, pinched his nose, then sighed, collecting himself. "Do you know . . . I tried to stop bullets." He stared into his glass. "These modern guns. The Maxim gun. Five hundred rounds per minute, did you know that? Do you know how many men get torn to pieces with five hundred rounds per minute? We couldn't do anything about the wounds but patch them up and hope. But I thought, perhaps, if I could stop the guns, stop the bullets. Freeze them in midair. Disintegrate them. Make them rust. But rust is a chemical reaction, not a biological one."

"Find some devouring bacteria, some gangrene for metal. *Clostridium perfringens*," Ava murmured. A bacterium often found in battlefield wounds.

Boyd pointed his glass at her. "Just so. But I couldn't do it. Couldn't jam the guns, wreck the bullets, or anything. Do you know what I think the problem was? I kept trying to stop just one side of it, just the enemy. But you can't pick and choose, can you? All or nothing. And if I stopped British bullets, that would make me a traitor. I was just so tired of trying to stitch up boys torn apart by bullets."

The bullets were only half of it. Just as many soldiers in the war had died because of disease. Typhoid, cholera, malaria, a dozen others that had plagued humanity for centuries. Which brought Ava back to the original problem.

"Harry Stanley," she said.

"Who? Is that . . . that . . . fellow who went after Livingstone, the explorer?" Dalrymple furrowed his brow in confusion. He was quite endearingly tipsy.

"That was Henry Morton Stanley," Ava said. "I met him, you know."

"Did you? Huh."

"Harry Stanley was my mother's first husband. He died of sepsis from a wound. I only got the whole story a few years ago. She blamed herself. She knows so much, can do so much, but she couldn't cure him. To this day, I think part of her believes she should have been able to save him."

"You mother's first husband, but not your father, even though you have his name?" Boyd studied her, curious.

"No, but that's a different story."

"Ah."

"I think . . . I wonder if she thinks I want to be a doctor because of what happened to him. But it was actually my brother. He nearly died from a case of measles. It was a lady doctor who helped him. She helped teach him how to get along when the disease blinded him. She was so very kind and practical. How nice, to be like that."

They were all in their cups. Ava was rather enjoying it, telling more than she should. She would probably regret these confessions in the morning.

Boyd drained his glass and thumped it to the table. "Dr. Miss Stanley, I believe your life is unnecessarily complicated."

"I would agree with you, sir."

"Arcane Taxonomy . . . is ridiculous. That's what no one tells you. We make it up as we go along, and it's *ridiculous* to pretend that any of it is quantifiable or predictable."

"But it must be, or we'd never have gotten this far," she said.

"And how far is that, really?" Boyd said, his edge of cynicism sharp as a blade.

She had the feeling he'd thought a lot about it, and that this might have been part of why he'd ended up an army physician rather than a famous Arcanist.

Dalrymple got up, and Ava and Boyd stared after him as he went to the shelf; Ava didn't see what he picked up until he came back to the table and set a candle in its holder in front of her. She stared at it, overcome by a haze of exhaustion. At the moment, she didn't even know what to do with a candle. The tent was well lit with kerosene lamps, and there was a fire outside where nurses were boiling water. The candle was useless, an affectation. What was he expecting her to do? Why did he expect her to care, after the last week of being overcome? An organism smaller than the point of a pin had them all on the edge of despair. The heat of anger overcame her.

"*Salmonella typhi*," she murmured, and touched the wick.

A flame sparked, flaring to the length of a finger joint and settling to a buttery yellow, an ordinary candle giving off ordinary light.

She'd lit a candle. She hadn't even doubted.

"Sometimes," Dalrymple said, "it's better to not try so hard."

Boyd laughed, clapping with delight.

She'd lit a candle. She hardly believed it and stared until the yellow light seemed to burn into her hindbrain. It was a fluke. She'd never be able to do it again, so to confirm it she blew the flame out, let the wick smoke, then touched the candle again. *Salmonella typhi.*

The wick caught fire. The candle burned. Simple.

She choked off a startled cry, then laughed. Here she was in the middle of a disaster, achieving such victory. A tiny, insignificant victory. And just like that, the whole world shifted.

Dalrymple patted his sides, searching the pockets of a jacket he wasn't wearing. Glancing around, he found what he was looking for and dug into the pocket of a white coat on the coatrack, producing a handkerchief, which he handed over. Gratefully, she took it and covered her face. He patted her shoulder companionably while the tears ran themselves out.

"Drink some water, my minions," Boyd said. "Get some sleep. Once more into the breach in the morning."

Torrance and West and the Terror of the Zambezi

"Which of you shall I choose as my mate?" the Deathless Queen purred. She stood from her throne, a goddess dripping with gold and diamonds.

She pitted the two friends against one another. They stood before the dais, weapons in hand—Torrance hefted a stone axe, West a spear made of obsidian. His attempts to break free of her spell using his Arcanist skills had come to naught. What else could he try? What other tricks could he avail himself of? The same anguished speculation played out on Torrance's face, his brow furrowed, his teeth gritted in a rage he was unable to turn against their enemy, this woman with honey in her voice and hypnotism in her glare.

She paced before them, smiling in victory. "Shall I choose the warrior? So strong, so determined. Or shall I choose the scholar and magician? Oh, you poor man, don't despair that your spells were not enough to break free of my power. No man has ever broken free from me! You failed before you even began!"

How could any man be unmoved by her feminine grace? The slender neck, the luxurious fall of hair, her perfectly made figure. Her allure was undeniable, supernatural.

"Perhaps . . . perhaps . . ." She stroked Torrance's shoulder, then stepped to West and touched his chin. All the time they remained frozen, their only reaction showing through the blazing fury in their eyes. "Instead of having you fight to see who will win a place by my side . . . perhaps I should allow you both to be my slaves!" She laughed, a musical ringing that was as unnatural as the rest of her. Her eyes shone yellow, reptilian. "But I would so enjoy seeing you fight for me, my slaves!"

Torrance and West had been on many adventures together. They knew each other better than anyone else in the world, better than most men ever know another. When their gazes met across the several paces between them, they knew with certainty that their minds were one. Wordlessly, they came to perfect agreement: They would not fight. Torrance would smash in his own skull, and West would stab himself with that stone blade before one would ever strike a blow against the other.

No woman could ever come between their regard for one another. And this . . . this the Deathless Queen had never encountered. This she could not defeat.

West dropped the spear. That simple motion, that simple action of denial, and the Deathless Queen's expression shifted from triumph to rage. She grimaced, all her teeth exposed; her nostrils flared—all her beauty vanished in the face of her anger, and in this moment the spell was broken.

Laughing, Torrance tossed aside the axe. "Our apologies, madam. We cannot accommodate you." They stood side by side, confronting their nemesis.

She tipped up her chin, attempting to disguise her anger with disgust. She stepped back up on her dais so that she could look down on them. Not that it mattered to them. They were secure. They had broken her control.

"You may think you can escape me," she said haughtily. "But you will find . . . you cannot."

She would show them the true terror of the Deathless Queen. She raised her hands and yanked down lightning from a cloudless sky. Thunder shook the cavern, raining down rock. She was impervious, for this was her realm. She sought to strike down Torrance and West.

West drew on the power of the armadillo's shell, the turtle's armor. A dozen creatures who had natural protection against their enemies. As the entire cavern rained down on them, the Deathless Queen's screams of rage shook loose the very stone—

When Torrance and West regained consciousness, they lay huddled together in the middle of a debris field spreading away from them. It was as if some great conflagration of dynamite had exploded out in all directions. Somehow, they remained untouched. But the cavern, the dais, the throne, the Deathless Queen and all her minions—they had vanished.

Had she been destroyed? Or had she simply gone to ground, hidden in her subterranean fortress, to emerge and wield her power another day? They did not know.

"Torrance?" West asked cautiously.

"West?" Torrance responded.

"Well then. We're alive."

"Seem to be."

"Maybe . . . maybe we should think about getting the hell out of here."

"I heartily concur, old boy."

The pair briefly gripped each other's shoulders and then trekked through the rubble, through an underground tunnel, to emerge back into the light.

TWENTY

Thiobacillus denitrificans

The next day, four of their patients died. The day after, only one, an old man who had already been weakened by rheumatism and a bout of pneumonia. The day after that, no one died. And the day after, no new cases presented themselves to the quarantine tent. That included the Black side of the camp, as reported by one of the missionary nurses.

Boyd insisted that it was too soon to declare the outbreak ended. They would keep up the habits of sanitation and quarantine for another week at least while they nursed the rest of their patients through.

Working on pure faith that the knowledge would do some good in the future, Ava got back to her lab work, sampling the local strains of *S. typhi*. The task was repetitive, precise, and therefore soothing. It was a productive distraction.

In the afternoon, a shout from one of the quarantine guards interrupted her. "Sir, you can't go in there! Stop!"

"Is she in there, then? Can you tell me where she is?"

Ava recognized the voice very well and ran to the front building as Charlie Hallern shoved his way past the guard, his hooked hand raised like a weapon. The gesture would have made even a hardened soldier pause.

There was Charlie Hallern, just as he always was, wearing a rough peacoat even in the heat, his shirt open at the collar and a cap shoved over his unruly hair, not any more or less polished, as if he existed in stasis.

He smiled when he saw her.

"Charlie," she breathed. He was evidence of the outside world, of her recent past, the voyage on the *Penelope* and the crisis that followed. She hadn't realized that she missed him. She ran toward him, reaching out, and was gratified when he caught her in an embrace. The physical sensation of being held up, secure, felt like warm sunshine and cool water all at once. And then she was horrified.

"Oh God, get away from me!" She shoved him and backed away.

"Why? What?"

"We've got a typhoid outbreak. At least we did. It could still be hanging around. I don't want you to get sick."

He apparently didn't care, because he closed the distance and grabbed her arm with his right hand, his left forearm resting against hers.

"Where is Diane Monroe?" he asked.

She needed a moment to sort out the question. It wasn't that she'd forgotten about Diane, but that was a problem she could do nothing to solve.

"Gone. She left last week."

"Don't trust her," Hallern said with the intensity of one delivering a dire warning. "She wasn't telling us the whole story about that disputed territory. Conflict of interest doesn't begin to describe the situation."

"She has the title to a mine in the disputed territory," Ava said.

He drew back. "Well, yes. How do you know?"

"How do *you* know?"

"Messages for her started arriving at the ship as word got out she was in Cape Town. It was all right there."

"You opened her personal messages?"

"Of course I did," he said. "I wouldn't have, except they were from the De Beers company and the Bank of England and Alfred Milner and God knows who else. She wants Britain to claim that territory so the army will defend it for her. And she and her husband make all the money. Where is she, then?"

From that perspective, Diane was determined to start a war, not stop one. Bending international politics to her own benefit. Her ambition was breathtaking. But after the last week, after Ava had watched children waste away with fever, that problem seemed small. Ava couldn't find the words to explain all that to Charlie. "We got here and Mr. Monroe was already gone. She went after him."

He huffed in frustration. "Does this Mr. Monroe even exist, or did she make him up as a front, so no one would question her?"

That was an interesting question. Meanwhile, Charlie was still holding on to her. She only needed to take a step, and she'd be firmly in his arms. It would be easy to do.

She took a step back and went to the sideboard to mask how flustered she was. "Did you just get off the train? You must be wrecked. Let me get you some tea. I've already got water boiled—we boil all the water around here."

His tone turned grave. "Ava. How are you?"

He had come all this way for *her*. Not to foil Mrs. Monroe's plans. But to warn Ava. Because he was worried about her.

Her voice choked off, her throat too tight to speak. "We've lost thirty-one patients to typhoid. I couldn't save them. But . . . but I learned how to light a candle. I don't know, Charlie. I don't know how I am."

"I'm sorry," he said plainly, sincerely.

She sat. The chair was right there, so she sat, and couldn't remember the last time she'd had a good night's sleep. "You know what? I'm not. I've done so much, learned so much. If I can't pass the medical exams after this, I was never meant to be a doctor."

Footsteps crunched in the gravel outside, so they were ready when Dalrymple came in. The lieutenant considered Ava, then stared at

Hallern. She couldn't tell if the challenge in his stance—rigid, hands in fists—came from his military training or something more personal.

"Miss Stanley, are you all right?" He seemed about to say something else, glaring suspiciously at Charlie.

"Yes," she said firmly, so that both men would believe it. "Lieutenant Dalrymple, this is Captain Hallern. And vice versa."

"You're not army," Dalrymple said, very nearly an accusation.

"Ah, no. Merchant captain. The *Penelope*, impounded at Cape Town right now. I'm up here chasing after . . . well, just after some information."

"I see," Dalrymple said. "Shall I . . . call for some tea?" As if they were in a parlor and not a thrown-together military infirmary.

"Something stronger?" Hallern suggested, and that won him a smile from the lieutenant.

Dalrymple said, "I don't dare break into the captain's supply without his permission."

"Captain Boyd," Ava explained. "You'll like him; he's a cynic."

"Well then—"

A round of shouting outside interrupted them. Hallern glanced toward the doorway, curious. Ava and Dalrymple stiffened, going on alert. The tenor of the cries meant casualties were arriving. This was always accompanied by an air of panic different from the slow desperation of illness.

They went out to see what fate had brought them as a wagon pulled to a stop in the yard, joined by a handful of British soldiers and a few armed men in civilian clothing. Private guards, hunters or miners carrying rifles, dressed in rough khakis with worn, sun-faded hats pulled low on their heads. It might be someone hurt in a mining accident, though the mines had their own infirmaries.

A woman wearing a familiar coat and gown was sitting in the back of the wagon, her face sunburned and stiff with anxiety. And yet somehow her hair was still neatly pulled up under her hat. Diane Monroe, entirely focused on something in the bed of the wagon.

The wagon's driver was a clean-shaven man with a bowler cap over flyaway dark hair, wearing a loose-fitting jacket over a dusty shirt and trousers. They were all dusty.

Then the driver looked straight at her and said, "Ava, we need help."

It was Gilda Bell, her disguise so complete Ava hadn't known her. Ava nodded and strode around to the back of the wagon, Dalrymple at her heels.

Luis Marchand sat propped up against the front boards. His right arm was in a sling, his right shoulder bandaged. His head was lolling, indicating he was half asleep, or maybe half dead. He opened his eyes long enough to meet Ava's gaze and chuckled darkly.

Diane was seated next to the supine body of a man Ava didn't know. Middle aged, sturdy build, his salt-and-pepper beard overgrown by a week or so. He was sweating with illness, his expression tight with pain, cringing in delirium. Holding his hand tightly, Diane stared at the man as if she was afraid to look away, as if he might vanish. This, then, must be Frederick Monroe. Pale, his cheeks sunken, he didn't look very much like his picture.

Diane glanced up suddenly. Ava almost stepped back, as if reeling from a blow. "You must save him," Diane said.

The bandages wrapped around Mr. Monroe's gut did nothing to stanch the bleeding. He seemed to be made of blood. Ava had no experience with such a wound.

Dalrymple was already up in the bed of the wagon, shouting at a guard to bring a stretcher.

"What is it? What's all this, then?" Boyd stormed up and got a look at the scene himself. "Right. Dalrymple, get him to surgery. You—" He pointed at a soldier. "Go tell the colonel his prodigal Englishwoman has returned. Stanley!"

"Yes, sir," Ava called back.

"You think you can handle this one? He doesn't seem quite so close to dying." He pointed at Marchand, who chuckled again, as if this were all some great farce that he had no part in.

The story of what had happened to them would have to wait.

The two officers, the bleeding man on the stretcher, and the gaggle of soldiers carrying him—as well as Diane Monroe, because no one dared tell her no—rushed off to surgery, leaving Ava and Hallern room to climb into the back of the wagon and tend to Marchand. He made a fuss about not needing help, he was fine, just a cut. But as they guided him off the back of the wagon, his legs gave out. Hallern caught him before he hit the ground.

Gilda rushed around to help. She was wearing khaki trousers, sturdy boots, a jacket and gloves. Among the rest of the men and soldiers, she would have appeared to be a young man.

"Gilda, what happened—"

"Gordon. I'm Gordon." She spoke with an air of pleading. Determined but uncertain, begging Ava and Hallern not to argue.

Ava tried out the name. Gordon Bell. "All right, Mr. Bell?"

Gordon Bell nodded gratefully. Hallern stared a moment longer but didn't argue.

Marchand leaned on Gordon and Charlie, and they followed Ava into the infirmary.

TWENTY-ONE

Chlamydia trachomatis

A reason many gave for not wanting women to be doctors was now before her: modesty. In the study of medicine, women inevitably had to see things that some considered too indelicate for their presumably refined dispositions. Some of those same people thought nothing of subjecting women to unspeakable disease, injury, and hardship in time of war.

Inevitably, a woman doctor must see men naked, or nearly so. Fortunately, Marchand wasn't at all squeamish about stripping off his shirt and dropping the bloody thing on the ground, leaving bare his well-muscled arms, his chest with a pattern of curling dark hair. Ava wondered if Marchand was ever squeamish about anything. Gilda—Gordon, Ava was going to have to keep reminding herself—brought him a cup of water, which he drank down.

Ava got clean cloths, a bottle of peroxide, and a set of sterilized tools and a tray and started investigating the wound. The shot had entered his right shoulder below the clavicle. There didn't appear to be an exit wound.

"The shot just grazed me," Marchand insisted.

"Mr. Bell's wound was just a graze," Ava said. "This is something else. I'm going to have to dig for the bullet, I'm afraid." She worked to sound confident and not at all daunted. "We don't have any ether or chloroform to spare."

"I only need a shot of brandy," he declared.

"Not sure we have that either."

Charlie dug around in one of the cupboards and found Boyd's bottle of whiskey. Unlike Dalrymple, he had no compunction about taking it. Marchand drank a couple of shots right off.

Ava scrubbed her hands and got to work. Gordon and Charlie held down his arms and distracted him with questions.

"What the hell happened to you?" Charlie asked.

Marchand shook his head and spoke around pain-gritted teeth. "Just like that colonel said. Boers, up in the hills. The last holdouts. We could look at the maps and argue that they were in German territory. But when you're there in the hills, how can you tell? Borders mean nothing. All they saw were intruders.

"Monroe had hired scouts to go with him. To survey and mark out the territory he wanted to make his," Marchand continued. "They were retreating when we found them. Monroe had already been shot. *Ai! Merde!*" The man bit out additional French that Ava didn't know the meaning of and knew better than to ask.

"Sorry. Almost there." The bullet hadn't gone far, but it had hit bone, and she had to remove shards that had embedded in the surrounding tissue. After easing them out with tweezers, she dropped them in a tin dish on the table. Everything was bloody.

"The rebels followed us. Shot at us the whole way. That's how I got this. But hey, our Mr. Bell here got off a few shots in return. Downed one of them, I think." He chuckled, then let out an exhausted sigh. "We got away. Too late, I think. I'm not sure Monroe even knew it was Diane leaning over him, he was so far gone. He will not live."

"You don't know that. Boyd and Dalrymple are very good," Ava argued, but Marchand shook his head. Finally, she got hold of the smashed bit of lead bullet and eased it out. The wet tissue squelched a bit, and seeping blood obscured her view of the wound, but she finally removed the bullet and set it in the dish.

"I've seen many men die of such wounds. You are so young—how many people have you seen die?"

Just then, she was furious. Full of rage. Marchand was so smug, so worldly, lording his experience over her. He had no idea what she'd seen. He bragged about death. Had he ever seen an epidemic?

"I don't know," she said. "We've just had a typhoid outbreak, and one tends to lose track."

He glanced sharply at her. He would live, she thought. He was awake, aware, ready to complain. He would live.

Marchand took another drink of whiskey and closed his eyes. "Diane, she says to us, 'Go back to Kimberley. Ava will know what to do. Go to Ava.' And so here we are."

When she was satisfied the wound was clean, she stitched it up as neatly as she knew how, wiped the incision with antiseptic, and scrubbed her hands. Now he needed to rest. They'd moved all the cots to the quarantine section, but maybe they could get him back to the guesthouse.

"How do you feel?" she asked.

He didn't seem as drunk as he should have been. He patted her hand. "I am very well, Mademoiselle Doctor." His eyes drifted closed.

Marchand was more hurt than he wanted to let on, but he wasn't feverish, and his breathing was regular. She decided to leave him in the chair. Gave his shoulder one more brush, got a blanket on him, then left him to rest.

Charlie and Gordon waited, pensive. At loose ends, without a task to occupy them.

"You should probably go see Colonel Harcourt," Ava said. "I need to clean up here. I'll follow along shortly."

Charlie was going to argue. He started to reach for her. Ava could still feel his arms around her. But all he said was "Are you sure you're all right?"

"Yes, I am."

Finally, they left. Gordon squeezed her arm on his way out.

For the moment, all was quiet. The building was empty, the infirmary peaceful. No nurse was calling for assistance, no patient was crying out for help. Ava sank onto a stool by a supply table, just to rest. She planned on checking in with Boyd and Dalrymple to see how their patient was and if they needed anything. Apart from that, the typhoid ward likely needed more help, or she could go see if Macintosh at the next camp needed a hand. There was always more work to be done somewhere.

But her eyes closed. Later, she wouldn't have said she slept. Her mind was too busy for that. Turning over what Marchand had said, the commotion of the last hour, the last week, and always, always going back to the microscope that revealed the secrets that made everything clear.

The malleability of borders. Maxim guns tearing boys apart. The wounds, the blood. Whoever the bullets didn't kill, bacteria would. Humanity carried the means of its own destruction with it everywhere. The vision fell on her: This was just a prologue. Battles would come involving thousands of men, tens of thousands mowed down in an afternoon, absolute carnage, to say nothing of the rot and death that would follow. And still, all these ridiculous weapons, all this power, the slaughter. All the knowledge collected by science, all the exploration, the labels on maps, the names that codified every possible detail in the world. And still they could not stop this destruction.

This was her imagination. And yet she could label the bacteria that would be present. *Clostridium perfringens*, *Shigella dysenteriae*, *Salmonella typhi*, along with the dozens of microorganisms involved in decay. An unbroken line, from that future imagined battle to the slides she studied now, on back through time to the first simple organisms that emerged to create life on earth. These, the ones reaching back to her, flourished, will flourish, on a battlefield between France and Germany, Somme, Verdun. She had seen nothing like it. No one had. Except maybe Captain Boyd, imagining what battles like the siege at Kimberley would produce after armies had time to perfect their methods.

Future terrors filled her.

The unending chain. The borderless life. Bacteria, stretching from the past into the future. And she was in the middle of it. Medicine would not keep pace. The stench of it, this thing pummeling her from some imagined future, overcame her. It wasn't real, and yet she could taste the rot in the back of her throat, the stench overwhelming the medicine sting of antiseptic fluid, bile filling her nose—

She awoke when she vomited, a thin stream of not much, because she hadn't eaten all day, and that might have been why she fainted. Had she fainted? Disoriented, surprised to find herself sprawled on the floor, the smell of old plank boards baking in the sun stinging her nose.

Hands clutched her shoulders, and she flinched. It was Dalrymple, kneeling beside her, his concern overflowing. His hands were washed, but streaks of blood stained his off-white lab coat.

Gasping, she pulled away. "What, what—"

"You've got to stop doing this," he said.

"Doing what?" Her mind was still in two places. More than two—strung across a path, an unbroken road paved by microscopic creatures speaking to her.

"Ava! Get ahold of yourself!"

She wiped her mouth on her sleeve and focused on breathing. Feeling the floor under her. Feeling her own skin around her body. "All right. I'm fine. I'm awake."

"Where did you go this time?"

"War," she murmured. "There's going to be a war."

"Already been one, I should think," he said.

"There's always another. A war with Germany?"

He snorted a little. "Some say war with Germany is inevitable."

"But what if it isn't?"

"One problem at a time, Doctor."

God, now he was doing it. Dalrymple kept his hand on her shoulder, and she leaned into the touch. "This keeps happening. Visions, whatever it is. It's just . . . if I can use it, if I can control it . . ."

"Whatever this *practicum* is, whatever you're doing, I think it's controlling you."

She was tired. Right to her bones. She patted Dalrymple's hand. Selfishly taking comfort. "This war . . . I would stop it if I could."

"Some things you can't stop."

She didn't believe that. She didn't accept that. "Someday . . . *someday* . . . we will learn how to cure disease. To stop these outbreaks. We've come so far, I must believe we can go farther."

"And meanwhile we build weapons that kill thousands. It's not the bacteria we're up against."

"War is a disease," she muttered.

"You should get up off the floor. Come on, then."

"Give me a minute." Getting up seemed like a huge task.

"Here." Dalrymple stood and offered his hand.

She let him pull her to her feet and held on to him. Dalrymple blushed. And then she blushed. They both stepped away, and she commenced to brushing dust off herself.

"How is your patient?" she asked, quickly looking around for a rag and bin to clean up her mess, finishing the job before Dalrymple could offer to do it for her. "Mr. Monroe? Were you able to do anything?"

He shook his head. Ava paused, taken aback.

"Perforated intestines," he said. "Not to mention blood loss. Nothing we could do."

Poor Mrs. Monroe. What must she be feeling? "I'm sorry."

"Part of the job." He looked down and suddenly seemed to notice the blood on his clothes. He stripped off the coat and threw it on the pile of outgoing laundry. "I suppose it's all part of the job."

They had laid Frederick Monroe out on a cot in a quiet corner of the recovery room. He had been cleaned, stitched up, dressed in a buttoned-up shirt to hide whatever destruction had ravaged his gut. His hair and beard were damp, and his face seemed flattened in the laxness of death, the life that had animated him gone. A pressed leaf, all color faded.

Diane was sitting on a camp stool next to him, one hand resting on his, which were crossed over his chest. She had taken off her gloves. She was dusty and disheveled from travel, one sleeve of her jacket torn. The grime of travel marred the color, which Ava thought had been dark blue. The woman had aged in the fortnight since Ava had seen her last. She was sagging, grayer.

Ava crept into her range of vision, not wanting to startle her. Still, Diane didn't move her gaze from her husband's face.

"I'm so sorry," Ava said.

Diane glanced up. Her smile flickered and her eyes were shining, but no tears fell. "That's very kind. Thank you."

"Can I get you anything? Tea?" Ava asked. The English response to everything. It sounded ridiculous. The offer was an affectation. A way to fill space. But maybe Diane really did want a cup of tea. "Or I could just leave you alone."

"No, stay. Please."

Ava found another camp stool and brought it to sit vigil with her, by her husband's body.

"He was so ambitious," Diane said, her voice soft. "I so admired him. I knew from the moment I met him he was going to do great things. Circle the world, climb mountains—do you know he was a mountaineer in his younger days? Mont Blanc, Kilimanjaro. At one point I thought he'd hare off for the Himalayas. But I'm glad he turned his attention to other goals. He could have done anything, you know. He should have done it all."

All this had depended on Mr. Monroe, Ava thought with some anger. Diane's whole part in the journey, the Brannocks' plot to steal her papers, the flight from Cape Town. So much had depended on reaching him. This whole plan had been his. Or had it? Well, it hardly mattered now. He was gone. Whatever plot had surrounded him was scattered to dust.

"You should have been with us." Diane turned to her, offering as kind and gracious a smile as she ever had. But the words cut like a scalpel. "If you had been there, you could have saved him. You should have come with us, Ava." This was an accusation.

Ava let the reprimand slide off her. Words, they were only words. And they were wrong. "It was his choice to be there," she replied. "Your choice to follow him."

"Ah. I see." A dismissal. An implication that Ava wasn't worth arguing with.

At one time, earlier in their acquaintance, Diane's tone would have inspired tears. Now . . . Diane's grief was speaking, that was all. And if her accusation was more heartfelt—well, Ava wasn't bothered. This wasn't about Ava, not really.

"Mrs. de Haas still has room in the guesthouse, when you're ready to get cleaned up and rest. Just call for one of the nurses if you need anything." Diane showed no sign of moving.

Ava touched Diane's shoulder and then left her alone.

TWENTY-TWO

Paenibacillus polymyxa

Captain Boyd lifted quarantine, and Ava returned to Mrs. de Haas's guesthouse. Diane and the others had taken up residence there again, recovering from their trials.

Ava found Charlie Hallern sitting in the backyard of the guesthouse, drinking something. A steaming mug rather than a glass of amber, so tea rather than alcohol, likely. She pulled a wicker chair closer to him.

"I have something of yours," she said, and offered him the handwritten journal.

He accepted it, chuckling wryly. "Ah, yes. Dare I ask what you think?"

She could barely remember being angry about his connection to Conrad Zane's novels. So much had happened since. She could admit he was a good writer with a flair for the dramatic. She could admit she was entirely incapable of being objective about the matter.

"I have to admit, Torrance and West have been keeping me company these last few weeks. I'd ask myself what they would have done, and the answer was always keep going. Just keep going."

"And the *real* Torrance and West?"

"They'd have been horrified and demanded that I come home immediately, where they could look after me." Well, to be fair, Anton had only asked in his telegram that she write home once in a while. But she was sure he would rush to her rescue if she asked him to.

Charlie laughed warmly, then turned thoughtful, his lips pursed. "Stories are easier, I think. They turn out the way we want them to."

"When we found out about the books, my brothers and I sneaked copies into the house, to read them by lamplight after bedtime. I'd read out loud, for Harry. We'd laugh about how fantastically untrue and melodramatic it all was. I'd try to put the book away . . . and one or the other of them, usually Archie, would demand to hear the rest. They'll be very jealous to hear I've read the new one before anyone else."

"You can't tell them you met me. That would take some of the mystique off it, don't you think? Conrad Zane should remain just as fictional as my versions of Torrance and West."

"Would you like to meet them? I can arrange it."

He hesitated, his expression freezing. Was that shock? Fear? "I'm not entirely sure that's a good idea."

"I promise I won't tell anyone about Conrad Zane. Though if you ever decide to give up shipboard life, your career as an author seems secure."

"Thank you, Miss Stanley."

Marchand went around with his arm in a sling, pretending that he wasn't injured, but he sat and rested more often than was usual for him. Though quiet and thoughtful as ever, Gordon Bell remained dressed in trousers and coat. He might have become Gordon, but he was as attentive as ever, bringing tea to Diane and keeping a watchful eye on her. Diane was restless, unhappy. Of course she was. Her husband had just died.

But there was more to it. With Diane, there was always more to it.

Here they were, gathered in the parlor of the guesthouse as they had been in the salon back on the *Penelope*. Something of that previous adventure continued to bind them together. Though now they spoke little. Marchand grumbled; his shoulder pained him. Ava had offered to get some morphine for him—Boyd had a small supply and might be willing to part with some of it. But Marchand refused, satisfied to rely on drinking to knock himself out. They finished supper. The lamps were lit, a coal fire burned in the grate against the nighttime chill, and the evening promised to be a peaceful one.

Until Diane stood and announced, "We must press forward, of course."

They all stared at her. Ava laughed. Then shut her mouth, cutting off the sound. *Press forward into* what? she wanted to ask. Where else could Diane go, and to accomplish what?

The silence stretched, until Ava felt she needed to explain. "I'm sorry. But . . . Mrs. Monroe. Your husband is dead."

"He would want me to continue his work."

"Would he?" Ava argued. "How many people have to die for this? And for what?"

Diane went to the base of the stairs, where they'd set their packs and satchels after their disastrous journey. After digging in one of the pockets, she drew out a familiar packet of papers, worn with folding and unfolding for frequent study.

She wielded them at Ava and the others. A cudgel, or a flag. Something like both.

"We got so close, Ava," she said. "We got right up to the mining claim, and it's so beautiful. You can tell the rift in the hillside is just full of minerals, for whoever can dig them up. We only have to survey the border to our advantage, and it'll be done! One more trip. This time we know what to expect. We'll be careful."

That innocuous sheaf of papers that the Brannocks had died for, diverted them halfway around the world for, that Frederick Monroe had died for, that they'd gone through so much trouble over. Those boundaries, those lines Diane was so obsessed with. They weren't real. They didn't exist, except when people like her made them exist by sheer will.

Migrating animals didn't care. The roots of the grasses blowing on the veld didn't care. Bacteria didn't care.

Ava stood, catching hold of that thread of anger, that longing to do something with her helplessness. *"Salmonella typhi."*

A crackle and hiss, the ignition of paper catching fire, the sharp smell of smoke, and the whole sheaf of paper burned, incinerating in one great orange flame, turning all to ash. Crying out, Diane dropped the fiery mess and stumbled back.

For a moment, it seemed the burning pages might set the floor, the furniture, the whole house on fire. Ava would have to remember some of those *practica* she'd done, summoning moisture from fungus, attempting to make rain fall indoors. But by the time the mess hit the floor, the flames were gone, only ash making a sooty mess on the rug.

"You—" Diane glared knives, daggers. Her lips parted, on the verge of curses. Her composure, her eternal calm, finally broke—but only for a moment. Briefly closing her eyes, she settled herself and brushed ashes from her hands.

"You've made progress," Diane said finally, glancing up, lips twitching. Not a smile, not a scowl. Neither, both. "But this won't stop me. Not for long."

Ava nodded in acknowledgment, one opponent to another on this very small battlefield. Maybe this would stop her; maybe it wouldn't. But she'd done what she could. Anything that came after . . . well, she couldn't save the world.

Marchand chuckled. "Eh, there is always something."

The next morning, Diane and Gordon set off by train for Johannesburg. They were going to look for some associates of Frederick Monroe's in the mining business. Ava didn't inquire too deeply.

Side by side, they made a startlingly good-looking pair. They were both dressed well in new clothes—Diane somehow knew where to buy a fashionable set of full mourning garb in a dusty mining town like Kimberley. She wore a black walking gown with a trim jacket, a black hat with a brim to keep the sun off, and a half veil of netting. He wore a dark-brown suit, tailored to make him look dapper, dashing, and male. A new bowler cap, polished shoes. Diane's arm hooked around his elbow. Gordon was the taller, standing straight, seeming happy to escort her. With his smooth, rather fine face, he seemed young. People would think he was Diane's son and not her friend.

Ava said goodbye to them at the house. Diane gave her a slight nod, as a duelist leaving the field might. Gordon clasped her hand and thanked her. For what, Ava wasn't sure.

Marchand went to the train station to see them off but didn't continue on to Johannesburg. "I get too old for this nonsense," he said brusquely.

Diane had paid him what her husband had promised him; they'd found letters settling the agreement between them among his belongings. He was off to Cape Town to recuperate in some nice seaside hotel, he hoped. His expression was set in a grimace with pain. He might never get the full use of that arm back. He didn't blame Ava, which was kind of him. She'd done the best she could with the wound.

"A more experienced surgeon probably could have done a better job of it," she said, by way of apology.

"Eh. I am not dead because of you." He tried to shrug and hissed in pain. "Safe travels to you, Miss Ava. Wherever you go next."

Back at the infirmary, the officers were in something of a rush. Dalrymple was being sent to Bloemfontein to relieve one of the army doctors there. He was packing up, with Boyd supervising and offering advice, perhaps not so helpfully. The banter gave Ava a feeling of comfort. No intrigues and espionage here, with the pair of them.

"You don't need to take *all* the bandages, surely," Boyd declared. His feet were up on his desk, and he was reading a medical journal. Dalrymple was moving back and forth between shelves and a leather bag. Putting things in, taking things out.

"You might help, *sir*," Dalrymple complained. "Pack up those bottles of peroxide, perhaps."

"I'm not giving you any bottles of peroxide, old chap. You'll have to make do with what you find there."

They paused when Ava entered. She regarded them with a strained smile. She was actually sorry to be leaving them. "I've come to say goodbye. I'm headed back to Cape Town."

"Huh, is that so?" Boyd asked.

Dalrymple's shoulders drooped. Did he seem sad, even? "You've decided to go back to London?"

"Yes. I think everyone's right—it's high time I take the exams."

"You'll do very well on them, I think."

"Wait a moment." Boyd set his feet on the ground, got out a sheet of paper and started writing.

The waiting was awkward. Better to make a clean break of it. Maybe she shouldn't have come to say goodbye at all.

"Do tell me you'll keep working on your bacteriological *practica*," Dalrymple said to fill the silence.

"I can hardly call one trick a *practica*," she said. But yes, she'd written it all down. She could reliably light candles. The fainting spells, visions, insights, whatever they were—she wouldn't go so far as to call it clairvoyance—she was still thinking about. It wasn't a *practicum* if you couldn't control it. But it was something.

"Linnaeus started with one trick, didn't he?" the lieutenant said.

"Well, if you put it like that."

"He's right," Boyd said. "Keep working on it. I expect to see your name in the journals in a year or so. Here." He both blew on the sheet of paper and waved it to dry the ink. When he was satisfied, he folded it up and offered it out to her. "Take this."

Ava accepted. "What is it?"

"For your exam board. Letter of recommendation. Highest endorsement. Well done, Stanley."

She doubted he could have given her a better compliment, and her relief and gratitude seemed like a physical weight leaving her body. She nearly started crying right there. "Thank you, sir."

"I'll walk you out," Dalrymple said. Boyd snorted at them and rolled his eyes.

For the last time, then, they walked down the lane between tents, to the edge of the camp. Slowly, on no particular mission for once.

"Miss Stanley, a question for you."

"Yes?"

He paused, lips parting—he seemed to be laughing quietly at himself. Then he asked. "May I write to you?"

How traditional. How charming. "Yes, you may. Lieutenant Dalrymple, I have a question for you."

"Anything."

"What's your first name?"

"Marcus," he said. Definitely smiling.

"All right then."

He waved a hand by his temple, almost a salute, and turned back to the infirmary.

The party broke apart, then broke again. One might look at it as damage, pieces of their group falling away. Ava was more inclined to use another metaphor: They were like *Amoeba proteus* reproducing, the body splitting to form a new independent life-form. Then splitting again. Increasing, rather than breaking.

Ava took the train to Cape Town with Marchand and Hallern. As soon as they disembarked, Marchand went his own way.

"It has been a great pleasure knowing you all! Au revoir!" He bowed himself out, perhaps not as grandly as he might have. His arm was still done up in a sling. Ava urged him to see a doctor to check the incision and change the dressing. He didn't promise he would. And then he was gone.

"The old mercenary," Hallern said, chuckling.

"You know," Ava said, "I'm not sure I ever actually met a mercenary before him."

"Most of them don't mention it unless you're the one paying their bills," Hallern replied, suitably wry.

The admiralty had finished its investigation, and custody of the *Penelope* was released back to the shipping company. Hallern—which was to say Suminwa—got command of the ship again. This was good news, of course. The shipping company was sending them to Nassau to pick up their original itinerary where they'd left off. Ava was taking another ship back to Southampton. Not quite full circle, then.

She saw them both off at the gangplank, on her way to her own ship.

"Miss Ava," Suminwa said. "I am glad you've returned to Cape Town in one piece."

"So am I."

He saluted, and walked back up the gangplank. Hallern lingered. Awkward, he took off his cap and scratched his already unruly hair.

"May I write to you?" he said finally.

Such a rush of feeling and affection and confusion overcame her then. Two men asking to write to her in as many days seemed excessive. She was past her schoolgirl days. Why should she blush?

"You may," Ava finally said. With no idea where it would all lead.

Torrance and West and the Pirates of Tenerife

Consider London through the eyes of a man who has never before been to the city. Who has never been to any city. The storm of traffic on the streets must seem savage; the tumult of people and creatures, the canyons of structures, and the smoke and smog settled over all like a blanket must seem as chaotic as any torrent. And to what purpose? How would they know? How could a stranger discern the meaning of it all? To those who call the far-off wilds of the world home, London must seem as distant and alien as the sands of Mars. What we call savage is home to them. What we take for granted as civilization is, to some, a wasteland of brick and noise.

Torrance and West returned to London. After their time on the sea, lost on the rocks of distant archipelagos, amid their strange and foreign struggles—after all that, London seemed alien. Incongruous, incomprehensible. The artificial suits and strangling ties of the men seemed constraining. The corsets and stiffened folds of the skirts and jackets of the ladies seemed outlandish, bending their bodies in unnatural ways that made no sense. They stood dumbly in the bustle of Trafalgar Square, and for just that hesitating moment, they wanted to flee. To return to that other world of adventure that they understood better than this one.

But the moment passed, and they had to admit that they were home. This, the great city of Europe, was where they belonged. They had to be grateful that they could navigate both worlds.

Side by side, they walked on to their favorite club in Mayfair.

"My good Mr. West," Torrance began. "I have received a letter."

"Oh? Anything interesting?"

Torrance glanced at him sidelong, eyebrow raised, a familiar expression. The pleasure and amusement of keeping secrets from his dear friend, knowing that he would both rile West up and draw him in, like a fish on a line.

"Have you ever been to the Grand Canyon?" Torrance asked.

West broke into a smile. "My old stomping grounds! Of course I have!" In fact, he had paddled a canoe for part of the length of the Colorado River, journeying into nooks and crannies of the canyon that no other man had seen, for no other reason than to say he had done so. Torrance well knew this.

"By any chance have you heard tell of a story that a small company of survivors from the legendary city of Atlantis fled its destruction and found refuge in the great depths of that region?"

On the face of it, such a tale was pure fancy, the worst sort of speculation and wish fulfillment, the spun-out fantasies of spiritualists and charlatans. And yet centuries ago—when the legendary city of Atlantis was at its peak, for instance—the climate of the world was different. Geologists have shown that there was an ice age, that glaciers covered much of the earth, that oceans and their sea levels drew different lines upon the map, and that even a place as ancient and formidable as the Grand Canyon might have drawn in such travelers and offered them places of refuge that later became hidden, and so slipped past the observations of modern man.

Both Torrance and West knew and heartily believed the words of Shakespeare, that there are more things in heaven and earth than are dreamt of in our philosophy.

West regarded his friend with a level stare. "They're only stories. Legends. Sheer fancy."

"And how many adventures have we pursued that began as only stories?"

Most of them, West knew. Most if not all of them. "When do we leave?"

TWENTY-THREE
Bacilli

March 1903
London

Ava's family wanted to wait in the lobby of the hospital to hear the results of her exams. She absolutely forbade them from coming anywhere near the hospital at any point that day. They'd make her nervous at the very least. At the worst, if anyone recognized Anton, Bran, or Beth, they might cause a scene. All with good intentions, but Ava didn't need her head filled with such chaos.

They wanted to show their support. To cheer her on. She understood this and appreciated them. Out of all those in the erstwhile company on the *Penelope*, Ava was the one who'd had a home, a family, to go back to. She hadn't really understood what that meant before.

After all was said and done, the medical exams were her own. Her own trial, and her own accomplishment. She would walk through the doors alone, and she would have to walk out alone. Wonder of wonders, Beth and Bran finally seemed to understand—that to really prove herself, Ava needed to choose her own path. They needed to trust that she knew what she was doing—or that she would at least learn along the way.

She did promise to come *straight* home after to tell them the results. Anton had decided to lease out Barleydale and live in town, closer to professional connections, lecturing opportunities, and gossip. Being in town suited them all better. Though Ava was likely to set out on another trip soon enough, to continue her research. That was for later. She found it encouraging that she was ready to set out again so soon after her adventures in Cape Colony. At one point, she had vowed to never leave home again. Wherever home was. London, New York, Colorado Springs. All of the above.

Might as well travel. One met such interesting people.

She'd received letters from both Charlie Hallern and Marcus Dalrymple. Hallern and the *Penelope* were back on their usual route between the Caribbean and Europe. He suggested they might cross paths one of these days, and Ava decided she'd like that. Lieutenant Dalrymple was in line for a promotion for his work in the war and after. He had a decision to make, then: Stay in Africa, travel to another colony. Or resign entirely. Go into private medical practice, or pursue academic interests. Too many choices, he confessed. She understood.

He also told her that the last of the concentration camps had closed in January. For him, that marked the true end of the war.

Ava didn't hear from Diane Monroe or the others. Dalrymple could only pass on rumors, that she had given up on pursuing the mining claim in German South West Africa, or that she was married again, to another diplomat and would-be entrepreneur. Or that she had returned to England to arrange her husband's affairs. Ava walked in the better parts of London sometimes, in Mayfair or Kensington, and imagined she saw an elegant figure in the black of mourning, with a familiar shape of face and perfectly arranged hair. She would be accompanied by a pensive, clean-shaven young man. Her nephew, maybe. Ava could never be sure. She didn't think she would ever meet Diane Monroe again.

True to her word, after the exams she caught a bus to Notting Hill, to Sir Archibald's town house. Tried not to be impatient with the horses jostling among all the other horses, buses, wagons, and carts. Once the bus got moving, they made decent time.

The whole trip to Notting Hill, she could barely sit still. Her heart raced. She wanted to scream, laugh, and cry all at once. This should have been routine. It wasn't like she'd saved a life. Or killed anyone.

She jumped off the bus while it was still moving and loudly wished the other passengers a very good afternoon. Someone muttered "Americans" loud enough for her to hear, and that made her want to laugh.

They were waiting for her in the front parlor, the whole lot of them, gathered before the cozily burning grate. The difference in temperature between indoors and out was pronounced. Anton was reading the paper from his armchair. Mother was at her desk, pen over paper, but she must have paused to listen to Bran, Harry, and Archie, all bent together in conversation.

Ava heard part of it as she came in through the vestibule and hung up her coat.

"Most families would be happy to have a son go into banking," Archie said.

Clearly pained, Bran said, "Surely you can find something more interesting to spend your time on."

"Oh, don't mind him," Harry said. "He's only saying that to rile you up."

"Next he'll say he wants to go into government," Anton said wryly.

That was when Ava appeared in the doorway. They all straightened. The combined force of their attention was overwhelming. Her voice dried up completely. All the words must tumble out at once, or none could.

"Oh, Ava, dear!" Beth said, standing, wringing her hands, much like Ava was doing.

"Well?" Bran said. He was gripping his knees.

Could have heard a pin drop, as the saying went. Ava had meant to put them on at first. To be very serious. But her smile broke out, too wide and relieved and happy to stay hidden.

Anton beamed. "Dr. Stanley, I presume?"

They all swept together in a celebration of congratulations, hugging, laughing, and more hugging.

"See, Archie, you want to make people happy, become a doctor," Harry said.

"That's just it, like you said—I want to rile them up! It's Ava's job making everyone happy."

Anton had acquired a bottle of champagne. That was how sure he'd been that she'd pass. They drank, gathering around, all of them chattering like starlings.

Dr. Stanley. It didn't quite feel real yet. Part of her wanted to reflexively deny it, as she'd done for the last two years. She also felt like she'd done it all backward. In Kimberley, she'd behaved like a doctor. The others had treated her like one. High time she owned the title.

And now that she had it, she could move on to other worries. Other trials ahead of her. One in particular—the vision had kept pressing on her. The weight of impending disaster. The certainty that she ought to do something about it. This was one of the precepts of science: When you made a discovery, you shared it.

While the others finished off the champagne, Ava leaned toward Anton, beckoning her stepfather into a muted conversation.

"What is it?" he asked.

She answered, "Who should I talk to about preventing a war?"

AUTHOR'S NOTE

All the usual thank-yous apply. Thanks to editors Marilyn Brigham and Clarence Haynes for their feedback and insights, and to the whole team at 47North for their work. To my agent, Seth Fishman, for fighting the good fight. To Daniel Abraham for a last-minute beta read he didn't really have time for but did anyway. To Yaz Campanella for the technical read (all remaining errors are my own). My family and friends kept me going during what turned out to be an unbelievably difficult time: Mom, Dad, Rob, Deb, Emery, Max, Yaz, Wendy, Anne.

While I was writing this novel, my mother, Jo Anne, was diagnosed with a brain tumor. Three months later, on Christmas Eve, 2024, she passed away. When I was sixteen and announced that I wanted to be a writer, she brought home a stack of books from the library about writing and publishing. She supported me every step of the way. Until now, she'd read everything I published. I'm heartbroken that she won't be reading this book. But she's still with me, every step.

The music that kept me company while I was writing was *The Armed Man: A Mass for Peace*, by Karl Jenkins.

I have a couple of primary sources to tell you about:

Bacteria in Daily Life, by microbiologist Grace Frankland. Published in 1903, it might be the first popular science writing about bacteria. Frankland also cowrote a biography of Louis Pasteur and was part of the first class of women admitted to the Linnean Society in 1904.

The Brunt of the War and Where It Fell, by Emily Hobhouse, from 1902, is an impressive piece of investigative journalism chronicling the conditions of concentration camps run by the British army in modern-day South Africa during the Second Boer War, after a scorched-earth policy displaced much of the population of Boer territories. She brought together eyewitness accounts, correspondence, testimony, and statistics. Around fifty thousand people died in the camps from disease and starvation. Hobhouse's work brought the plight of the camps to the attention of the British public.

I was also inspired by the work of Joseph Conrad, and by University of Colorado professor Kelly Hurley's seminars on Victorian literature, which I've clearly never forgotten.

Wash your hands and get vaccinated if you're able.

ABOUT THE AUTHOR

Photo © 2020 Lucy Tuck Photography

Carrie Vaughn is the author of more than twenty novels and over a hundred short stories, two of which have been finalists for the Hugo Award. Her most recent novel, *The Naturalist Society*, received starred reviews in *Library Journal* and *Booklist*. She's well known for her *New York Times* bestselling series of novels about a werewolf named Kitty, who hosts a talk radio advice show for the supernaturally disadvantaged. In 2018, Vaughn won the Philip K. Dick Award for the postapocalyptic murder mystery *Bannerless*. A graduate of the Odyssey Fantasy Writing Workshop, Carrie is also a contributor to the Wild Cards series of shared world superhero books edited by George R. R. Martin.

Vaughn survived her nomadic childhood as an air force brat and managed to put down roots in Boulder, Colorado, where she currently collects hobbies. You can visit the author online at www. carrievaughn. com. For writing advice and essays, check out her Patreon page at www. patreon. com/carrievaughn.